DOUBTS
of the
Heart

Eva Shaw, author of *Games of the Heart*

CRIMSON
ROMANCE

F+W Media, Inc.

This edition published by
Crimson Romance
an imprint of F+W Media, Inc.
10151 Carver Road, Suite 200
Blue Ash, Ohio 45242
www.crimsonromance.com

ISBN 10: 1-4405-6828-6
ISBN 13: 978-1-4405-6828-2
eISBN 10: 1-4405-6829-4
eISBN 13: 978-1-4405-6829-9

Dedication

Chapter 1

I put on a coconut bra. Don't tell me you've never wanted to do that because down deep every woman has. But you know what the scary part was? It fit. For coconuts.

Turning around in the shop's microscopic dressing room at the International Market Place in downtown Honolulu, I tried to scrutinize my reflection in the fuzzy, fun-house mirror.

"And what's become of your pride, Nica Dobson?"

This was not a rhetorical question because I really did ask myself that. Self didn't answer, which is a good or a bad thing depending on where my psyche was living at that second.

I slipped out of the bra and back into shorts and yellow t-shirt, sandals, and Cubbies baseball cap. What had happened to me? Who was I? What was my purpose in life?

Sorry, if you think I have any of these answers, I don't, so quietly close this book and check out the ones on the self-help shelf. Life is a big, fat mystery to me. That's why I found myself in Honolulu, a year after surgery for breast cancer, six rounds of chemo, and then seven weeks straight of radiation. I was on leave, not from my senses, but as a confidential consultant for the Federal Bureau of Investigation. It's like being a temp, but I got to carry a gun if needed, and an ID card, and swore to uphold apple pie, Mom, and the American way. But as a consultant, I could give my opinions, but had no clout when terrible things happened and received no pats on the back when things went well, which often made it tough to tell the difference between a good outcome of an investigation and a rotten one. Want details? Just ask my cousin,

Pastor Jane Angieski about that. She exposed all sides of me in her best-selling memoir *Games of the Heart*. Alas, I was okay with me for about ten years, but then this cancer diagnosis happened.

My co-workers at the Bureau thought it was for the medical reasons that I was on leave. Made sense, since I did need time for my body to get stronger, but honestly, I'd begun thinking the leave was necessary for emotional ones. Could I continue to fight their fight? Who was I fighting? Could anyone ever win?

Not being clear why I was a consultant, I knew I'd become a danger for my partners, citizens, and even the criminals. Yes, for myself, too.

Don't misunderstand. I believe in truth, justice, and John Wayne. However, doubts clustered and squawked in my brain like greedy pigeons in Central Park. For some consultants and agents, it takes a bullet for them to examine their lives and their bucket lists. For me, it was a nasty swarm of cancer cells right near my heart that made me wonder if the absolutes shared by my fellow team members and agents could ever be mine again. The treatments for breast cancer, to me, were a blessing because after years of being undercover as a wealthy patron of the arts in Las Vegas, I was free. Of course, I'm still a wealthy patron of the arts, thanks to marrying the late George Wainwright (oil importing and banking) and the late Clayton Dobson (family fortune with the smarts to get into Microsoft in the beginning). You won't be tested later and I'll try to remind you if I bring them up again.

I loved them both and they loved me. Yet, I think they wanted a trophy wife rather than a life partner and because of my cover for the Bureau, I gave them what they wanted. These men always got what they wanted. George died of a heart attack when he was "away on business." Yes, even the death certificate had quotes around that. Clayton? Who knew that a bee would sting him when he brushed it off his face with golf towel before selecting a five-iron at the eighteenth hole at Pebble Beach? Who could imagine that an insect could end the life of a billionaire who even the president didn't call by his first name until he was asked?

Within twelve short months, I went from living in a mansion the size of Oprah's in Montecito, California (and yes, I have been her guest) to living at the Hilton in Honolulu. My friends who'd been through it and the counselors in the support group said, "Cancer changes things," but apparently not everything as I quickly found out.

I put on my hot yellow "I Love Waikiki" T-shirt and denim capris. I wasn't ready to buy or be seen in public in a coconut bra, well, quite yet. Then the second I flung back the fitting room's curtain, I was knocked back and then teetered forward. Blame it on the high-heeled sandals. I grabbed a chunk of a green Aloha shirt and snapped. "Listen, pal, if you take off the dark glasses and realize there are other people in this market, maybe you wouldn't be a menace to society," I barked.

"Me? You could get yourself killed moving like that, you know," he growled, but took my elbow as if to steady me. That's when I saw the two goons standing on each side of him. In the Bureau, I've heard that described as "packing muscle," and these guys looked like poster boys for that.

"No need to assault me, you creep. Take your grubby hands off me or bring on your buddies here because I can make them uncomfortable enough so they won't forget me for a long time." I growled the threat and yanked my arm from his grasp. It was then that I saw the spot where I'd previously been standing now housed a novelty cart pushed into place by two teenagers still texting and oblivious to who or what was in their way.

Before I could save the little dignity I had left, the man squinted, blinked, and then stared into my eyes.

On a scale of one to ten, I would later tell my cousin, he came in at a firm seven, about three inches shorter than me but I'm five foot ten inches without the wedge sandals. Even though I had taken a course to profile suspects, honestly? I was never good at it. This guy was about twenty pounds overweight, but broad shouldered and muscular. His short dark hair was receding a bit at the forehead, yet with that cool bristly haircut head look, it didn't matter. He was wearing glasses with dark rims and a crooked smile. His features were the typical melting pot of locals with more Chinese than Hawaiian, I thought. I did like what I saw even if he was annoying as all get out.

Apparently he did too because he kept staring until I wanted to poke him. Then the next words from his mouth made mine open.

"Nikky? Nikky Wikiwiki Ticky?" He grabbed me with the arms of a weightlifter and yes, lifted me off the ground. He swung us around. "Of all the people in the entire world, you are probably the one I would never have expected to actually run into. Wow, right here in town." Finally he put me down, and I'm no lightweight, and stepped back, obviously to get a better view as his eyes did that once over you see in movies or by players in the dating world—at least according to Hollywood.

Here's the scoop. Wikiwiki was not a name in any way connected to either of my late husbands. It was the appalling nickname I was given in high school. My given name is Monica, but I have always been called Nica. The jocks and the cheerleaders at my high school ruthlessly changed it to Nikky because my last name was, unfortunately, Ticky. Plus wikiwiki in Hawaiian means fast or hurry up, something I certainly wasn't, but it was the butt of a three-year joke for the cool crowd. The geeks, who also sort of ignored me, but let me hang around with them anyhow, told me to pay no attention to it. I thought I had let that painful adolescent wound heal, until that second, standing there looking eye to eye at someone who knew of my high school trauma. He was now spouting it like he'd just heard that haunting rhyme for the first time.

"I cannot believe it. After all these years. Nikky Wikiwiki Ticky in the flesh."

"Yes, all of me and in person," I responded and jerked myself out of the forthcoming hug that I could see was about to pull me to him.

"You don't recognize me, do you?"

Of course I didn't, but the guy certainly knew me. So I bluffed. What would you have done? "You must be here for Kukui High's twenty-year reunion, too. You and your buddies." I nodded to the muscle behind him.

He tilted his head. He looked squarely at me. Then he smiled, and this time, the crooked front teeth gave him away. I'd seen enough of that smile in homeroom when he was flirting with any girl who would look his way and also as my lab partner in chemistry, when he wanted me to complete whatever assignment we had. I never knew why he joined Chemistry Club, except that our teacher suggested that if he wanted to graduate, it might be a good idea. Yes, I had heard and remembered that conversation.

All that ran through my mind before I said, "Payton Yu. If it isn't the most legendary all-time superstar football hero ever to grace the halls of, and somehow graduate from, Kukui High? Well, how about that?" And then to myself I thought, *And the biggest pain in the butt I ever had homeroom with for three straight years. If I never saw this jerk again, life would be grand.* Except my patron of the arts persona kicked in. "How lovely to see you again." But of course I didn't mean it. Would you?

"You've changed, Nikky Wikiwiki Ticky, and yet I can see the old you is right there, wrapped up right inside this more-than-hot package," he said, walking around in a circle as someone might drooling over a new Corvette.

"You always were observant, Payton."

He came to stand inches from me, winked, and added, "And you're older."

Talking as I might to my late husband Clayton's elderly great aunt Gloria—that is, slowly and clearly, bless her little heart and deaf little ears—I said, "Some of us have grown up in the last twenty years, Payton."

"Whatever you did about growing up, you've excelled—and in the right places. If it weren't for those crystal blue eyes and the way you crinkle your nose when you're angry, which always made my heart go wild, I wouldn't have recognized you. Wow, little Nikky Wikiwiki Ticky all grown up."

"Payton, I'm now called Monica or even Nica, like I preferred in high school. Others call me Ms. Wainwright-Dobson." And for your information that sentence did come out with icy indignation plus a righteous tilt of my chin. Remember how the popular kids in high school could be brutal when they found a victim? Imagine starting high school at thirteen. Imagine being twig thin, taking advanced academic classes, especially excelling in math, and graduating when I was sixteen, when I was recruited by MIT. Did I mention thick glasses, frizzy hair, and, since my refuge was reading, my tendency to trip over things since my nose was always in a book. Doesn't take a genius, does it, to see that I had "target" emblazed over me every single day at Kukui High School. Okay, coupled with my teenage looks, if you must know, life was tough until the best parents on the planet Otis and Jean Ticky adopted me when I was seven. They were in their forties, but that didn't matter. Mom and Dad knew I just needed a safe home and plenty of love.

Does the name Kukui High sound familiar? You're right. Kukui High School is the same one that Commander Steve McGarrett of *Hawaii Five-0* and "Book 'em, Dano" fame supposedly attended. Unfortunately, that fine-looking hunk is a fictional character. But if he had been real, he would have been in the same ultra-hip crowd as the above most-annoying person I had ever met.

Even without my inelegant looks, my adoptive last name would have caused any socially ill at ease teen at least a bit of mortification. Otis and Jean had been parents to other foster kids, but Mom always got so serious when she'd tell me, "When we hugged you, sweetheart, Dad and I decided you were the one… the one we were to never let go." Hence when the official adoption papers were signed, I got great parents and Ticky became my new last name. From Dad, I learned to fish, camp, and cook pot roast worthy of a five-star restaurant. From Mom I learned play a mean game of poker and the piano, and I was good enough that during college, I worked summers at supper clubs and did weddings and anniversary parties in my spare time.

My cousin Jane, who seems to think she's an expert on such things, says, "That's why you keep pushing yourself. That's why you over-compensated and became a FBI confidential consultant."

She calls me a "McAgent," like a fast-food variety of the real thing. She says I don't trust people. Whatever. I certainly was not going to fall into that Nikky Wikiwiki Ticky jab again. I squared my shoulders and forced my eyes into "interrogation" mode, which is what I always tried to use when grilling a suspect. I waited for it to come. It was the barely perceptible nod of acknowledgement from Mr. Big Man on campus. It came from Payton Yu, an heir of the gigantic Yu shipping and transportation dynasty and one of the largest employers in the State of Hawaii and Pacific Rim.

"Nica. Yeah, I remember. I heard from the grapevine that you'd done well in life, but a hyphenated last name is something the old gang forgot to mention." He stood there shaking his head with just a hint of a smile.

"Nice to see you too, Payton." I looked at my wrist, which fortunately did have a watch on it. "I'm late, or we could spend more time catching up on the good old days."

"How about coffee? A shave ice? Rainbow always pleases the returning *kama'ahina* and you're definitely a local. We can go to that cart." He pointed across the crowded market. "Like the same one that nearly rolled right over you if I hadn't saved your life. But you can thank me later."

I didn't care if he looked like a younger, shorter Asian/Hawaiian American George Clooney, which he did. I didn't need to rehash the good old high school days with a boy, no a man, I'd only one meaningful conversation with during that torturous time and the person who had personally crowned me with that offensive nickname. Besides, he was definitely playing with the wrong crowd now. If he needed protection during the middle of the day in downtown Honolulu then whatever his career had become beyond shipping, I'd bet my FBI badge that there was a rap sheet with his name on it in the system. I always knew that some of the football players were going to end up on the opposite side of the law than I had, however it still disappointed me. I looked again at the two huge men and thought, *Payton, you've grown up to be a bigwig with the Pacific Rim mafia or you're running drugs.* But I said, "Not possible. I'm really late." I backed away.

"Hey, Nikky, um, Nica, you'll be at the reunion dinner tonight, right? I'll see you then?" he asked as one of the muscle men with him whispered in his ear. "Looks like this isn't a good time for me either, Ms. Wainwright-Dobson." He bowed like Sir Lancelot straight from a play. "Promise you'll save a dance for me this evening." He took my left hand. "You really did grow up and fill out well, Nica."

For a split second, I wanted my right fist to collide with that crooked smile and those white crooked teeth. I wanted him to have a taste of the hurt I suffered because he and his hipster gang had tormented me with that nickname and their ugly jabs. But good manners and the examples of honest parents kicked in. Okay, you want the truth? I knew if I took a swing at him, his bodyguards would definitely win the match. "See you there, Payton," I muttered, spun around, and dashed toward the parking lot.

Attending the opening events at Kukui High's twenty-year reunion was now so not going to happen, or so I thought, until I was getting into my car and my cell phone rang. "Hello, this is Nica." It was a number I didn't recognize.

"Is this *the* Monica Wainwright-Dobson? Are you the FBI agent?"

"Well, that is my name...but an agent...actually, no..." I replied cautiously. "Who are you?" But as I asked, I knew this wasn't any creative sales pitch. In my ten years with the bureau, I had heard that catch before, the catch of desperation in the woman's voice. "I'm not currently with the Bureau."

"It was murder," was the next sentence.

"Are you in danger right now?" Old habits die hard and I scanned the parking lot to see if I was being watched or stalked by the men hanging on Payton Yu's every word, but pretended to be involved in the phone call. Best to get the facts straight. Not the time to flinch.

"No. No danger and you don't understand," the woman said.

"I don't. The word murder pretty well defines danger for me."

"You have to find who murdered my daddy," came the next breathy sentence. An audible and rough, raspy swallow followed. "I read about you on the Internet. Then I found out that you're there in Honolulu."

I waited, having learned early in my career that with silence people often feel uncomfortable. Then suddenly they say what they really mean and more.

"I am so sorry to intrude, you don't even know me. This all seemed logical before when I talked with her, when I told her I need help and when she gave me your number." There was a slight German or French accent beneath the woman's perfect English.

"Her? Who is the 'her' you're referring to?"

"I knew it was foolish. I told her so, and I didn't want to call. But she insisted I contact you. She gave me your private cell number."

I leaned against the white BMW, looked out toward the crashing waves on Waikiki. And waited.

"I got it from your cousin Pastor Jane Angieski-Morales."

"Cousin Jane. Of course," I replied.

Okay, take a breath, because it's time for a quick explanation. It's convoluted, but since the day I collided with *the* Pastor Jane Angieski-Morales during an undercover op in Las Vegas that went horribly wrong, at least at first, my life had not been the same. What happened left me so disenchanted with law enforcement, I tossed down my badge for a time.

But back to the above mentioned cousin. You see, Jane Angieski-Morales and I are related by a bizarre, somewhat stretched throw of the genetic dice. Jane's grandfather, the fine musician and university professor Dr. Henry Angieski and my birth grandmother were cousins.

While Jane was working on the family's genealogy, she found the connection, contacted me again through the Bureau, and insisted that I attend the Angieski family reunion. Little did I know at that point, Jane, Henry, and I were the only members of the clan. Her methods of getting people to do things were familiar to me and the Bureau. When she nearly destroyed five years of painstaking undercover work the Bureau had carefully prepared, I wanted to wring her neck. It all turned out well, but for months the very mention of Pastor Jane Angieski-Morales's name made my stomach churn. That was two years ago, before Jane and her Las Vegas police captain husband Tom Morales married and BC for me, before cancer.

To say it was a shock to become part of their family, after what was a jarring start, is an understatement. Yet, I've grown used to Jane's ability to jump to more conclusions than a frog on Red Bull. She's got a good heart, I keep reminding myself, and she's the reason I agreed to return to Honolulu for my high school reunion. When I was diagnosed with Stage 3 cancer, Jane stayed by my side, holding my hands and head through chemo and radiation. When the email came that Kukui High was holding its twenty-year reunion the same day that Jane was asked to temporarily pastor the Church on the Beach, a mission that helps the homeless in Waikiki and holds Sunday services in front of the Hilton Hawaiian Village, she flatly said, "Nica, you know I'm bigger and far more annoying than you are. We can argue about this or you can pack some clothes. You need to be someplace where you can figure out your future, rest, and have fun. And besides, we're all going."

"Even the dog?" If you've read her memoir, which is now on the *New York Times* bestseller list, called *Games of the Heart*, you know all about *the* dog, Toughy.

"Hush your mouth, Cousin. He's family. What a silly question."

Even with my meager combat, martial arts, and interrogation training, thanks to the Bureau, I've learned when Jane has made up her mind, it's impracticable and totally useless to argue. Don't misunderstand, I like Jane and admire her. You'd better not tell her. And I'll swear I didn't say it if you post a message on her Facebook page. It'll just encourage her to continue to be my BFF, not that it's a bad thing, but I've never had a BFF or been that close to a woman whom I wasn't wrestling to the ground.

Hence, my new, entire family from Jane, Tom, Henry, Jane's foster child Harmony, their rather cute little dog, had all taken up residence in suites at the hotel thanks to the generous funds I had received after Clayton's death. Tom and Harmony were in Maui snorkeling and. because Jane's baby was due any day, I hoped he'd make it back or she'd probably volunteer me to be a birth coach. Enough said.

As I heard Jane was involved with the caller, my sigh probably rippled the coastline from Waikiki to the North Shore. I formed my words carefully. "Yes, Jane gave you my number. What is it that she said I could or would do for you?"

After a long pause, the woman's voice went up an octave. "You know people who knew him. That's why I am calling, because you're the only one who can help me. Please, Ms. Dobson, help me find Daddy's killer."

I leaned back against the car and watched the slivers of sun bounce through the mimosa tree that was shading the parking lot and honestly wished I had a mimosa in my hand.

"I think you'd better tell me what you're really talking about?" In the time it took to ask that and then wonder just what an on-leave and possibly former FBI consultant could do about a murder, I knew, somehow, I was already involved.

"Jimmy March. Jimmy March. People sometimes called him the March Man."

The name took a long moment to register. I shook my head. "Jimmy's been gone a long time, since the late eighties, I think. Everybody knows. He killed himself. I remember reading his work in college literature courses, right there with the Beat Poets and Jack Kerouac. But murder? That's not the way I remember it."

"But it was. I know the truth."

"Wait. Let me finish. I've always been a fan of his music and some of his novels about the convoluted sixties and seventies. I liked his wacky memoir of the people he hung out with such as Mick Jagger, Janice Joplin, and Brian Wilson from the Beach Boys. I remember reading an essay he'd written about the colorful underbelly of Honolulu, with surfers, pickpockets, and gambling dens that were about as hidden as my nose. I even studied his novels in college. But I remember that my professor clearly said Jimmy took his own life. Although, I some tabloid of the time said he became a hermit while another said he was in the witness protection program." What I didn't say was that same teacher of mine explained how Jimmy liked to play Russian roulette, so if he was dead, it because he'd been exceptionally stupid and perhaps so drugged out that he thought he was immortal. It happened in those times.

"That's not true!"

I pulled the receiver away from my ear. The woman could scream. "I'm sorry, whoever you are. I've listened to the stories about him; my literature professor mingled with the same group of writers; my cousin's grandfather Henry knew him, too. When we got to Honolulu last week, Henry even drove us around to some of the places where they'd hung out. He talked about Jimmy's reckless streak and how he'd go off without telling anyone and disappear for months on end. Jimmy, I heard, would go skydiving one day and then drive fast cars the next. I even remember an article in *Rolling Stone* about how he loved to play with a pistol."

Henry had certainly never idolized him and I trusted Jane's grandfather's take on life.

There was a bit of static and then she said, "He was like Hemingway. He was a man's man. But his death is real and his killer just made it look like Russian roulette. All lies. I can prove it. Just listen. Remember, his body was never found. Oh, Ms. Dobson, did you know that? Won't you please listen and help me?"

"Hold on, now. Let's review reality here. I don't know you and you don't know me. I don't see why you called." I opened the car's door, swung in, and flicked the key so the windows could roll down.

"Doctor Daddy, that is, Professor Angieski, I mean, and the Slam Dunk band are going to do a benefit concert at the newly renovated Hawaii Theatre. The money is going to help build a cancer ward for at Queen's Medical Center. You're going to be there, too. Jane said so."

Once more, I knew that dear Cousin Jane was guilty of sharing too much information.

"Honolulu is where my father was killed, six days before I was born."

"But I read that his body wasn't found. Hence, there was no killing."

Some people, as you may have experienced just today even, sometimes don't listen when others are talking and I knew this was the case with me and the caller.

"The article said that the band is going to give a charity concert. I have an elderly aunt who lives in the city, but when I called Auntie, she didn't know about your arrival." The woman's attempt to chuckle came across brittle, and without taking a breath she continued faster. "She never cared much for authors, especially novelists, or singers for that matter. She's not fond of Christians either—oh, that slipped out. I know Slam Dunk is a Christian band."

My mouth squeezed into a straight line. It's been my experience that when people are stressed, like this woman seemed to be, they blurt out things. In the agency, this is useful, but now, well, it was creepy how she talked as if she'd been stalking me, Jane, and Henry.

Henry spent the academic year teaching music, and his fellow rockers were entrepreneurs, a doctor, a mayor, and a retired Marine from San Diego. When they got the platinum record for "He's Alive," a song which Henry wrote forty years ago and again recorded last year, it could have made news worldwide. Anyone could have tracked down the band, made the connection with Jane and Henry's last name, and since Jane's a well-known author and trouble-maker, she'd be pretty easy to find. Somehow, it all made sense.

"From what I've read, Jimmy pretty well had an entourage of willing women, and I believe he was an all-star when it came to romance. If you can prove you're his offspring, what makes you think that there aren't a dozen other half-siblings out there?"

"Because he only truly loved my mother," she said with a sigh and muffled a cough.

"That sounds noble, but from what I've read about the nineteen-eighties, love had little to do with procreation. Besides, Henry and a few of the guys in Slam Dunk have talked about Jimmy in passing, especially after that special on *Access Hollywood*. Henry told me something like, 'Guy was a wild man. Too full of himself. Last I saw of him, I gave him a week to get sober and find some rehab or he'd be out of the band.' Jimmy couldn't or wouldn't, Henry had said, and that's the end of story, or so I've heard."

There was a long pause and I would have sworn we were disconnected or her cell died, but I could hear a gulp and then a squishing sound, like she was blowing her nose. "There's no statute of limitations for murder, Ms. Dobson, and I have to know who killed my father."

Chapter 2

"Anyone who clicks on Google can find this out," I wanted to tell the caller. And yes, there was crankiness in the comment, which I blamed on the Playboy Payton encounter.

But instead, I took a long breath and realized that if I were trying to find who killed my biological father, which was highly unlikely since my biological mother refused to name him on my birth certificate, I would plea, bargain, maybe blackmail if that is what it would take to find the truth. So I listened. At least I could do that.

I looked up at the incredible blue sky, breathed in the smell of plumeria in the breeze, saw the swaying palms brought to life by the afternoon trade winds and thought, *Could Jimmy have been murdered? Why wasn't his body found? Did anyone really care after he disappeared, other than that woman, and only now?* But it was over. Old news, ancient history, well, at least ancient for that group of teenagers crazed then by bell bottoms and tie dyed shirts. Now? They were Baby Boomers more interested in their 401K and upcoming grandbabies than what had become of Jimmy March; the original bad boy of music, who in a blink, seemed to have fallen off the planet. Sure, there could be a cult out there that thought his disappearance was a government conspiracy, but I'm not even going to go there. You'll have to Google for that if you want more info.

Finally, I said, "Police take care of things like disappearances, kidnapping, and murder. I don't care or have time for something that happened three decades ago. For now, I'm on leave from the Bureau." Then I realized this woman was recounting March's fame, listing the novels, quoting his poetry, and I was thinking of quitting the career I'd spent ten years with.

"Shoot, who cares?" I muttered. In a split second, I knew the desperate woman cared. Deeply. "Okay, I'll listen with an open mind," I replied and was about to give a warning that I doubted how I could help, but she interrupted me.

"Henry, and now you are the only link I have with my father. You have a connection to the bands and musicians who played with him while he was in Hawaii. They'd never tell me anything and when I make inquiries, I'm treated like an outcast. My mother never came forward to claim paternity even after the seven years when he was officially determined to be dead." There was a long silence. Then she said, "How could she? Mother was Lanie Dupris."

The caller choked the words, waiting for recognition of the name. I didn't respond. The name meant nothing. She cleared her throat with a shallow cough.

"Mother's family used to own half of Honolulu and a major part of Hawaii, before statehood. Her family tree dates back to the original white settlers. When she met Jimmy, it was love at first sight even though she was already engaged to a distant cousin. He was a young businessman in Honolulu, and I think his name was Harrison Yu. Mother said she could never love him since it was always just a business deal, like a merger of two affluent families. Then her true soul mate came into her life, my father."

That made me stop. The Yu family, Payton Yu, et al. Would I ever get away from him? What were the odds, after all these years, to see him and then hear the family's name all in a matter of twenty minutes? This time, it was my turn for those steady breaths. I put Playboy Payton out of my mind and said, "Honey, you know that out of wedlock babies weren't anything new, even in the late eighties, and even in some circles today."

I knew privileged trust-fund debs who hung around *and* fooled around backstage listening to rock and roll certainly found themselves pregnant, just like the penniless groupies. Those same wealthy girls surely didn't have their children without lots of fuss from both sides of the family.

I formed an image of Lanie, a supposedly prim and proper child of Hawaiian old money, and the shock on the faces of family when she strolled home with a rocker wearing some psychedelic shirt and with unkempt hair. That is, if he really did look like the photos I'd seen of him. "Are you telling me because of true love that your mother threw over all of her social breeding for Jimmy?" Yes, that did come out as rude as it sounded.

The woman gulped. "I was raised in Switzerland and that's where I'm calling from. I'm standing here in the Geneva airport. My flight to New York, then Los Angeles, and finally Honolulu leaves in a few more minutes."

"Miss Dupris, save time and heartache. You can't do this on your own. Bring your mother. That way she can talk with Henry, the older guys in the Slam Dunk band, and anyone who knew Jimmy. She needs to tell the Honolulu PD the truth. All that she remembers and maybe even things she had heard about that night. They'll need to talk with her."

"That's not possible."

"Of course, it would be embarrassing if she's been estranged from her sister, your aunt, but sometimes we have to face down our fears," I said, thinking about how I was absolutely not going to attend the reunion after meeting Payton. And then I heard the hypocrite in me have the gall to say, "Yes, there are times when we have to do the things that are the hardest."

"You don't understand," she protested.

My laugh was brittle. "You might be surprised." I looked at my watch—the reunion dinner and dance started in three hours.

"Mother died two weeks ago."

I half expected her to stop talking. I wanted to express my condolences. In the Bureau, I had to do my share of that and while actually pretty terrible, I was good at it. When word spread to the other agents and my supervisor how "great" I was sitting with a victim or their family and telling the worst, I got elected. It helped that I was a Christian, they said, and as a Christian I knew they were right.

"Until a month before she died, she refused to mention my father. Now I know and I have to find out who killed him. You see, Ms. Dobson, Mother was in the dressing room with Jimmy, in the theater, right there in Honolulu on the last night he was seen alive. She heard the shot."

"Just yesterday, I was in one in those dressing rooms, and if someone came into kill your father—if he was your father—then why didn't he or she kill your mother, too?" Here's the deal. Picture a room so small, you'd have to go out in the hall if you want to change your mind.

"She wasn't hiding, exactly, she told me because she was getting dressed. Mother said she had been watching Jimmy's door and waiting for a groupie to leave. As the hussy strutted down the hallway, Mother slipped in to be with Jimmy. She was going to go away with him—he'd promised to make everything okay. They had plans. They would have made it work. Mother had so much love for Jimmy. She said they were soul mates. She just wanted to be his wife."

I could hear the muddled sounds of an announcement in the background.

"That's my flight, hold on so I can get my ticket out."

I waited and wondered: where *was* this going?

"There, okay, yes," she said and then returned to me as if there was no interruption. "Mother was eight months pregnant. She was a large woman, traditionally built like many who share Hawaiian blood. I was only four pounds at birth, so there wasn't much pregnancy showing. Our family would have disowned her if she had left Honolulu with Jimmy. It was because he wrote avant-garde novels and sang in bands and surfed. Mother said, 'Our difference in social status never mattered.' However, they did anyhow. Disowned her, disowned us. Grandfather saw me only once when I was in the hospital and called me a bastard. How can a grandparent call an innocent baby something like that? That's who he was, Mother told me, and never criticized him."

I could hear her breathing. I stayed quiet attempting to wrap my thoughts around how this woman and Jimmy's X-rated poetry and novels meshed. I'd read an online article from an ancient *People* magazine that he was reportedly stoned when writing most of his work. They said the writer's work was avant-garde and I remembered chuckling. Personally, I found the characters fascinating, but I didn't get some of it.

After a deep inhalation and she continued, "The night of the murder, Honolulu had one of the gusting storms that I'm told blow dash over the land. Mother said she was drenched to the skin just running from the car into the theater. Of course, she'd been hiding in the alley as she waited to be with Jimmy. Jimmy wouldn't even speak to her, she said, until she changed out of the soaking clothes—he called her his 'precious Hawaiian diamond.' He handed her one of the male dancers' shirts that he'd snatched off a hook in the dressing room, one that could fit over her baby bump, and told her to change into it. She said she was behind a changing screen in the corner of the dressing room as the door was opened and closed and then she heard whispers. How could she be found there? The publicity would have killed her father. She just wanted to go away and let the family make excuses of why she wasn't at the latest social gathering."

"And?"

The caller swallowed. When she talked again, that squeaky voice sounded dead serious. "Then there was commotion, a door busting open. There was a terrible bang. A gun had been fired. Then more screams. She flew around the screen, straight into the chaos. Jimmy was lying in a pool of blood. A pistol, a small one that looked like a toy, was next to him. Dozens crammed in the room. Everyone was shouting."

"Are you certain of this?"

"Ms. Dobson, please let me finish. I've been rehearsing what I was going to say to you for days. Mother was terrified, but she reached down and begged Daddy not to die. Daddy said something like, 'Go with the guys from the band. I'm going to be okay. Go now.' And one of the band, she didn't remember who, dragged her from the room. She was sure Daddy would call her, but she never heard from him again. Never saw him again."

"That's quite a tale you have. Why now, so long after his disappearance or death?" I longed to hang up, sip forever on one of those ice coffees that Jane guzzled prior to her pregnancy, or even if I could, throw out a bible verse like my cousin loved to. But I couldn't spout a verse or stop listening.

"It sounds mercenary. Money. I need it."

"At least you're honest."

"Mother was ill for years. Her heart was never strong. The Dupris trust fund took care of most of her medical bills even after the family disavowed any knowledge of us when I was born. I teach French and English at the same school I attended as a girl, but Mother and I barely made ends meet. Now I'm ill." The words came out flat, as if she was resigned to a death sentence. "I'm heading to Honolulu to plead with what's left of the Dupris family to continue the trust until Mother's final bills are cleared. Most of all, I need to find out who holds the copyright on my father's writing and prove that I am his daughter, his only child."

I wanted to say, "Good luck with that, kid," but said, "What is your name?"

"Diamond, Diamond Dupris. Mother named me Diamond because of my father's pet name for her."

"Ms. Diamond Dupris, I cannot make any promises. You're asking me to dig up ancient history. I'm staying at the Hawaiian Hilton and you can find me there. I'll ask a few questions, but honestly, please do not get your hopes up."

"Oh, thank you. I just knew you could help me. I have to hang up now, the cabin doors are closing. Thank you and God bless you."

A kidnapping gone wrong administered by Lanie's family or even the Yu dynasty? Or just a forever-under-the-radar-for-whatever-reason disappearance? Or a murder? Or bad odds while playing Russian roulette? Was the March Man dropped into some black hole? Where did the greedy little heiress and a wealthy family that seemed to be dripping with money fit in? And who was lying?

Holey moley. This sounded to me more like a Lifetime Original Movie than real life. Phew. Even without meeting Payton again and now being obliged to reconnect with dozens of Kukui high school grads because otherwise I'd be a hypocrite, who wouldn't have known me then if their lives depended on it and wouldn't know me now, my day was made.

• • •

I pulled my car up in front of the Hilton Hawaiian Village time share properties where I'd rented four suites; for me, Jane and Tom, Harmony and the dog, and another for Henry. Henry was close to Jane, but at least for me, she was best in small doses. I thought perhaps Henry might like a bit of breathing room, since Jane was even more high strung than when I first met her…and that says a lot.

I was walking through the lobby when I heard, "Not literally, but speak of the devil." It was Henry.

Henry's good disposition and gentle nature showed all over him and his ready smile was tough not to immediately duplicate. "You look exhausted, Nica. I thought this was a holiday?"

"The truth is, Henry, I'm conflicted. Jane's to blame." Not really, you understand, but it felt good to say it.

"Jane? Since she and Tom conceived that little one, she's become the energizer bunny. I thought she could run rings around me before, but now the girl never stops. What is this about, honey?"

"I'm troubled about two things, which are polar opposites. One? Am I totally crazy go to the dinner and dance tonight for my high school reunion? I'm inching toward forty, yet inside I often feel like that same geeky kid. Will I regret it if I don't go? Will I regret it if I do?"

Henry motioned me toward the lobby where there was a group of delicious, big red rocking chairs begging for us to relax. I sat down and could feel my breathing slow as I looked past the beach and to the bluest ocean on the planet. He rocked for a bit and knew I'd go on, I realized, when I was ready. Finally, I said, "When I was at the International Marketplace earlier this afternoon, I bumped into this guy, who happens to have been the superstar quarterback from high school and my senior class. He'd changed and yet, I could see that boyish part of him."

"Then go. You'll meet some others you haven't thought about since high school and gosh, you might even have fun. Remember what you told us when you finished the treatments?"

"Yes. I was no longer going to live with regrets. I was going to reinvent myself if I had to and choose happiness."

"So?"

"Well, he was the guy who spread the word about campus that I was one of those fast girls, you know what I mean."

Henry took a measured breath, smoothed the front of his Hawaiian shirt that shouted "tourist" and he looked like he bought it for that reason. Henry knew how to have fun. "Look inside you.

What would you tell that beautiful lady who is you to do if she were your best friend?"

"Are you always this astute? I'd tell her to go and kick butt if anyone was rude to her."

"That sounds like smart counsel. You need a date for tonight?"

"Date? Why, I rather doubt if I could find…oh, you mean you. Professor Angieski, would you do me the honor of attending what will be one of the most boring but soul-satisfying evenings of my life?"

"Thank you, Mrs. Dobson-Wainwright. I would love to." We shook hands and laughed.

"Now that this is settled, Nica, what else is up? I can see it in your face."

By now, we'd walked over to a coffee cart and with tall iced coffees in hand, we headed toward the beach. I slipped out of my sandals, as did Henry, and we stood in the shallow, warm waves and let the foam tingle our ankles. "I just heard from a woman who swears she's Jimmy March's daughter."

"Quite possible, wouldn't be the first, would it? So?"

"She's sure Jimmy didn't commit suicide, even though she doesn't know where he was buried. She seems certain that he was murdered."

"Hog wash," he sniffed.

"That's what I thought, too, but this woman knows more than regular people might. I could tell. She really believes what she's saying. She wants me to find out how Jimmy died—well, more honestly, who killed him and where he's buried."

"May I be the voice of reason? Have you thought what could happen if the Federal Bureau of Investigation got wind of how you may be interfering in a case that has long been buried? They might frown on what you're doing, especially since you're on medical leave."

"Henry, what do you believe?" I asked, dodging children dashing into the surf, then heading back toward the hotel. "What if I were to ask a few questions—which was all I planned to do? Could I sleep at night with Diamond fresh on my conscience if I didn't at least do that?"

"Yes, you could, but do you want to?" he asked.

"What is it called when Christians only come to the aid of another when it's easy?" I wondered out loud, wondering if I was in that group.

Henry nodded. "Convenient Christian. Be careful, will you, honey?"

"I'm careful."

"You are trained for investigations. Can you stop yourself with a few questions? Besides, who are you going to ask?"

I dusted the sparkling white powdery-soft sand from my feet. "Maybe I've been hanging out with Cousin Jane too long, but would you introduce me to any musicians who are still hanging around the Island—that is, those who may have known Jimmy March after you kicked him out of Slam Dunk? Maybe some will have a different view on what happened to the infamous March Man. Maybe he really did orchestrate his disappearance. Maybe he really didn't want to make Lanie Dupris his bride? Maybe others were after him? Will we ever really know?"

He nodded and shrugged. "I do know one thing…I'm still in touch with a couple guys from the old days who live in the Islands. But let's deal with that tomorrow because we're going to a high school reunion. Shouldn't I pretend to be your sugar daddy? Or I could be some foreign dignitary who doesn't speak any language that these folks could possibly know. Better yet, since you've got more money than you know what to do with, how about if I'm a gigolo?"

As we waited for the elevator, I gave my gigolo-for-the-evening a daughterly hug. "No wonder Jane, Harmony, and that little dog are nuts about you. You can make even my bad moods turn around."

"That's my job, honey." He chuckled.

Chapter 3

Have you attended your twentieth reunion yet? To call it "interesting" doesn't even cover it, does it? It's actually like being on the freeway, seeing a fender bender accident and watching the two drivers get into a fist fight. You don't want to look, but you know you have to.

Henry, my self-appointed gigolo for the evening, and I waltzed into the auditorium at Kukui High School arm in arm, as all good committed, even for the evening, couples should. The room felt about half the size as when I graduated two decades before. But instead of the senior-prom crepe paper streamers and tables with cheesy decoration, the place actually was decorated to look like a supper club, if one stretched their imagination. A lot.

A case on which I was assigned before the one Pastor Angieski nearly blew, a sting operation that took years to set up, was to investigate a talent agency in Vegas that bilked pretty little high school girls out of their parents' money. They even had pre-teen girls supposedly filming parts in a bogus soap opera to swindle more money, insisting if these children had just a bit more training they could be stars. Of course, the company sold this specialized training to the girls and their mommies and it certainly was not cheap. Back then, I'd been on more than my share of photo shoots and dumpy TV sets, and this looked just like one. We scribbled our names on badges. I placed mine beneath the square neckline of my little black dress and Henry's went on the lapel of his dinner jacket. Surrounded in a sea of aloha wear, we stuck out, and in this crowd, I was relieved to see I had grown up.

"Nikky? Oh, my, how you've grown. It's Nikky Ticky right?" A bald man, round as he was tall, pulled me into an embrace and I thought Henry was going to get in there, too. But Henry was agile and smart, taking three steps back. The man continued laughing and talking. "I would have recognized you anywhere. You look just the same, except I think you're taller. Oh, ha, ha, ha. You don't know me, do you?" The hulk kept his hand over his name badge, then pulled it down and grabbed me closer. "Eddie Munro. I was on the football team—okay, I warmed the bench, but I got a jersey. And I was on the team with your sweetie, Payton Yu."

"Eddie, my goodness. It has been forever, and to put the record straight, I've never been nor will I ever be Payton Yu's sweetie." I stepped back and God bless Henry, he took my arm. Mind you, Henry is about three inches shorter than I, but he's older and apparently Eddie respected that.

"Not what he's telling everyone." And he pointed across the room.

I could see his back, see him glad handing our follow graduates like he was running for election, and of course, there were a half dozen women around him, one with her arm over his shoulder.

"Steady, girl," Henry yelled over the band. "I'll get us something to drink. Sparkling water, as I remember for you?"

In the other direction, pulled away from the in-crowd, I thought I recognized a few of the kids in my nerd squad, and as I was about to head that direction, someone pulled my arm. "You made it," Payton said.

"Wouldn't miss this for the world. I can't promise I'll be at the picnic and the beach day this weekend, but since I was in town…"

He was wearing Teva sandals, dark slacks, and a white silk aloha shirt that played up the amber color of his skin. In my four-inch strappy gold high heels, I towered over him and that, honestly, felt good. His face seemed to be glowing, probably from the idol worship he'd just lapped up.

"You look wonderful, Nica." He gave me the once over, not like a piece of meat, which I expected, but like a human person. That was a first.

"As do you, Payton. Enjoying yourself, as always."

"As always? These are my people, you know. These were your people at one time," he said and looked into my eyes. For too long, actually.

"Lots has happened since high school," I replied and tried to break the spell, but in my heart, a tiny cloud of doubt formed. Had I, in my haste to leave all things troubling from my time in Hawaii, forgotten about the precious things I had learned?

As if, darned it all, he was reading my mind, he said, "You might find a piece of yourself if you hang out with us. Besides, there," Payton pointed, "is Skeets, I mean Brandon Breckenridge. He was valedictorian, remember? He's now a pilot for Hawaiian Air and he and his wife, Maggie—think she graduated a year after us—just started a shelter for battered kids even though they have three of their own. And over there? Remember Cords Mueller? He's a dad of six keikis, um, kids that is. Imagine having six little ones and he works for the Navy out of Pearl Harbor and married D'Sheila Walters, that girl he was always drooling over in homeroom and chemistry class. Ronda Yamaha is standing next to him, you've got to remember her. She was a cheerleader, the one that did cartwheels down the hall? Now she's a cardiologist at Queen's Hospital. Mini Pohaku, think he played guard on the team, yeah one of those guys who tumbles into everyone and he's still bigger than three of me, well, he took over the family child care business when his dad retired last year and the company's doing better than ever."

"Then there's you, Payton," I said, and since my cancer I try to always tell the truth so that *is* how it came out. The comment hung in the air. If Payton wanted to be rude, he could. I probably would have if someone had said that to me.

His lips moved into a crooked and charming smile. His forehead crinkled and he winked at me. "Yep, good for nothin' as always, Nikky. I think in the yearbook my title was: guy who would amount to *li'ili'i* or 'little' as we say in other official language of Hawaii—that is, English."

I happened to look across the room and there stood the two bodyguards from the earlier encounter. "Those guys must think you're important."

"Naw, they're here to humor me, but if you have about a week I could explain everything."

"I think I'll pass on that," I replied and started to turn away. Whatever Payton Yu had or had not done with his life in the last twenty years had nothing to do with me. I was going to find Henry and leave. Enough of the good old times. But that idea came to an abrupt halt because Henry was walking right up to us, with two glasses of something bubbly.

He handed one to me and reached out his other hand to Payton. "I'm Henry—"

"Henry Angieski, wow. *The* Henry Angieski of Slam Dunk." Payton shook his hand so fast I thought Henry's arm might be thrown out of its socket. "I cannot believe this. I've been buying your CDs for years. It was my sister, Alana, who turned me on to your music. What are you doing here?" Payton looked around and gestured at the high school auditorium.

"I was getting this lovely lady a drink," he said and then laughed. "You've got to be Payton Yu. Nica mentioned you."

And if you wonder, I wanted to sink right into the floor. Payton's ego didn't need to know that I'd discussed our meeting earlier that day and I actually saw the man's chest puff up a bit. Could this evening get any more embarrassing? Don't even ask.

"Me? She talked about me? Oh, sure I was taken aback when we bumped into each other, especially here in Honolulu, but of course she's here for the reunion." Payton slapped his forehead.

"She's here for a holiday, too," Henry said, and I felt my breathing regulate again. "I'm just happy to meet you, Mr. Yu."

Why on God's green earth was Henry being so formal with this smart aleck who could barely pass chemistry—and I should know because I was his lab partner. But he just kept it up.

Payton took a business card out of his shirt pocket, scribbled a number on it, and handed it to Henry. "Call me Payton. Everyone does. I know this is presumptuous of me, Henry, but if while you're in the city you could do me a huge honor, I'd be really grateful. Alana, like I said, is a big fan. Could I have a car pick you up and you could come to the house to meet her?"

Oh, goodie, the light bulb just went on. You see, since I arrived on the island and in my effort to totally relax and find myself for myself, I'd refused to watch any news programs or log on to MSN. But I'd seen the signs. They were everywhere. They screamed: Yu for Governor. Or: Make Yu Your Choice. Or: The People for Yu.

Alana graduated from Kukui High two years before we did. She was the perfect blend of geek and society charmer. She was striking with long straight black hair, big almond-shaped eyes, and true joy about her. I thought back about when I was a freshman. My adoptive dad was a petty officer in the Navy, and we'd just arrived in Honolulu. Me? I was sporting a very bad attitude as a thirteen-year old that was so smart she was attending high school in a place she didn't want to be. On the first day of school, when the dreaded lunch period arrived, Alana spotted me, came over, and I expected her to be rude, like the other cheerleaders were. Okay, like the entire student body of the high school seemed to me, but of course that was my insecure perception.

Alana walked up to me, put out her hand, and said something like, "Gosh, I love your red high tops. You're new, aren't you? I'm Alana. Come on, Nica. You have to have lunch with me and my friends."

You could have knocked me over with a palm frond. She picked up my cafeteria tray and together we walked not to the cheerleaders, but to one of the other cliques, if a science club can be a clique. Within four hours of hating Kukui High School, I found a niche, and while it wasn't easy being three years younger than everyone, it was because of her that I coped. Until she graduated, she always sought me out if I was alone and made sure I felt welcome whether she was hanging out with the cool kids or the geek squad.

I finally made the connection. Of course Alana was running for governor of Hawaii. She was smart, I heard she graduated with a law degree from the University of Hawaii, and went on to Stanford for a doctorate international business.

I realized while I was visiting Memory Lane, Henry and Payton had just made plans for a visit the next day. I didn't want to wrangle an invitation, but you can be sure I was going to ask Henry all about Alana when he returned.

"Come on over to the table, Nica and Henry. We'll make room." Payton motioned to where there was a gaggle of admirers turning to look and beckon him back.

God bless Henry. No wonder Jane was devoted to the guy because when he said, "Sorry, man, Nica and I have other plans. And we don't want to be late," I wanted to kiss his wrinkled cheek.

I couldn't read the expression on Payton's face, and remember I had tried to become a profiler. Maybe it's because I still saw him as an obnoxious football player. Yet, for a second, I swear he looked let down. Then it fluttered away and back came a broad smile. Probably disappointed because he couldn't introduce his new BFF Henry Angieski to his chums? That was my thought, too.

"Then tomorrow, Henry. Nica? I hope you'll let me take you to dinner while you're here in Honolulu," he said.

I racked my brain for a good excuse. *I'm having a yet another frontal lobotomy. Or, I'm on the next Mars mission and gosh, it leaves tomorrow*. And then out of nowhere came, "I'd like that, Payton." Honestly, it was all I could do not to throttle myself.

"It's a date then. You're at the Hilton, Henry said. I'll call you." With that, he shook Henry's hand once more and leaned forward to kiss me on the cheek, and I leaned into receive it.

It was official. I was smitten and bitten by the spell of Payton Yu. "Aloha, Payton," I managed but only felt the warmth linger.

Chapter 4

The breeze, the ocean, a view of Diamond Head, and a mug of Kona coffee should be the way to start every single day. I was in paradise. Actually Honolulu, but it's the same thing, right? I tried to chase away the thoughts the reunion. Not one of the kids I hung out with in high school was there. Do geeks congregate, except maybe at Comic Con and an opening of a new Apple store?

After sipping my seltzer and witnessing the anything-but-reserved chatfest with Payton, Henry and I escaped to Bubba Gump's at the Ala Moana Shopping Center to ingest enough fried food so the combined number on our cholesterol levels could circle the universe five times. Sure, it was yummy and Henry's company was so easy on the soul. He's one of those older guys you feel safe with and if he weren't involved with the flamboyant Geraldine English, Senator for California and ultra-liberal livewire, I might consider making a play for him. Okay, not really, but I love being around him.

Full disclosure? Henry couldn't stop talking about Payton. I wonder if they were already friends on Facebook? No big surprise there. Payton was a charmer. Yet for me? That charm wore off at the speed of sound, as I told myself.

The trade winds skittering around my lanai made the curls tickle my forehead, but tickles were better than not having hair, which was true when I was undergoing chemo. I looked down at my unpainted toenails and thought how my plans for the day were shaping up nicely. I was going to call the spa for a facial and pedicure for later that day, because as soon as the sun came up, I was headed for a long walk on the beach. Maybe a short swim or a nice time stretched out on one of those inflatable floaties. Nothing too strenuous. Then it would be straight to a lounge chair with umbrella, my e-reader to keep me company, and perhaps a nap.

Lunch? Poolside served by a handsome hunk. My biggest decisions would be whether to have a shave ice, an island treat like a snow cone, or stroll to the ice cream shop for something creamy and tropical.

If I were on assignment, I would be going over scintillating files like ten years of tax returns, financials, or cell phone records. I might be sitting at a stake out waiting for a crook to show up, my gun holstered and probably cutting into my hipbone. I would fluctuate between praying and sweating, and if others in law enforcement were honest, they'd say the same things, except those who don't pray, and then they would complain.

I closed my eyes. I sighed and thought about the pedicure.

Well, those *were* my plans. Even though I started my day with devotionals and thanksgiving, I should have remembered Proverbs 2:18 (Make plans by seeking advice) because I only had myself on my agenda. Should have known better.

There was a knock from the adjoining suite. I could tell by the rat-ta-tat-tat it was Jane and she called out, leaving the door open and not waiting for my response, "Cousin? You decent?"

"On the lanai, Jane. Get some herbal tea and join me." It wouldn't have done any good to stop the woman, especially with the determined pregnancy hormones kicking her nosiness up a notch.

She moved quickly, especially for a woman heavy with child. "You know, Nica, I can't get that gal, Diamond, out of my mind."

"Don't start worrying over it," I said, but in my mind I was poring over that phone call, too. "Maybe when she gets to Honolulu—if she does come—she'll forget all about me."

"You heard her voice. She was desperate when she was pleading with me. And besides…"

"Get the hotel phone, Jane honey, will you?" This came from Henry and from the next lanai. "I'm on my cell and can't grab it. The door's unlocked."

Luckily she was still standing because it would have taken her ten minutes to move from the lounge to get the phone. If there is one thing about Jane that people notice first, it's that she is not quiet. I could hear the conversation through the walls even if the door wasn't ajar.

"Felix, you sound awful."

The person named Felix must have responded because then Jane said, "That hacking cough makes me want to Lysol my cell."

Another pause before she said, "Sure, I'll tell Gramps, but he's not going to be happy. Besides who can he find at this late date to fill in on keyboard? I know that's not your problem now. Okay, well yes, if you're sick you're sick. You take care, Felix, and go to the doctor." All quiet, and then Jane gave the scoop to Henry, again loud enough so the neighbors on the floors below and above now knew that Felix had been hit him by some bug. A fever and nagging wife was going to keep him in Pittsburgh.

Henry stomped into my suite, obviously back from a morning run, because of the damp t-shirt and shorts. "Fiddle sticks. And cheese and crackers." He slumped into the deck chair. "Fiddle sticks again, my girls, what are we going to do? We can't just call in to the musician's union and get a sub."

"Do you know anyone here in the Islands who could fill in?" I offered.

He wasn't listening. "How in the world, for heaven's sake, can we find another piano player at this late date? We've got to practice—we're all rusty and we're on in three days." The words barely got from his lips when he stood up, eyes and hands raised heaven bound. He smiled. Then he gallantly bowed to me. Have you seen that picture of the Cheshire Cat in *Alice in Wonderland?*

Then you know exactly what Henry looked like, a dangerous look indeed.

"Oh, no, not me, nope, you said it yourself. Remember when I tried to jam with the guys when you did that charity gig in San Diego? I believe you managed, 'Stick to Mozart, baby,' as you choked on a gulp of soda."

"That'd never happen again, my girl. You just weren't prepared. You really do play well."

Have you ever seen a Cocker Spaniel with those huge pleading eyes? That's what Henry looked like as he waited for me to cave, which I did. "The only time I've been in front of a crowd was when ushering a protected witness into Federal court. What's wrong with Jane?"

You must see the irony in this. Jane was currently as comfortable as a hippo on roller skates. Of course, I would have never ever said this to her face and if you repeat, I will swear that you're pulling her puffy pregnancy legs.

"Oh, Nica, I love the idea," Jane gushed, allowing me to help her get comfortable in the lounge chair. "Sweetie, you've been a fan for how long? Forever. And I've heard you play the piano. You know the music by heart." She bounced up, as best as someone currently her size could and hugged me.

"I don't think I can." I tried to pull back, but if you've ever been in gale-force winds, seen a tornado on the Weather Channel, or attempted to get close to a display during a Nordstrom's shoe sale, all combined, that's what hit me.

Then Henry hit it fast and hard. "What about Matthew 18:22, missy? Didn't Jesus advise us to forgive seventy-seven times? Besides, I promise never to drink soda while you're playing. No wait, seriously, I was overtired that night. So how many times shall *you* forgive me? I'll stop throwing Bible verses at you if you'll just listen."

I flopped back in the lounge chair, folded my hands serenely on my lap and waited, after I finished what was cooling in my coffee mug. *This better be good*, I thought. From my perspective, I was about to make a donkey's backside of myself in front of thousands of Slam Dunk's fans just so the group didn't have to find another keyboard artist. Or that's what I was telling myself when Henry said, "Nica, it's a match made in heaven. You know the music, you know the guys. They will whine and fuss like a bunch of five-year-olds if they must play with someone they don't know. They're really a bunch of bashful old bruisers. They aren't regular musicians. They're geezers like me, grandfathers, and suddenly we've found ourselves to be hip again. You can bet we never thought that would happen, and we're all a bit shy."

Could you really protest after all that? What I managed was a lame, "Shy?"

I could see the runaway freight train that was Henry Angieski and he was just getting started. In my time knowing him and staying with Jane, Tom, Henry, and Harmony as I got through my treatments, he rarely argued and was superb at winning his point—whether it was what to have on pizza or how to decide on the charities Slam Dunk gave their profits to.

"Sure, you'll have to practice a bit and we won't get you to do that tricky number, the solo, but it'll work. It'll be fun."

"Fun? Besides, I'm not hip or cool or whatever the current word for trendy is." Yes, that was a wimpy protest even to my ears.

"Get something." He handed me his wallet. "There's money in it. Get some skinny jeans, you've got the figure. And a t-shirt. Maybe a long vest or something in black would be good with your blond hair, or—" He saw me cringe. "Okay, about a red or yellow or blue, you look good in blue."

"I'll help you, Nica." Jane was there with her iPad, already looking for coupons and sales. "This is the perfect solution. You need to get out of your FBI reserved personality mode, honey, and get back with the living."

"The living, breathing, pulsating crowd that will be at the benefit?" I shuttered.

Then, when I thought he'd pulled out his biggest gun, I watched as Henry looked down toward his sneakers. "No, you're right. This is too much to ask."

I jumped up and hugged the guy. "Guilt? You can do guilt?"

Jane was laughing, I was laughing, and Henry was already calling the other guys in the band to let them know the show would go on.

Half of me was terrified at the thought of performing in front of rock fans, even if they were plump Boomers revisiting their youth. But the other side, well, okay, truth be known I was excited. Yep, I was to be part of the band. Ohmygoodnessakesalive. What a hoot.

"We'll practice a few times, the guys will love having you there, and then by Friday night you'll be ready."

Sure, they were older men, "old codgers" Henry called them, and they could all lose ten or twenty pounds, but it would be thrilling. Never in my wildest dreams did I think I'd be playing with Slam Dunk. Yes, I was scared.

Suddenly, it was as if a jack hammer hit the hotel door. "Let me in, man. You have got to let me in. They're after me."

I jumped, and Jane attempted to rise from the lounge chair. So it was Henry who got to the door first. He laughed and pulled it open all the way.

"Henry—Jane—oh, hello, pretty lady." The man stopped and looked me over and after all the commotion of the morning I realized I was still wearing a short, Hawaiian printed bathrobe and my shorty PJs underneath.

"They're after me," he said, flailed his arms and circled the room, my suite, like he'd had a few too many cans of Red Bull.

I recognized him at once. We'd met the year before at Jane and Tom's wedding. Max Robertson was, by reputation, the best bass guy in the business, when he took off time from being mayor of El Centro, a lush farming community east of San Diego.

Everybody marveled at how he played; true musical genius, they said. Also a true pain in the backside with all the drama that he could dish at the group. I had heard this from Miss Pollyanna herself, Jane Angieski-Morales. I wondered how he ran a city when he couldn't even handle any relationships with women. I knew he'd never married, didn't play the field, but there was a quality about him that made him a chick magnet.

My mom would have described him as "a wiry little fella," and she would have been right. Max just a bit shorter than me and with quaking, nervous energy. He was quick, but apparently not swift enough to get away from whomever was after him this time.

In the instant it took Max to throw his body behind the heavy drapes, the hammering started again. I yanked the curtains closed and pulled a chair close to the window, trying to hide his form, as Henry opened the door.

A poker face I do not have, but I did my best to look as if I were sitting and chatting with Jane while studying images on her tablet so intently it could have melted the frame. As the door opened, the threshold was filled with the largest blond woman I'd ever seen, and trust me, I am a large woman, too. Her voice was hands-over-your-ears big.

"That weasel's here. Yep-er-ee, I can smell him. I'm going to wring his skinny his neck." This came out in a booming German accent, fist punctuating the sentences.

"Oh, no, he's mine—git outta' my way," said another blond who had apparently lost the elbowing match to be the first in the room. "All the way over here, Hilda, you promised I could get my fingers around his neck first. I was to git him before you. 'Sides, if anybody is going to teach that slippery scoundrel what happens when he tries to two-time an Alabama gal, it's going to be me," twanged the second with a bouffant style that was so big it could have been picked up by air traffic controllers.

As they bounded into the middle of the suite, Henry jumped back. The man wasn't a fool where angry women were concerned.

Jane whispered to me, "I know after a few adolescent and college age tangles with my own grandmother, who had Polish ancestors, was raised in the south, and was one of those steel magnolias, you just don't mess with a southern gal. If you did, you don't get away with it for long. I'm not budging. Better than TV."

If we were characters in one of those sitcoms, the canned laughter would have been echoing. The camera would be looking from the big, beautiful beauties to Max's foot that protruded out from below the drape. In that sitcom, you might see the camera pan to me attempting to cover the toes of Max's shoes. If a trade wind puffed into the room, it would be all over. Well, they would have been all over Slam Dunk's bass player, that's for sure.

Then the fuming stopped and it got deadly quiet as the women, in unison and as if again we were transported to some sitcom, looked at Jane, and dismissed her at once. Too pregnant.

They checked out Henry. Too straight.

Then, as if they'd just seen Goldilocks, they focused on me.

Have you heard the expression, "Their eyes could cut you to shreds"? There's truth to it. I was not getting involved in this, not by a long shot. "I'm an innocent bystander. Truly, ladies, don't misjudge the situation. I am no competition to you. And while I can understand your feelings—I've had a few go-rounds with men myself—you'll just have to be patient. He'll come out of hiding. Eventually." I got up, crossed the room, scooting the chair an inch back toward the curtain. Okay, I'll admit it. I found perverse pleasure in hitting a foot as I moved that overstuffed chair.

"Ladies, come. Sit down. My granddaughters and I are just planning our day. You're welcome to wait here for Max. He'll show up when he comes to his senses," Henry said. And with a straight face and sparkling eyes he added, "There's coffee, enough for everyone since room service provided extra cups, and we can all have a nice chat and wait together." Henry turned away because I knew he was going to laugh when he added, "Yes, we'll wait here for as long as it takes for Max to appear."

Hilda plopped down in one of the easy chairs and said, "Ja, thank you."

I swear she stared at the drape and I wondered if she saw it quiver. But after she blinked a few times, she said, "Max told us about you. So we came here. He is so handsome, but what a rascal man. Gloria here says so, too."

Gloria nodded, turned her full lips into a straight line, and paced between the drapes. Finally, she leaned against my chair and fingered the fabric covering their quarry.

"I would have given him everything," Gloria said, wiping a tear. "And that dinky slime ball couldn't even tell the truth. I'll fix him good and plenty if I get my hands on him." Absently, she bounced against the curtain, apparently not feeling Max's body collide with her shoulder. But then, I heard a groan. It was Max. I coughed, but heads turned my way and I left the chair. If Gloria found that Max guy hiding behind the curtain, I was not going to be caught in the middle of what could get ugly fast.

Henry patted the sofa where he was sitting and I sat on the edge. This was like being an actor without the other players knowing what could happen next and one part of me was anxious to see what would happen when the ladies sniffed Max out.

Picking up his guitar and plunking out the theme song from *Jeopardy!*, Henry said, "Max is quite the crafty guy, ladies, and rumor has it he can slip out of nearly any squeeze. Why, he could be anywhere in this hotel including sitting right under one of those umbrellas they're putting up on the beach. Why," he chuckled, "for all any of us know, he could be right behind a curtain in this penthouse."

Chapter 5

"The beach—yes, that's it." Hilda clapped her hands. "I'm going down there."

Gloria sprung up. "Not without me, honey. I'll check the lobby on the way and we'll make them open the bar. He could be hiding in there, under the counter, in a storeroom, and just maybe under a rock. That tricky rascal is around here." She sniffed.

And with that, only their syrupy perfume remained. The room felt spacious and quiet, like being in the eye of a hurricane. Still, Max didn't appear. Jane made sure the door was secure and then twisted the lock. "Who knows what they'll do when the latest goose chase ends without their amour in their clutches?" And she threw back the drapes. "As amusing at it might be, and trust me, I plan to make it plenty funny when I tell the guys in the band later today. Oh, Max, it's really useless to explain."

Max extracted himself from the drapes and I watched as he stretched. Now that he wasn't running scared, I really looked at him. He was in his mid-forties, I guessed, and had the chiseled features of a Native American with those gorgeous high cheekbones, much like I imagined on an Inca priest. Lots of jet black hair was conservatively cut and the aqua golf shirt was neatly tucked into tan Dockers. He was trim, like a cyclist, and with that underlying structure of well-toned muscles. He studied the toes of his conservative brown wingtips. "I swear that's the last time I'm going to get myself into…"

For some reason, even to my jaded but tender ears, he sounded slightly troubled by just how close his ladies had gotten.

"Come on, Max. You're just fooling yourself, because Jane and I don't believe you. Nica does not even know you that well and she's laughing," Henry razzed him.

Max flopped onto another sofa, but his feet kept jiggling. "It didn't get complicated until last night. Hilda and I had some fun in New York." He looked at me and added quickly, "No, not that kind of fun, just enjoying being together. It was only fun and fun was all it was meant to me with a little kissing, a little snuggling, nothing more.

"But then a nasty coincidence happened. Hilda's a flight attendant and was scheduled to be on my flight back from Washington where I was at a conference for mayors. I mentioned to her I would be here in Honolulu and maybe I laid it on a bit thick, like Slam Dunk couldn't get along without my superior musical talent, but it was all in good fun." Max turned to Henry.

Jane shook her head and held onto the baby protruding from her middle. "You see, Nica, my grandfather is even more straight-laced than me. And one day, Max's string of lady friends is going to be his demise." She turned to Max. "Oh, Max, stop looking at Nica. She cut her teeth in the FBI on deviants like you."

"Thanks, Janey, now Nica'll never fall in love with me." He pouted. "Yeah, I told Hilda Slam Dunk was playing here, told her we'd be at the hotel. Man, I never thought she'd really show up or that who else would appear on the scene? Gloria." He gestured, indicating her ampleness. "Well, Gloria accepted my offer to have a little fun, too. She was a passenger on the same flight, but in coach. We met as I walked down the plane aisle, just to get some exercise, mind you. I invited her to the hotel for dinner and to come to the concert."

Since it had only been after my cancer surgery that I had accepted Jesus Christ as my personal savior and only then started to read the bible, I didn't dare spout, "Proverbs 31:30." But it seemed to me that this guy Max summed it up pretty well with,

"Charm is deceptive and beauty is fleeting." Max was Jane and Henry's friend and fellow band member, so I simply didn't open my mouth, much as I longed to.

Max nodded to me, but continued straight into his flimsy reasoning to be caught in the cross hairs of two women seeking revenge. "Then it all started to fall apart. We went to that club, the Glass Slipper. You remember it, Henry?"

"It's a dive, Max, but we're all going to meet there after the concert, if you can stand to face the place again?" Henry teased.

"Yeah sure, but back to me, man. I nearly had a heart attack as they came in after one another. Thought this'd be the end of Mayor Max White Eagle Robertson, I tell you, but the club was so crowded I ushered Gloria to one side and settled Hilda at the other. Then I prayed for the best."

"You prayed?" Jane asked, blinking in disbelief. "Did you hear that, Gramps? Praise the Lord, this has to be a first."

"Yes, thank you, Jane, I do pray and besides, I'm not the heathen you picture. You and your never-at-a-loss-for-the-Good-News grandfather over there along with the band have been trying to convert me to a believer for most of my life. And you can praise God because some of it has worn off. The truth is, I thought I could get away with spreading myself between them. But when one of the guys in the band asked me to jam with them, and you know I can't refuse that, well, they both came up close to the bandstand. After the final set, the guys and I went back stage. And they followed me."

"And you've been running ever since?" Henry asked.

Max jumped up and walked a wide circle around the room. "I paid a taxi driver four-hundred dollars to drive me around all night long because I was scared to come back to the hotel. But then—"

"Okay, Casanova. Think we've heard enough," Henry interrupted the saga. "And stop fidgeting, man. You always make me nervous. Now listen up. I want to tell you something. Nica needs your help."

"Nica? What's wrong?" Suddenly all the mischief was gone and Max's forehead was a mass of wrinkles. The boyish charm had disappeared.

I knew that was a face I could trust, especially after what Henry had previously told me all about the guys in the band. I remembered that Max was the youngest, just a few years older than me. Jane thought of him like big brother or an uncle and had said, "He's a mayor right now with aspirations of becoming the governor, if he can settle down in his skin. And stop pretending he's the Brad Pitt of public servants."

Henry started the tale of Diamond Dupris with me and Jane interrupting to add more details until the story was finished.

Max tied, loosened, and then retied his shoes. "Don't get involved in this, Nica. Sure, you're savvy with crooks and criminals, have to be with the bureau, but I don't like the feeling. Yes, okay, granted this comes from a man who feels like a fox forced to ground by the hounds. But Henry is right. Wait, get those hackles down. I remember Jimmy March. Henry and your grandmother, Jane, were married and happy. I was this skinny high school kid who hung around hoping that Slam Dunk would let me carry their equipment. That's when I met Jimmy. We spent some time together. Never did understand his novels and his poetry stunk, but that's another story. Hey, you think I'm a wild and crazy guy? No way, I'm a regular Goody Two Shoes compared to that man."

"Henry and Jane have told me about your exploits, Max. Well, at least the exploits that happen when you're away from El Centro. You of all people should have insight on what motivated Jimmy March and caused his possible death. I can't turn my back on someone in need." I didn't realize until that second how strongly I felt, how involved I already was. While this was a far cry from the parable of the Good Samaritan, helping a Christian sister was something I knew I needed to do, if I were going to call myself a Christian. I stopped and wondered out loud, "Is Diamond Dupris a Christian?"

"Nica." Jane took my hand. "It doesn't matter. If you need to help, that's it." Then she turned to Max and tilted her head. "Max, if you do not help my cousin, I will blackmail you," she said in the sweetest little girl voice I thought possible and thought impossible coming out of pushy, assertive Pastor Jane Angieski-Morales.

"Two can play at this game, Janey," he said and then turned to me. "Jimmy March was bad news and digging up that time just seems like a wish for heartache for the woman who thinks she's his long-lost daughter."

I hoped my voice would come out calm and level, not the infuriated way it sounded since, as Jane says, I'm in touch with my softer side. "No, I will not. I cannot turn my back on her." I expected Henry to frown and Jane to question me. But they both had a look of approval and contentment.

Max grunted, slipped down into an easy chair, and slid lower, nearly disappearing in the folds of his clothing. For a long time, he fiddled with his outlandishly large watch. Or maybe it just seemed like a long time that he was mulling whether to put Jane to test if she'd blackmail him or my staunch position on helping a stranger. He flexed the fingers, but froze when we heard a knock. I had never seen a man dash into another room so quickly.

"Room service," came the voice from the other side of the door. We laughed and I nearly spit coffee all over my silky bathrobe.

I waited until another breakfast was placed on the table and wondered if Max was going to say more about the illusive novelist Jimmy March. Would he tell me the truth? Max was a good politician, maybe the last of the honest ones, Henry had said, but I had been around Washington D.C.'s movers and shakers and fixers, enough to know that they often preferred their own agendas over what others needed. Was Max this way? Could he lie?

Once the man returned and caught his breath, I asked, "Do you really know or have an itching feeling, or any other suspicions about what happened to Jimmy March?"

"Heard the gossip and I've got my theories." Max didn't look at me, jingling the change in his pocket before he leapt across the room, picked up the newspaper, flipped to what I could see as the stock market report, and ran a finger down the columns. His finger stopped and he smiled.

"Okay," Henry said. "Your investments can wait until you answer Nica. Sit down, Max and tell us your theories. Spill it, Max."

"Yeah, okay, Henry. As to Jimmy, well it all just seemed a bit too, well, fishy." His back straightened with the words and he cocked his head toward me. "Whole mess was just too odd. But, hey," he chuckled, "I'm the guy who reads lots of conspiracy theories. Besides, I'm suspicious by nature, and remember, two generations ago, my ancestors were living on the reservation without running water or heat, after being forced to accept the government's perfect relocation program that was to help the Navajo. Okay, honestly? Maybe I just wished something was up. Yeah, fishy, it seemed to me."

"Like maybe Diamond is right? Jimmy March didn't disappear, but he was murdered? So then, what happened to his body? If he wasn't dead, why go into hiding all this time? His last novel became an instant best seller after his 'death,'" I said and watched for any change in the size of Max's pupils and realized Max was watching me as I studied him. "Did the March Man stage his disappearance to gain that fame or escape the wedding altar?"

He looked away first and said, "Jimmy was doing some business with heavy hitters. I heard that he got roughed up a few times. Never really saw it myself, mind you, but I had a knack to hear gossip. Still do. But with Jimmy, I didn't know if it was drugs or gambling or just big talk. I never found out and truly, never tried very hard. I kept a low profile, since I was barely a teenager. But Honolulu was my home turf, I grew up here, and I just ate up that rock and roll stuff, even though my church-going mother said it would lead me to hell in a hand basket. Besides, I was a footloose guy, enough money in my pockets to make me happy, a gal on each arm, and the world on a string."

"The difference now is…?" I said, shaking my head, and I'm embarrassed to say that I started to giggle, imagining what might have happened if Gloria and Hilda had found him. "Well, except those two hunting you down right now while we're talking."

Max scowled and then laughed at me, a kind and honest laugh. Perhaps if he were younger or I were older…then this train of thought crashed when I remembered that Jane told me he'd been engaged five times and nearly married twice.

"The difference, my dear, is that I now know when things are unsavory. Even though I was a kid, going through the agony of adolescence, I knew better. Jimmy never did quite catch that drift, I heard. Rumors, right after the night that he disappeared, or was kidnapped or murdered or whatever, were that it was a hit man who got him. Or else, someone with a score to settle. Jimmy cared about people, most of them anyhow, but I've heard he sometimes cared for the wrong people and in the wrong ways."

Henry touched his fellow musician's arm. "You mean Jimmy March had enemies."

"You tell me. You seem to know as much as I do."

"How do you know all this, Max?" I leaned forward, wondering what other chunks of the puzzle Max wasn't revealing.

"Folks generally ignored me since was I was such a skinny, little Navy brat, whose dad was out on a submarine, surrounded by a bunch of honest-to-goodness real rockers with plenty of muscle lest I forget my lowly place in life. I was this twerp of a kid who somehow was accepted, yet they knew no one would believe any story I told about any of them. They said things in front of me.

Most of the stuff was way above my head, like insider talk about managers and club owners and who was sleeping with whom."

Henry nodded and Max continued, "I vaguely remember hearing Jimmy telling one of the dancers that she should let him know if anyone was asking for him. Then the accident happened."

"You were there that night?" I thought I'd heard all of his stories.

"I got out quick. There was so much chaos after I heard a bang, which I assume now was the gun being fired. I figured the police would eventually show up. I'm not stupid now and wasn't then. A stagehand sent me packing with the first dancer who would take five bucks to drive me home. Imagine what life would have been with that getting back to my mother if she'd learned I was frequenting a rock concert. A few days later, I went back to the theater and saw a few of the crew packing things up—since when Jimmy wasn't there, they cancelled the concert." He whistled and made his eyebrows go up and down like Groucho Marx.

"Did these guys say that Jimmy died? Or did they say they saw him running from a group of crazed women, like someone else we know? Seriously, do you know what's happened?" I asked.

"Don't know, but I came out of it a changed man, or boy, depending on who's telling the story. Yep, reborn you might say. No, I guess by that frown that's not something you'd say, Nica, but I did clean up my act and got serious about college. You might not remember, Henry, but Mom was on the losing side of her battle with heart failure. Dad was deployed. Sick or not, she was good with the guilt. You don't know guilt until you heard how my mama could do it. Guess I should thank that manager at the club. He thought it was better to drag me out of there before the police arrived than to have to relay to my mother that I was caught up in the incident. I just never told her I was there. She went to her grave never knowing."

"Who would know more about Jimmy and that night? Do you suppose the manager might still be alive? There's got to be someone. It's been a long time, but you stayed in touch with the musicians around here. Think, Max, you have to know someone," I asked after a long moment.

"There is this guy, but Nica, it's a long shot. Been a lot of years, you know. His name is Babes. Babes Waller. He's still here in the Islands, according to the grapevine. Last I heard, he was locked away in an assisted care center or nursing home, one of those old folks places." Max cringed. "He never could save a penny, the geezer. I've bucked those odds. Plan to be rich and old at the same time. Yep, investing in mutual funds, growing an IRA, watching the CDs increase in value. Got a good pension plan going with the city. Being mayor has its perks. And when you good people elect me as governor of our fine state, well, financial worries will be history." He snapped up the business section of the paper, rolled it up like a horn, and punctuated his sentences with it. "Want the name of my stockbroker again, Henry? Did you ever call her when I gave you the number last summer? Now I do a lot of e-trading, but she's good. Mighty sharp lady."

"What's the name of the retirement facility where Mr. Waller lives?" I asked, already tired of Max bragging.

"It's not a Hawaiian word, or even island sounding. It's Compton, no. Carlton Towers…no, Villas. Carlton Villas. Crazy how they give those places pretentious names when it's probably some flea-infested ghetto for poor unfortunates who didn't invest their money. When I'm sixty, with the investments I've made now—"

I turned to Jane and Henry. "I'm going to ask Mr. Waller a few questions and I'll be at the concert hall in time for the practice session. My heart will be in my throat, Henry, but I'll be there for you. And Jane?"

"What? I can't go with you to Carlton Villas. Sorry, but I'm meeting with the ministry staff for the Church on the Beach. I need to make sure that their permits are correct. And make sure they have my grass skirt ready."

"You're kidding, right?" I asked, but while Jane has been known to stretch truth to get a better effect, I knew it was true since she didn't laugh.

Max stopped telling Henry about which stock would secure his future. "Nica, if you need a man to help you make a decision on clothes for the gig, you just call me. Legs as long as yours shouldn't be covered. Hey, they should be registered as a lethal weapon against all red-blooded males."

I pulled down the bathrobe and headed toward the bedroom, but Henry caught up to me.

He whispered, "Nica, be careful. You don't need to save everyone just because you've been saved by our Lord and Savior. Does that make sense? You need to take care of your body and your mind right now. Where will it leave you if something goes wrong?"

I started to protest something about the Good Samaritan, but Henry hushed me as I said it. "Yes, I know. I have no jurisdiction here, I'm on medical leave, but I can ask some questions."

Henry was about the best Good Samaritan around. If that were really true, and I was being honest, why was he so concerned about me reaching out to help Diamond? No, she wasn't left by the side of any road to die, but she was in a pickle, had just suffered the death of her only parent and in need of financial help. Could I say no to this, even if, as my friend Henry inferred, it might turn out to bite me on the backside?

Chapter 6

Picture one of those dashboard bobble heads. That was me. "This is nuts," I said, pulling into the parking lot. I wanted to smack my GPS, but the address I'd scribbled down and then given to the device was the same. I sat there, staring at the front doors of Carlton Villas, because that was what the discrete sign did say, and then bobbling more. I asked myself, "How can this be the place?"

Max had said, "Babes is destitute." These digs didn't look like a home for the hard-up.

Max had told me, "Babes called me for money about three years ago. I'd just taken a wallop on my portfolio and still wanted to close on an office building that needed renovation, but when I got his note, the squiggling handwriting of someone who might have had a stroke, I sent my old pal a few thousand. Not a loan, mind you. How could he pay it back living hand-to-mouth as he does? Told him it was a gift for old time's sake. Last I heard from him."

Something had to be wrong, if what Max said was true. Was it true? He gave me the name and address, so why would he lie? There it was, staring itself in my face. The building was a three-story, ultra-modern affair, with a citified Hawaii-style that included flowering gardens of petunias cascading over balconies. Masses of well-trimmed, scarlet bougainvillea in king-sized pots shouted for attention as the palms swayed in the breeze and clusters of plumeria plants the size of oak trees perfumed the trade winds. Purple orchids filled terracotta planters that lined the path to the front doors. As the winds blew that morning, the rustling of perfectly manicured palms shouted the fact that this was no flop house for seniors. Oh my goodness, no.

I set the parking brake, withdrew the key, gathered my purse, and asked a groundskeeper if I was at Carlton Villas. "Yes, ma'am, that's what the sign says." He smiled.

I swept my palms over the front of my coffee-colored linen slacks to smooth out the wrinkles and tried to straighten my posture as well. I knew by putting one foot in front of the other, I'd be inside soon and this mystery would be solved. I'd get the info on Jimmy March, I'd share it with Diamond, and I'd play a benefit concert with a rock band. Just an everyday deal for a FBI consultant. Not.

If Carlton Villas was the "skids" as Max implied, I could only pray that should I find myself old and alone, I'd skid into the same set of circumstances. Dear old Babes Waller seemed to have skidded quite well.

As a consultant to the agency, I'd once headed up a fraud case in Florida involving nursing homes, care facilities, and group houses that didn't report the deaths of their residents. Rather, they buried the folks who had no family in the Everglades. Then, they'd keep reporting to Medicare that the residents needed various medical services, covered by our taxpayer dollars. It worked for about five years, until the sting in which I went undercover as a long-lost daughter busted it. Really sad. So, when I entered the grand foyer of Carlton Villas, I was thankful that there was none of that sweetly sour old-people smell. What I breathed instead matched that of a five-star hotel.

The front door opened and closed without a whisper and at once the receptionist looked up from filing her nails and balancing her cell on her shoulder. She smiled. Note: it was a genuine smile, not a sarcastic smirk. I liked her, or actually, I liked the woman whose nametag announced she was Tina. I nodded and stood discretely away from the front reception desk, waiting while

Tina whispered into the telephone. I turned and pretended to be intent on the oil painting of exotic villages that decorated the reception area. I wanted to eavesdrop on the conversation, but because Tina continued to murmur I gave up. It's the truth. Your taxpayer dollars fund programs and the bureau trains consultants to eavesdrop and there's an art to it that I never really picked up. Instead, I thought of Babes Waller and what Jane had told me before I left the penthouse.

The last time Jane had seen Babes, she said, was as a teen and attending some kind of rock revival festival in Chicago, sponsored by PBS. She told me, "Gramps and the band played before a performance by retro groups such as Peter, Paul and Mary. Slam Dunk hadn't hit the big time yet, but still all the profits went to charity and then the band founded the Slam Dunk Foundation." I already knew it provided care for children and adults who were terminally ill, whether that was housing, jobs, or outlandish wishes, much like Make-A-Wish Foundation does.

Jane explained, "At that concert, Babes had been there as a substitute drummer with another group that came on before the Slam Dunk. He'd been good, but even then they said he kept forgetting things, little things, like his music, that drove the band nuts. I remember Gramps taking one of the guys aside because they were teasing Babes bad."

I could only imagine because when I'd been backstage with Jane before one of the band's performances, the joking never stopped. Jane then said she'd heard Babes fell into tough times and Henry tried to find him, to give him a hand, but the drummer seemed to have dropped off the planet. "He was a good guy to me, Nica," Jane said just before I left the hotel. "When you see him, tell him I miss him and will visit as soon as that Morales kid makes his appearance." She patted her bundle of humanity.

Waiting for Tina to finish her marathon personal chitchat, I heard, "Oh, he didn't." And, "Who told him that?"

Tina smiled again, and apparently thought I might be tired, so she motioned me to have a seat. Babes had not been as imprudent as Max and Henry had imagined. Yet, then why did he ask Max for money? Why had he contacted Max at all? And for that reason, why hadn't Babes asked Henry or even Jane for it? The why, of course, was that he wasn't in financial jeopardy by any stretch.

"You know about how complicated families can be, and I come from a *big* one," Tina explained, replacing the receiver. "So sorry to keep you waiting."

Now that I looked at the young woman, she was shockingly stunning and with Chinese and possibly native Hawaiian ancestry. I thought of Diamond Dupris. Would the woman whose father was the novelist and gadabout musician and mother who was from a respected Hawaiian family be as lovely? I guess I was staring because Tina cleared her throat.

"Babes?"

"Ma'am? No, babies here. Just old folks, really old ones, older than you. Oops, that didn't come out right." She giggled, looked horrified and then concerned for me. She came around to the front of the desk as if to help me to one of the guest chairs. She was dressed from head to toe in black, and about as big as a minute.

"Oh, no, not babies. Not women. I would like to visit with Mr. Waller, Mr. Babes Waller, a resident here."

"Ohhhh, I am so sorry." Tina laughed, producing a million-dollar smile and a voice like trickling water. I liked her even more. "Let me see which campus he's in and his suite number. They just made some room transfers this morning." She pulled up information on the computer, ran a manicured finger down the listing that was in front of her, and said, "New program, although all these changes make me crazy. Oh, don't misunderstand, I like it here…gosh, who wouldn't, at least until I can get a toe in at the TV station. I'm going to be a news anchor."

Tina had me sign in using an electronic keypad. She waited as I hesitated next to the square, asking my connection to the resident I was visiting. "Are you related to Mr. Waller? He's not to have visitors who aren't related because, well, he can get a tad upset at times."

"It's really vital I speak to him," I replied and if I hadn't been on medical leave, this would be the time that I'd pull out my badge. "Does it help that this visit could involve something that the Yu family needs to know? I was just talking with Payton Yu yesterday." Yes, I had just used Payton Yu's connection and inferred that Payton wanted me there. So what if I was about to get the truth of Jimmy March's death? Besides, what good are enemies if you can't use them, right?

"The Yu family? Payton Yu?" she said, and seemed impressed. "Of course, and why didn't you say so? Did you say that Mr. Waller was something like an uncle?"

Tina had been friendly, but when I mentioned the Yu name, she practically sparkled. I didn't realize they had that much clout. "Like an uncle? Yes, yes." Okay, if that works, I'll get to visit Babes.

Tina handed me a visitor's badge, picked up the phone again, asked for a concierge to come to reception and at once a young man in a crisp gray uniform came through a set of doors behind me.

The man made practiced small talk while keying an entrance code, then he escorted through the halls. Yes, I did mentally make note of the code. I didn't plan to come back when the coast was clear or anything, but old FBI habits die hard. I couldn't help but wonder at the plush royal purple carpet muffling my steps, the original art on the walls, and the conversation nooks complete with antiques, or at least excellent reproductions. But it all looked surprisingly real.

The staff members were fashionably dressed in business casual attire and the smell of a scrumptious lunch wafted through the hall. Roast beef or chicken? I felt my stomach rumble, but I wasn't there to eat. Instead, I needed a hearty meal of information.

If the opulence of this place meant anything, Babes's problems didn't involve money, even thought he was kept behind locked doors. We stopped in front of another carved set of doors. The attendant keyed more numbers, which I memorized, and the door unlocked.

"Please take a seat, ma'am," he said, motioning me to one of the sitting room's overstuffed chairs. Within moments, Babes came in and I recognized him from the old photos Jane had once showed me.

"Hello, Babes. It's Nica. I'm Jane Angieski's cousin. I'm Henry Angieski's niece." Well, sort of and that was easier than second cousin on my biological grandmother's side, right?

"Jane—my little flower. You're still as beautiful as..." Babes said. His faced glowed and he tried to finish the sentence again, but stopped with "as."

"Babes, I'm not Jane, but she asked me to visit you," I said.

Whether or not he understood, he reached out and pulled me into a bear hug. I bent down to the man in the wheelchair and realized this was going to be okay. This was going to be a cake walk compared to the interrogations I have done, but it was the first time I had asked questions, albeit unofficially, since my cancer treatments.

Babes pulled me closer. The arms trembled, but his grasp was shockingly strong on my shoulders. Then he pushed me back to look me up and down. A city street map of wrinkles were etched into the ancient, milk-chocolate colored face. The skin from his chin rested on the collar of his open necked green golf shirt, and the once bushy eyebrows, that Jane said where his trademark, were now sparse wild gray hairs each with an agenda of its own.

"Seems you've got a good life here," I said, looking around. Tchaikovsky played softly in the background. Arrangements of hibiscus in shocking yellows and reds were displayed here and there, and a baby grand piano waited for attention in a corner of the room. The furniture looked like it had come from ads in *Town and Country* magazine and was nicer than the pieces in my condo in Washington, D.C.

"Yeppers, but these digs jest temporary, girly, as I'm headed back to the road next week," he replied, patting my hand vigorously, almost like if he stopped that action, I would disappear. He didn't attempt to lift himself from the wheelchair and an attendant pushed him over to a corner so we could sit. Then his eyes hazed over and the ability to talk with me vanished at the same time.

"Going to play in Atlantic City. New group forming there. Called me the other night. Asked all pretty like if I come down. Going to strut my stuff all around the eastern seaboard. Maybe a tour, even. We'll really make hot music. Yessiree, got the call last night. It was from Buddy Holly, the man himself, asking for me and my drums."

I scooted a chair closer. Could he remember an event that happened years ago if his mind had gone so far as to think that a rock great from the nineteen-fifties was alive—and would settle for a so-so drummer?

"How are they treating you here?" I knew enough about Alzheimer's not to try to upset patients with the facts. No need to burst a bubble or insist that Buddy Holly was singing in Heaven, that he'd died in a plane crash in a cornfield in Iowa decades before.

Babes chuckled. "Treating me?" His belly jiggled, like he relished secret joke. "After every gig, you'd never believe it, honey girl, well that little guy who's in charge of the bell hops, yeah, you saw him, he takes care of me, all personal like. All the time like he's assigned to me alone. And never once complains about bringing up the drums from the limo downstairs, never once does he say nothing. He's a saying, 'Mr. Waller, it's my pleasure to serve you.' Serve me? I like that guy. Wants to get into music someday, he says. Yes, he says that. Says he can sing. Told him just yesterday that I'll call some friends, my agent and people at RCA Records. Get him to record a demo and I'll pay to have forty-fives sent out to the rock-and-roll radio stations. But he won't hear nothin' about it."

It took me more than a moment to figure out a forty-five wasn't a gun, but you know my background. Just for history's sake, at one time vinyl records came in two sizes; forty-fives, about the size of a sandwich plate, and seventy-eights, about the size of a dinner plate. "You're a good man, Babes."

"They're all pretty nice kids for hotel folks. No, this ain't the Ritz, but it'll do." He waved his hand in the air.

Yes, this wasn't the Ritz, but it was the right place for Babes.

"Yep, Jane. The hotel workers are mighty kind to this rocker."

"Babes, my name is Nica. I'm Jane's cousin." I tried to look into his brown and glassy eyes, but I could tell that it would be easier to pretend I was Henry's granddaughter, especially if I wanted to know about Jimmy March and the old days.

"Listen, Jane, I just give them a buck tip and they take notice. A silver dollar is still big money in this part of town. Yep, that's why I keep these silver dollars in my jacket pocket." He handed me a red bingo chip from the handful he had extracted while talking. "Here's one for the subway ride home. Honey girl, you need two?"

"Money…" I murmured and took the chip and twisted it in my fingers. This visit certainly was about money and the mystery of how a down-on-his-luck drummer with Alzheimer's disease was living in the lap of luxury.

"Been in swankier places, but it'll do. For now."

I held his hand and said, "Yeah, it's a good hotel. You're a blessed man."

"Amen, Jane. Hey, you see that wild cat Henry anymore? He was always asking where you were. Never seen a grown man act more like a protective mama than Henry. You remember him at all, Jane? It was a tall, white guy, played guitar in a band. Thought he could play the drums, too? Can't remember what that skinny guy's name was who replaced me, but Henry said soon as I got my drinking under control, I'd get my old job back. Henry's a good man. If you see him again, you tell him I'm not drinking none now. I'm AA-ing it. I'm reformed. You remember Henry? A tall guy with blond hair? You remember him at all?"

"Henry is Jane's grandfather, Babes." It sounded like I was talking to a child, and in some ways, he was. Perhaps, he'd always been. It hurt to know that this was no longer the Babes who had treated my cousin like a princess.

Once, when I was recovering from a treatment, Jane and I flipped through old photo albums. She got a faraway look in her eyes and had said, "Babes taught me to play poker. Pretzels were the stakes. But within one week, I was beating my teacher and he wouldn't play anymore. I remember vaguely, just a child at the time, the smell of 'cough medicine' on his breath and so did the bottle that he kept in his back pocket. And then he was out of the band and out of my life."

"Sure, sure, I remember, Jane's grandfather." Babes's eyes fogged and his chins sagged. All three. He stared into memories I couldn't see and his eyes blinked and then closed.

I watched his chest go up and down, hoping when he opened his eyes, we could continue. Yet, as I touched his hand, he flinched and yanked it away as if I'd hit or he'd touched a hot stove. When he looked up at me, he didn't know me. However, it was as if he were gazing right through me. A tear slipped down his pleated cheek. Then another. I reached up and he allowed me to blot them with a tissue I'd fished out of my purse. This time, Babes didn't flinch. Whatever had made him cry was not going to be voiced to me and that was even more heartrending because I could not comfort him.

A long minute stretched to three or four and I waited. I just prayed Babes would be returning shortly.

In the adjacent dining room, I could hear the sound of flatware and plates being divvied out. Now I heard Broadway hits coming from the sound system that was piped through Carlton Villas. I watched as other family members started congregating in the visiting room to share a meal with their loved ones. And I waited for some flicker of recognition from Babes.

He blinked, sat upright, and his eyes cleared. Now was my chance, now or never. "I thought of a friend of ours the other day," I began slowly, falling over my words. "Yes, Henry and I were talking about him." I prayed for direction and this was not the direction I anticipated but it was the best I could do. "It's someone from the past."

"Hey, I 'member the past good, honey girl. Do I know you?" he asked, squinting and rubbing his eyes.

"I'm Nica. I am Jane Angieski's cousin and I'm visiting you."

"Janey. Sure. I know who you are, Jane. And say, just look at you. You're a pretty girl."

I was not going to correct him again and lose the possibility and reason for my visit, so I just nodded.

"You met somebody? Who? Was it one of the guys? The guys from the old band?"

"Jimmy March."

"Noooooo." It was a long drawn out and painful moan of a word. Babes's eyes didn't move from the folds of his belly. We both watched it rise up and down.

Chapter 7

"That's right, Babes, you remember Jimmy March." I tried to calm my voice as if I were calming a panicky witness to a crime. "I am certain if Jimmy were here, here in this room with you, he'd be putting a new act together. I love his music, especially now that they're on CDs, um, records, forty-fives and seventy-eights, I'm sure."

"No, no, no, no," came in labored, anxious puffs of denial. About what, I didn't know, but was the "no" edged with fear? Or was I suffering from an over-active imagination and having withdrawals from being on active bureau duties? The circle of his mouth, as he said the word, still lingered in a huge, quivering oval. Did his eyes grow with alarm or was I jumping to conclusions again?

I smiled and calmly said, "Yes, Jimmy March. I bet he's got contacts in clubs, like those in Vegas. He's as famous as—" Suddenly, I couldn't think of any rock stars that Babes might know. Then "Love Me Tender" came on the elevator music that was being piped into the room. "As Elvis Presley."

"No, no, no." This time he was not moaning and he was not quiet. He yelled. Visitors and residents stopped their conversations and stared. Sounds from the dining room stilled. No one was breathing, including me.

"Hush now, Babes. It's okay," I cooed and patted his knee, afraid that the staff would kick me out for harassment.

He smacked my hand away. Then he stopped with his beefy fingers in midair. Babes looked across the room and I tried to follow his gaze, but in the next instant the buttons on his golf shirt took all his attention. He twisted them so tightly I was afraid they'd pop off and then noticed two were already missing. He started on a surviving one as a gentle-faced nurse who was talking with a patient sitting at another window looked our direction. She smiled at me and nodded as if to say, "That's why he's here," and that Babes's outburst was expected. The noises from the dining started again and visitors went back to their quiet, soothing conversations. Babes just buttoned and unbuttoned his shirt. I started to breathe and waited. But not for long.

He craned his neck forward, looked both directions, and finally whispered, "Jimmy's gone. Guess you didn't know. Guess you didn't read it in the paper. Sorry to have to tell you…most of them are gone. All gone."

"Yes, I knew he died."

"Gone, all gone," he repeated as if he were convincing himself.

"You do remember Jimmy March?" I spoke quickly, so I wouldn't lose Babes to the memories he was silently chewing on as if they were a wad of gum.

"I saw him lying there." Babes's eyes cleared and the triple chins wiggled. He shuttered.

"Where did you see him?"

Again in a whisper and only after looking around the room, he said, "I saw the blood. Plenty of blood, too. Red and sticky." He trembled to the point that the wheelchair wobbled. "I touched it to make sure it wasn't catsup. Guys were always pulling pranks on me. But this time, it was different. It was the real deal."

I whispered the next questions. "You did? You saw blood?" *Now the truth, or never*, I thought.

He grabbed my hand and squeezed the fingers hard, and said, "Dead. But don't you go and tell nobody. They said not to tell you, not tell nobody and I never did. I seen it was him dead. I practically seen it happen—well nearly did." Babes released my fingers and then wrung his. He pushed up and tried to get out of the wheelchair but flopped back in the seat. He kept saying, "Don't tell. Don't tell. Never tell," as he massaged his bulging, arthritic knuckles.

I watched him relax and I smiled and nodded until he looked at me again. "Babes, you can tell me about it, about when you saw the blood. You can tell me since I know all about Jimmy."

"Well, cuz you already know. I guess it's okay. But I was afraid, let me tell you. Heard the shot, too. Loud."

"Did you see Jimmy fire the gun toward his chest?"

Anger exploded. "Who told you that?"

I'd seen Alzheimer's patients become instantly violent as if something just pops inside them, and I prayed I hadn't pushed Babes that far. Apparently, my mouth hadn't caught up to my brain because then I said, "Everyone says Jimmy killed himself."

He pushed his hands into his cheeks and then covered his eyes as he said, "Never seen so much blood," like he was reliving it. Then he turned toward the window.

"Babes? Did Jimmy shoot the gun at his chest? Was he playing Russian roulette? Was Jimmy holding a gun?"

"I hear the phone. Who are you? I'm waiting for Buddy to call, you know Buddy Holly, right? He's the greatest, man, the greatest. We're planning a gig—going to L.A. Yep, Buddy Holly. Would you ask the bell captain or the clerk at the front desk if that call is for me?"

"No, Babes, it's for somebody else. I just saw the woman over there getting the call. It's not for you. Besides, I have a few more things I want to talk with you about. Babes?" I was too late. His eyes had glassed over and his chins sagged. Even the button, which had held his interest, was forgotten.

I lifted his hands from the handles of the wheelchair and folded them across his belly. His cheek was cool to my touch, but his breathing was slow and even. I bowed my head, rested my hands on his fingers, and did something way out of the Old Me character. The New Me whispered, "Heavenly Father, please care for Babes. He's a good man. He was good to Jane when she was a kid. He needs you now, Father. Watch over him and be with him as he plays his final songs. In Jesus name I pray. Amen." Out loud I added, "Good bye, Babes," and kissed his wrinkled cheek.

. . .

Slowly, I returned to the reception area thinking more clearly than ever how not one of us knows the number of our days. The years are kinder on some than others. My adoptive parents, in their late forties when we became a family, had been gone five years. Babes, I thought, must be about Henry's age, but life hadn't dealt him an active body and a clear mind like Henry.

I tried to focus on what I knew, rather than the tough things that can happen to people. Babes said Jimmy March was lying on the floor and there was blood. But can one with dementia lie?

In case you hadn't noticed, I'm always suspicious of people. It is my job, or at least was my job. Bad things happened to musicians and flamboyant novelists like Jimmy March and out of loyalty or fear, Babes could have been told lies then and now believed them.

I slid a finger on the edge of the reception area, waited, smiled, and waited. I needed a bit of breathing space and Tina obliged, again eyebrow deep into a personal phone conversation. After a few moments, I coughed quietly.

Tina beamed at me like an old friend, a friend who understood that a girl had to make personal phone calls; and chatted some more. And frankly, I didn't care. But then, I whispered, "My adopted uncle, Babes Waller, seems to be doing well. He was glad to see me."

The receptionist held up her index finger and said into the phone, "If I go to that club, will he be there? Are you going to wear that halter again? Okay, yeah, someone's here and I need to go. Later."

Tina finally gave me her full attention as I lied, "Since I live on the mainland and it's impossible to visit regularly, I wonder if you could tell if he has other visitors? I just want to make sure he's not lonely."

The receptionist's was still excited and a bit squeaky from her clubbing plans. "Mr. Waller. He's my favorite resident. He's like this big old teddy bear. Before I started here at the front desk, I worked part time with the caregivers. I'd turn on the music at night and he and I would dance. Yes, he can walk, but chooses not to…or some of the nursing staff say he forgets how to walk, from time to time. And when I work nights, I sneak away from the front desk and talk with him. He gets lonely at night, just like me. I like to hear him play the piano. Sometimes, well, you know, sometimes he forgets how to play and just bangs the keys." She laughed again, a gentle sound that told me oodles about her kindness to Babes. "Sometimes, he plays the same song over and over. I can handle that for about twenty minutes and I'm out of there." She stopped abruptly and covered her mouth.

"I assume the costs of his, ah, residence here is still covered by…"

"Apparently the company that owns the facility gets regular payment or he wouldn't be here, that's for sure," she said with so much force that there might have been problems with other residents. But I was here just for information about Babes.

Tina didn't seem at all troubled by her honesty, picking up her cell and looking anxious to make another call. Yet, since she was used to being with "old" people, she was a patient woman with me.

Tina offered, "You'll want to talk with Mr. Quinn. Oliver Quinn. He's the manager. Would you like me to see if he's available?"

I nodded. I was about to meet the manager of the care facility as Babes's loving niece and since was my first visit ever, I was a darned neglectful one.

It took barely a minute before the door marked "Private" swung open. Oliver Quinn appeared.

Tall, lean, and tan, he looked exactly as if a Hollywood movie producer had cast him to play a professional administrator. He even had a goatee and the perfect amount of gray at his sideburns.

If he were part of an official investigation, I would put his name to the "not to be trusted" category. He had that look and I had to force down my FBI training because I hoped he'd tell me how Babes Waller was able to live in such a luxurious situation when what I heard was that the elderly man didn't have two pennies to rub together.

He smoothly chit-chatted about the weather, producing the brightest teeth outside a toothpaste ad, and I realized that he'd had plastic surgery or at least Botox. His face just didn't move like a normal human.

With the smallest gesture, he ushered me into his office and with a whisper, the door closed.

The man was first-rate at his job. As much as I wasn't comfortable there under these circumstances, false ones, he gushed graciousness, offering me coffee, then a tropical fruit punch or water. There was a hint of a South African accent as he said, "My, my, so good to finally meet you, Miss Waller." He licked his lips as his moist fingertips again touching my hand.

He stepped behind his desk, but waited for me to sit first. Time to correct the Waller/Dobson connection and while, to some, not telling all the truth is as bad as lying, you've already recognized that I'm above saying things to get the information I needed. Besides, Diamond's future depended on me and perhaps whatever information I could extract from this superficial guy now sitting behind the maple desk.

"Dobson, my last name is Dobson," I corrected and I wanted to say, *I've come here to get information about a death Babes may or may not have witnessed back in the nineteen-eighties. I didn't know he'd lost his memory, but what he told me might have merit. And now I want information as to who was paying his bills.* Yes, that's what I would have said if I had a badge on my hip and the sanction of the Bureau.

I racked my brain for some method to say these things when Quinn broke the ice. "Ms. Dobson, thank you for clarifying that. Let me assure you, it's been a pleasure to serve your uncle's needs all these years," he said.

"He seems contented for the most part," I replied, wondering if Babes often had outbursts like he just had with me, when I asked him about the past. I honestly doubted Mr. Quinn knew about Babes's behavior, or that of any of the other residents. I'd give good odds to the fact that he rarely, if ever, entered the residential portion of the building. "He seems to be doing well, considering. But I'm troubled, really because, well…" How did one ask if her "uncle" Babes was a donut short of a dozen? "How is his, well, his…"

"Memory. Of course, in cases like Mr. Waller's, memory challenges are hard to confirm without a full medical work up, which we can do at any time, if you'll just sign some forms and give your approval," he added as dollar signs flashed in his eyes.

"No, I don't think that would be necessary, unless the doctors feel it needs to be done." Who in the world was I to manage Babes's care? Yeah, I knew the answer, too.

"He is content, and like many of our guests, he prefers to live in days gone by."

"What about those memories, Mr. Quinn? Can he remember, say, when we were much younger?" I asked, and as much as I hated it, my voice sounded petulant and childlike, even a bit whiney. I clasped my fingers to look demure, which was tough for me because I wanted to blurt out: "Okay, Quinn. Let's have it. Can Babes remember being at the scene of Jimmy March's murder or suicide—depending on which story one wants to believe?" But of course I couldn't and wouldn't say *that*.

Mr. Quinn's smile was sugarcoated as he purred, "Your uncle's long-term memories seem to be excellent." He turned slightly and keyed something into the laptop computer. "Yes, Barnabas has been with us for awhile. Just a moment, okay, yes, here is Mr. Waller's file.

"Barnabas." I said it out loud and it almost came with a snap. "He's called Babes, Mr. Quinn."

As if I hadn't even spoken, Quinn continued, "Unhappily, Ms. Dobson, his short-term memories are often foggy. You understand at his age, the treasured memories we have are the ones we are able to revisit, but the daily ones for the moment are often lost. As family, I'm sure you're aware of it."

"So could he recall when I was young, perhaps when I was a girl? Could he remember the people we both knew? Could he remember incidents that happened, say thirty years ago?" I asked and counted to ten to curb my excitement because I was this close to demanding: "Could Babes be telling the truth about how the novelist died and about that pool of blood?"

"Most likely, he can recall when you were younger, yes. But please be aware that I'm talking from an administrative capacity." He repositioned the fountain pen set on the corner of his desk and leaned back in the leather chair.

"And from a medical viewpoint?"

"Naturally, you'll want to know that, since you're his niece. If you'd like to speak with his physician, Lillian Lamont is in on Fridays. She can give you the immediate physical diagnosis. We have everything here in the file." He patted the laptop in front of him. "However, it's our policy to have each physician discuss the condition of residents personally, with their next of kin."

Quinn flipped open his gold trimmed, leather-bound daybook, and looked at his Rolex as if checking to see whether he could spend more time on this family member. Then he said, "Oh, yes, right. Dr. Lamont is here from ten to five on Fridays. We schedule weekly appointments with the physician. Shall I e-mail her and ask her to set up a personal appointment? Or perhaps you'd like to talk with our resident psychologist? She's here Wednesdays. The physical therapists visit Mondays, and the various therapy and activity groups assist our residents on the other days, including volunteers who bring in children and babies. Our residents especially enjoy the entertainment from a juggler to the magician and especially Dr. Funny Fingers, a big burly clown of a man. Sundays, we have nondenominational services as well as Mass. Our Jewish, Buddhist, and Islamic residents have services, too, of course. It's an active schedule, but I'm won't bore you. I'm sure you know all this from…"

He waited. He seemed to expect me to fill in even more about the wheelchair-bound musician. He had all the records on the little computer screen in front of him, but unless I dashed around to the back of the desk and knocked Quinn to the floor, which would have honestly delighted me because of his cheesy, ingratiating smile, I wasn't going to see it from where I was sitting. Hence, no way was he revealing who footed Babes's bills.

Was his unfinished sentence a ploy? A test? Did he suspect that I was fishing for specific information or that I wasn't some distant relative to the aging musician?

I looked down at my fingers. God help me, I thought, and then words sprang from my mouth. Maybe it was a Heavenly Nudge. "The trust."

From the smile that just slightly tipped the corner of his perfectly Botoxed mouth, I was on target. "Yes, the trust," he repeated. "As I'm sure the attorneys have explained, we keep the trust informed of Mr. Waller's condition and specific needs.

I assume that the trust informed you that Mr. Waller is being included in a drug trial of a new memory-enhancing medication that has been extremely successful already throughout Europe. From the notes here, it seems he's becoming more active, asking to play the piano, and even making conversation with the staff."

"As his 'adopted' niece," I started, and yes, the word "adopted" did sound like there were quotes around it. "I'm not informed as to the day-to-day business the trust does, so I appreciate your update, Mr. Quinn."

I was about to ask more about the trust, such as the names of the attorneys, but something stopped me. It was Quinn. He'd scooted around the desk and snuggled up in the guest chair next to me. He placed a moist hand on my shoulder, which I could feel straight through the fabric of my linen shirt. All I wanted to do was get out. Fast.

As a ten-year veteran of the Bureau, not showing discomfort was drummed into every agent and consultant's head. I was not going to flinch or be intimidated with Mr. Quinn's clammy fingers sticking to my skin (through fabric, but you get the idea). I stood and disconnected from the hand. "You've been kind." I slipped the band of my purse over my shoulder and inched toward the door. With fingers on the handle, I said, "May I come back in the next few days? I'm afraid I barged in today. I was so anxious to see, um, Uncle Babes and he and I got a bit emotional, I'm afraid." Although I doubted that Oliver Quinn felt emotions, I was being charitable.

"Yes, my dear. And if you'll call ahead, perhaps we can have lunch or some coffee," he replied and if I hadn't scooted out of the chair, the guy would have placed a "comforting" arm over my shoulders and I would have had to burn my favorite Jones of New York shirt to get his creepiness out it.

He beamed like I was his. I followed his eyes as he checked my left hand for a ring, and opened the door to the reception area.

Tina was there just clicking off her phone. I thanked Quinn with a forceful handshake that would have done a professional wrestler proud. From the glint in his eyes, Quinn seemed pleased wherever his eyes wandered over me.

There could have been a slim chance that I was mistaking the wandering eyes and the lecherous grin for one of manly appreciate because I'd been out of the dating scene a good nine years. But I didn't think so.

Tina whispered to someone on the phone and slammed it down. Mr. Quinn and I snapped to attention. Had I actually been smiling back? I'd save the shiver and ponder this later, right after I gargled for twenty minutes with Listerine.

I realized at that moment, I had to see those files. You've heard on TV cop shows how they say, "follow the money"? It's true, and by looking at the records, it would be clear who was footing the bill for Uncle Babes's care. I checked my watch. I didn't have to be at the concert hall to practice with the band until three. I had a good two hours to snoop and not get caught. No, I didn't concoct a fancy plan. I'd been in situations tougher than that and knew one would come.

Quinn held the door for me as he put two fingers on my forearm. "Family is always welcome, especially since you're the first true family member to have visited Mr. Waller since, well, my, since his arrival, according to our records." No guilt attached to the words, but then again, Quinn had the science of not ruffling well-heeled feathers down pat.

I couldn't come up with a logical justification as to why I hadn't visited before. "So good to see for myself how well Uncle Babes is, especially since I haven't, well, been able to visit like a good niece should. Thank you for your time."

"No need to explain, Miss Dobson. You see," Quinn added with just the appropriate measure of sympathy and apology, "the trust administrator explained everything."

He smiled, glanced at his watch and said, "Oh, I must run, my dear lady. I've got a two o'clock tee time with our governor, Margaret Flint, and oh how Miss Margaret hates it when I'm late. You do understand."

I nodded and realized Quinn was fine at his job—which was catering to the rich.

Whatever the trust had discussed, I was glad to get out of Quinn's office and into the tropical air.

As I headed to the street, I started thinking about how different life was for me now. Otis and Jean Ticky had passed on after I finished my master's degree, but love 'em or not, I had family again, as frustratingly busy as Jane was, as warm and friendly and genuine as the others. Yes, they were family. Babes? None, or at least no one who cared enough to visit.

Because of the cancer, the New Me understood that being a consultant for the FBI didn't seem glamorous or fascinating as it once had. If it hadn't been for breast cancer, my backside would be glued to some office chair in a closet-sized and windowless cubicle poring over some crook's financial records or filling out reports that I wondered if anyone, other than my boss, ever read.

What happened in the next stopped all of this maudlin reflection. Fear can do this to you. Bet you knew that.

Chapter 8

My mind was fully focused on gaining entry into Mr. Quinn's office to read Babes's file and while there was no plan, as of yet, I knew one would come. That was what was on my mind turning the corner toward Ala Moana Boulevard.

I thought about driving around the city for old time's sake, but it was a good day for a walk, so I left my car in the lot and headed toward the big mall. I'd get something cool and tropical to drink, have lunch maybe, and then enjoy retail therapy at Neiman Marcus and DKNY. Hey, I had to wear something band-ish, even if I planned to hide behind the keyboard as I filled in for their ailing keyboard player.

Thinking about the event, I tried to block their fans out of my mind. I'd faced down serial killers, stood with SWAT teams before raiding a hedge fund office, been a hostage in a high-end home invasion, and told countless people that their loved ones had met with some terrible end. In college, I'd played at a few supper clubs and for weddings. "A group of clapping Baby Boomers—heck, it'll be nothing." Okay, the truth? To say the idea of being in a rock band on stage seeing all those people made me go weak at the knees was the understatement of the century.

I really should take Jane's advice, I thought, *and fortify myself with chocolate.* I knew I'd seen a café and bakery on that block and I was halfway there when something skittered up my spine. It wasn't an insect.

A survival instinct told me to stop. Across the street was a man, dressed in a silk shirt the color of a tropical lagoon, black slacks, neat haircut. Nothing odd. He chatted on a phone, leaning on the planter not far from where I'd turned the corner. He looked like everyone on the street, coming from or going to lunch. Yet, he had looked directly at me and I'd seen that connect. If he was police, he wouldn't have made eye contact and he glanced down. If he was an everyday nut-job stalker, he wouldn't have cared. I stopped in the shade of a royal palm and pretended to make a phone call, but I didn't have any backup. I didn't have anyone to call. Jane? At nine months and counting with her pregnancy, she was actually slowing down a bit and also fighting with city hall about having the church services on the beach. And Tom and Harmony were on Maui snorkeling near Molokini. Henry? He was off visiting with soon-to-be famous Alana Yu, sister of the infamous Payton of course, and whose last name was plastered everywhere since she was running for governor. Max? I didn't know the guy well enough to share a laugh. So much for a safety net; I was on my own.

From where I stood, I could see him. I thought about the gristly description of Jimmy March lying in a pool of his own blood which Babes had detailed and tried to attribute my creeps to that. Horrific things did happen in broad daylight, don't ever forget.

As I moved up the block, slowing to peer in the shop windows, he kept pace, walking close to the buildings. I slowed, he slowed. I stopped. He stopped. Always looking away and keeping the cell to his ear.

Then I did something brave, or supremely stupid. I turned and walked straight toward the man. He turned completely and moved away. I walked into a shop with forty zillion t-shirts, trying to be interested in one that shouted, "Surf's Up, Dude," as I tried to shake off the spooks. I'd been pretending to be back on top of my game as a consultant, and the truth was: Now I was nothing. Except as a rider on an emotional rollercoaster. Where was that always-in-control person? Fear was a whole new sensation. One I didn't like.

"Keep walking," I told the New Me, knowing with enough right turns I'd get back to the parking lot. No matter how fast I walked, the creepy feelings didn't stop. I was on the brink of getting panicky. "You're never afraid," I told myself, hearing the false bravado in that declaration, but new self just clutched her purse closer to her body. Stopping in front of a window displaying pearls, diamonds, and sapphires, I tried to calm the terror. I didn't need to turn around. I knew. He was there on the cell phone. Still.

I tried to memorize what he looked like. Nothing special. He was medium height, with spiking jet black hair, flashy diamond in his ear glittering in the morning sun. The wind ruffled the collar of his shirt and he fixed it while still looking at me.

I straightened my shoulders. "Nica, knock it off and get a grip," I ordered and then disobeyed that order. To my right was the little café and bakery I'd seen earlier and I dashed inside, thinking, "I'll call the police if he's still there in five minutes." Somehow that slowed my breathing enough to get a few dozen cookies to take to the rehearsal, but moments later, now loaded down with a pink box, I stepped through the bakery's door. Lots of people, many with packages, briefcases, and more cell phones crisscrossed in front of the shop. A few well-dressed children were being dragged along on a buying trip and one little redhead was stamping his feet and yelling, "No!" I knew just how he felt.

I slipped on my sunglasses and looked to where the man had been standing. Gone. Finally, he was gone. My cheeks puffed out in a sigh. "Okay—just an over-active imagination." Except that discomforting feeling would not go away.

The sidewalk was busy and in the distance I saw him watching me.

I balanced the bakery box, fumbling in my purse for the car keys. Then for the second time in less than twenty-four hours, I ran smack into Payton Yu. Plunk.

This time, he grabbed my shoulders, but not before handing me the bakery box that was about to tumble to the sidewalk.

"We've got to stop this. One of us is going to get hurt and as a tough law enforcement expert or agent or whatever you are, I have a sinking feeling it'll probably be me."

"Oh, Payton, I don't care if you get hurt, but I'm really thankful to see you," spilled out and once out, the New Me was glad his hands were holding me up. Every ounce of courage disappeared. The counselors in my cancer support group said personality changes were normal after everything I'd gone through, but becoming the Cowardly Lioness was a total shock.

"Nica, come on, honey, what happened? You look like you need to sit. Okay, come on this way. Look, here's a café. Sit down and catch your breath." His voice was so warm, his arm on my back was comfort and safe and okay, I'll confess, I followed like a confounded kitten.

I put the pink box on the bistro table, caught my breath, and then asked, "What are you doing here, Payton? Following me?" I huffed, which even surprised me, but the acknowledgment of being a lost little kitty made my bluster sound hollow. Because it was.

Payton's island tan never looked better and the cream-colored aloha shirt looked like it was custom made. He waved to a couple across the café, pulled his chair closer to me, and whispered, "My tutu, um, that's aunt to you mainlander types, is Tina's second cousin. Tina—you remember, the receptionist at Carlton Villas. Well, she sent a text to her cousin saying that she met a relative of someone who was somehow connected to Slam Dunk. She told her your name. Tutu knows Alana loves Slam Dunk and thought maybe Tina could ask you if you'd introduce my sister to the band. Then Tutu told me. The Hawaiian grapevine is speedy, although not always correct. For all I know, you could have been doing some charitable duty and visiting because you are such a noble woman."

"So you drove across town to meet me here?" I was totally confused.

"No. Not exactly. Tina also mentioned that she left for lunch just after you did and thought she saw someone following you. She followed the man, medium tall and pointy hair. Then she called Tutu again. After that Tutu called me because I'd told her we were friends and mentioned that you were at the reunion."

"And you dashed in on your white horse to rescue me?" I looked around. "To rescue me without your hired muscle?"

"Yeah, I left them at the office. Aren't you glad I'm here?" He smiled, that crooked melt-a-high-school-girl smile and darn it all, a little something in me seemed to be defrosting.

I took a long drink of the Kona coffee. "There was someone following me, Payton. Who would want to find out what I was doing? Who would even care?"

"Want me to ask some questions? You know, I've got a few connections here in Honolulu—and in the state."

I shook my head and snapped. "I'm a big girl, in case you didn't notice. Sorry, I haven't been myself lately."

"You look better than yourself, Nica. Whatever you've done since you left us locals to head to Boston and MIT agrees with you. Henry told me about your job, um, career, and about your marriages. I'm sorry. It's rotten luck to have to bury one husband, but two? I really am sorry."

"Thanks," I replied.

Payton gazed across the street, then said, "Do you remember Courtney Osaka?"

Having one of "those" minds that lets you keep all the useless and useful information stored for further need is a gift, so I immediately said, "Yeah, head cheerleader, cute as all get out, and as I remember, told everyone she was going marry you straight after high school and bear your children. And that was in tenth grade. Did she?"

The server offered more coffee. Our quick chat stretched to a half hour, which was fine by me. Better to have Administrator

Quinn out for his golfing date with the governor and away from the building.

Payton laughed, but it didn't sound like he enjoyed this walk down Memory Lane. "Sort of. We did get married."

"Hey, congratulations. That's great," and I meant it. They'd been sweet together. Courtney was pint size with thick black hair that fell to her waist and every guy on the football team willing to do her beck and call. Even then, with Payton's huge, chocolate colored almond-shaped eyes and a smile that could make anyone fall in love with him; she did, of course. *Now where did that "fall in love" memory come from?* I thought and shoved it to the back of my brain. "And I bet you have more than your share of little ones, right? You two always made a cute couple and your little ones have to be darling. What's children in Hawaiian? Keikis?" See, I can be polite even though I was still thinking about the hopeless feeling I had for Payton when Courtney made it well known he was taken. As if there'd been a chance for me, right?

"Not exactly. I was in my junior year at the university and had already been accepted to Stanford with their MBA program. Courtney, who was finishing cosmetology school, came to my apartment one day and announced that she was pregnant, very pregnant, eight months. She demanded that we get married."

"Okay, well, that's still good news, right?"

"The folks weren't that excited, but they accepted her. We made it legal, she quit beauty school, and I had an official roommate." He stopped abruptly. "Do you really want to hear my tale of woe, Nica? Don't you have better things to do today?"

Wild horses were not going to drag me away from hearing Playboy Payton's romantic downfall, because I could read on his face that all wasn't Jim Dandy in his world, and besides, he wasn't wearing a wedding ring. More so, there was no line where one had been in the recent past. Okay, it's horrible for me to say this, but a microscopic part of the Old Me felt that maybe he was getting as good as he had given. The New Me, with my now forgiving heart, said, "I'm a good listener."

He puffed a great breath, leaned his chair back to balance it on its back legs, just like I'd remembered him doing in homeroom so many years before. "The baby came, healthy, and Courtney did well. Cute little guy we were going to name Patterson, after my *anakala*, um, uncle. The baby also had red curls."

"But how?" I understand procreation, yet I must have missed something.

"Red curls, lots of them." Payton shrugged. "You know that my heritage is Chinese. Courtney's is Japanese. There was the dilemma."

This time, I just nodded.

"I didn't know what to do. My parents were in Hong Kong visiting my mom's side of the family. The day "our" child was born, I asked for a paternity test. No weird DNA discovered. Little Patterson wasn't my biological child. Courtney and I had a tear-filled talk and she admitted she'd been seeing a few guys at the same time we'd been dating. When she found out about the pregnancy, she went through the list, told the others, and each denied the possibility. Good old Payton Yu, Mr. Stand-Up and Honorable Guy, regardless of how shifty you may think I am, did the responsible thing."

I patted his hand. We both looked at our hands touching and in the same instant drew apart. "That was the respectable thing to do since you didn't know."

"Long story about to be over…Courtney and I filed for divorce and she sought out Patterson's biological father who married her and accepted Patterson. It's complicated, but we've stayed friends, us three adults and Pat. He's eighteen and a great guy. Plays football, we surf almost every Saturday morning together, and he calls me Uncle Pay."

"That's a happy ending, right?"

"Yeah, sure, Patterson's a great kid."

"So, you're not married?"

"I don't think that's in my future, Nica."

I sipped the smooth coffee. "Life is complicated. It certainly has been for me."

"Henry told me when he was at the house today. Oh, don't look at me like that. He explained about the cancer and your treatments because he loves you. When changes happen in life, it takes time to adjust. I know that." He looked at the tablecloth, twisted his coffee mug, and then re-arranged the orchid in the tiny vase.

The only changes I could imagine that could or should trouble playboy Payton Yu would be the fact that his hair was getting thin and that he'd never get into a thirty-two waist pair of jeans again. Then I wanted to slap myself. The guy just so was kind to me. Apparently, I could think I was grown up on the outside and hold a responsible position with a federal agency, but Payton turned me into a caustic, sarcastic adolescent. However, wonder of wonders, at least this time I didn't bark out those words.

"So, Alana had a chance to visit with Henry. Good time was had by all?" I asked, and yes, I did want to change the subject. If Payton needed those bodyguards, then he was playing in a league I didn't want to know about.

"She did. They talked for a long time and that's good for my sis. Life's been grueling for her these last months." His cell buzzed. He didn't answer and immediately turned it off.

I was stunned. "Running for governor is a big, complicated deal. All of your family must be proud of her. I knew, even in high school, that she'd be important one day. Planning to run for president in the future? She'll certainly get my vote. Wow I cannot wait to tell the people I worked with in the bureau that I went to school with the next governor of Hawaii." I waited. And waited a bit more.

Payton didn't even smile. How could he not be tickled three shades of pink for his sister? They'd always been close. What had happened?

"I thought you knew," Payton said, twisting the coffee mug. His brow was etched in lines I'd never seen before.

"Knew what, Payton? Your last name is everywhere. I've seen the signs that shout 'Yu for Governor' all over Honolulu. I've been avoiding watching the news since I'm trying to think only cheery thoughts to get over the constant edginess, like the doctors had advised me to do. What about Alana?"

He looked up and gently placed his hand over mine. "Thought you knew that just before Christmas, Alana was cycling on the Big Island—some charity race—and a fan thought it would be helpful to offer her a cup of water. He stepped out too far, she swerved to avoid hitting the kid, and at the same time a branch from one of the palms lining the highway fell in front of her. She flipped the bike, went down a cliff, and hasn't walked in eight months."

"No, oh, Payton, I am so very sorry. Alana was my hero. But she's still active, right? She's running for governor, so she must be," I offered, but the words came out tinny because his face was clouded. I knew worry and fear when I saw it.

"Wrong Yu, Nica."

"But your father is elderly? Oh, of course, one of your other relatives."

Payton tried to smirk, tried put on the crooked smile that melted high school girls, but it didn't work this time. He was serious. "I'm the Yu whose name is plastered around town."

Chapter 9

"You? Oh, no. You're kidding, right? You? No." The mouthful of Kona coffee that was nearly down my throat, nearly was spit all over the next hopeful governor for the State of Hawaii.

"What's up with this, Nica?" Payton handed me his napkin which I needed to blot coffee from my chin that got there when I gasped the above words. "I wouldn't have taken you for a staunch supporter of Margaret Flint. You are aware that she's the incumbent and my opposition. She has aspirations of running for president in the next decade, all backed with shady funding?"

"Not at all, Payton. I just am having a hard time imagining you as a politician," I replied and then thought back to the reunion dinner where Payton was glad-handing everybody from the catering servers to the guys in the slack string guitar band and all of the alumni, too. I prided myself on being aware of my surroundings and I had missed that. Totally. "So, who were the protectors surrounding you at the International Marketplace?"

"Protection, you're right, actually. Even this early in the campaign, the Flint camp has started to throw some mud. And it's going to get dirtier. I'm running on the Green Party ticket, which is actually strong in the Islands. Our current governor, Miss Margaret as she likes to be called because she traces her ancestors back to the original missionaries, inadvertently let it slip that if elected for another term, she'll lobby to bring in nuclear power to the islands. I heard that she's planning on selling some of the park land on the big island, too. I am dead set against all of this, as are the majority of voters."

"That's good then, I mean for your campaign, right?"

"Yes, it is, but Miss Margaret isn't a fool. Any hint of inappropriate conduct on the part of my group or me, for that matter, would be just what the Flint people would love to get to the press. Honestly, Nica, that's why I came alone today. My manager fears that if someone saw me and you meeting, you an FBI undercover consultant, they'd concoct a story that would have even level-headed Henry screaming at the top of his lungs."

"But you're above reproach, Payton," I said, but then added, "Unless they can twist something about you and Courtney and Pat."

"That was already tried. However, Patterson's dad is one of Hawaii's largest cattle ranchers on the Big Island and Miss Margaret back peddled when they tried to disgrace him. Suddenly my month-long marriage to Patterson's mom was a non-issue."

I shook my head. "Politics."

"But you know this stuff, being in Washington and everything," Payton replied. "Now tell me how I can help you with whatever this undercover op is that you're on."

I didn't want to trust him, but as one friend to another, he'd just revealed private matters to me. He didn't have to and I knew he was doing so to gain my trust. "There's no 'op.' Someone Henry once knew, a novelist and rocker from the eighties, fathered or didn't father a daughter. She contacted Jane—wait you haven't met Jane and that's not a bad thing because my cousin will take your breath away at the speed she moves—and I got nudged into trying to find out the truth."

"No reason why a paternity test can't be done now, even with long-standing family connections, you know, oh, yeah, you know this," he said, putting his hand over the coffee mug as the food server offered more.

"The problem is that this woman's father was murdered or took his own life. The body was never discovered. She needs to establish that she is his only issue, his only offspring, so that the royalties will justly go to her."

"That I get, but why was some creep following you?"

I saw a true look of concern in those dark chocolate eyes, ringed by eye lashes that would make a runway model drool, and yes, I did remind myself to stop looking at his eyelashes. "The only thing I can imagine is someone didn't like me talking with a resident of Carlton Villas."

Payton took a twenty out of his wallet and slipped it beneath his coffee mug. "But it's not like you were visiting someone in witness protection."

"Thanks." I nodded to the server as she cleared our coffee mugs and smiled at Payton. I was surprised she didn't scribble her phone number on the receipt. "The woman's name is Diamond Dupris. Do you recognize it?"

Payton shoved his chair back and we stood. "Dupris? Sure, another old island family. Once thought of pineapple royalty, I remember. I haven't heard of a Diamond. My mom, I think, had a girl friend named Elaine, from the family. I seem to recall some photos of them going to dressy debutante balls, but Mom isn't one to hash over old times. Want me to ask her?"

"Could you? And could you ask her if this old friend Lanie knew Jimmy March?"

Payton's eyes blinked and blinked again. "*The* Jimmy March? That's the connection? He's been an island legend for years, Nica. Folks swear that he shows up at rock concerts. A month back there was something in the *Honolulu Advertiser* that said he was reported to be seen on Waikiki or surfing on the North Shore."

"Like Elvis sightings?" I slipped my purse over my shoulder and we walked to the sidewalk.

He laughed and touched my elbow. "Yeah. Like that, I suppose, except the King *is* alive and everyone knows that. If March isn't alive, the royalties would be something else. Heck, everybody from

Aretha Franklin to the Black Eyed Peas has recorded his songs. There'd be a pot of cash for this woman if she can prove herself to be his daughter." He flicked on his phone, sent a text, and said, "I'm not going to have you walk back to wherever you parked your car, am I? Better yet, my driver will be here in a second and we'll drop you off. Why people think that Hawaii is too much like paradise not to have its own share of folks who are *maika'i'ole*, that is, bad, I have no idea. We do—plenty of losers just in case you haven't yet consulted with local HPD, yet."

A Lincoln Town Car pulled to the curb and Payton opened the door as I said, "This inquiry is strictly personal, Payton. There's no connection to any law enforcement groups; it's just me asking questions."

We settled into the deliciously cool leather backseat. "Then tell me," he said, "who you were visiting at that assisted care facility?"

"It's an old band member with Henry and a friend of March's."

"If you tell me more maybe I can help. I'm well—"

"Well connected, I know," I replied and this time, unlike the last, it didn't come out snippy. "No need, not yet, at least." I gave the driver the location of my car and when we arrived, Payton slipped out before I could. "Thank you. This was nice."

"Was nice, and it's our first date." He smiled and reached to give me a hug.

I took a step back. "Aren't you afraid someone might spot up and snap your picture with a FBI advisor? Wouldn't it be splashed over every local news program throughout the islands by eleven tonight?"

"Changed my mind. Crime-fighting superstar, hometown girl, long-lost love from high school is back for reunion and just catching up? I am actually going to tweet this from the car as we head back to the office. What could be better than the hometown jock stomping for governor to be seen out and about with a drop-dead gorgeous, all-American woman who happens to be linked, in a good way, with the FBI, and someone who at one time had eyes only for him. Yeah. I can handle that heat. Now if you get arrested? Well, that'd be another matter."

We laughed, easily. I accepted the hug and smiled, but then softly punched him in the arm and said, "Eyes for you? If you even noticed mine, you would have added 'Four Eyes' to the list of nicknames I was called in high school."

Payton's eyes flicked down to the sidewalk. "I did notice you. I'll tell you about it sometime." And he was off, which was good for me, because right then I knew Quinn and Governor Margaret should be standing on the first tee at their country club. But how was I going to get by Tina before she could text her tutu, who would email Payton that I'd returned? Right then, I had no strategy to get into Quinn's office that wouldn't alert everyone in the Yu family. Within minutes.

I got into the car, let the windows down, and hoped a plan would appear. It didn't. But I did see a clothing consignment shop directly across the parking lot with a rack of glittering t-shirts displayed in the front. I needed something for the next night's performance, whether I wanted to be there or not. Just maybe I could get some information too, I thought as I headed into the shop.

I pulled two black t-shirts from the rack and the clerk came toward me. "I'd take the smaller size, honey," she said. "With a figure like yours why waste it with extra fabric."

"Agreed," I replied. "And maybe I'll take one in red, and would you mind if I wear it? Hey, I was wondering. I think a girlfriend of mine works in this neighborhood. Tina Yu? Do you know her?" I handed the clerk a fifty and dashed into a curtained dressing room. I didn't want to give her added info from my credit card, just in case she was related to the Yu family.

"Oh, yeah, Tina Yu comes in here once in a while. She's a cutie, so full of life. Went to school with my son. I thought for a while they were going to marry, but she's got aspirations to be a journalist or a writer or something like that. Yes, she works across the street at that care facility. Want me to call her?"

"No, just curious and I thought I might surprise her and take her to dinner later. I know you're really busy here, but you wouldn't have any idea when she leaves for the day, would you?" It was lame as plans go, but the clerk was only too happy to help. On the dot each evening, Tina left at six.

"Mahalo," I replied and suddenly I knew exactly how I'd storm Quinn's office, but first I had to make believe I was a keyboard player for the boomer band Slam Dunk.

• • •

The Hawaii Theatre Center on Bethel Street felt like an old friend when I walked inside, grand but not stuffy, even though there was a musty smell in the air. It was the musty smell that brought back the memories. I looked at the blue padded chairs and the gold leaf on the architectural details and fell in love with it once more, just like I had when, as a youngster, Jean and Otis brought me there to see Peter Pan. The band wasn't there yet, but I knew I was in the right place for the practice session with Slam Dunk because the sound crew and technicians came and went. I attempted to be patient, something I'm not particularly good at, and with the music already in place at the keyboard I ran through the songs. This held my attention for another half hour and then I'd officially had it with the guys.

At ten minutes to four, I walked down the block to the ABC store for a bottle of ice tea or water and came face-to-face with Max Robertson. Naturally, there was a woman hanging on his every word and his arm. I backed out, thinking that I really didn't need water. But it was too late.

"Hey, Nica, wow, it's you," he called, extracted his hand from the blond who seemed to be fixing the collar of his Hilo Hattie bright red flowered aloha shirt.

"Hi Max, I've just come from the theater."

He took my arm and steered me to a buxom redhead who seem entranced by the sunglass display. "Nica and I and the band are playing at the Hawaii Theatre." Apparently the near lynching earlier that morning was forgotten because he said, "You'll be there, Angela, won't you?"

"Oh, Maxie, honey bun, this is so exciting," she purred. She looked to me to be about sixty and like she had enough money to stay that age.

"Maxie," I mimicked her, which was rude I know, but felt good. "Are you going to come to the theater at all? Are we having practice this afternoon?"

"Nica. Angela. Hey, it's not even one yet." He flashed his Rolex and if I hadn't been there to make sure he didn't just reset the time, I would have sworn he was pulling a fast one.

"Did you neglect to adjust your watch? We're not Pacific Time, Max. Here in Honolulu, we're on Hawaiian time." I rolled my eyes, shrugged, and nodded goodbye. "I'm going to get a couple bottles of water and head to the theater. When will you join me and the band?"

"Wait up, Nica. Sorry, Angela baby, got to run. This gal is a slave driver." Then he pretended to have a moustache to twist and added with a glint in his jet black eyes, "See you later, baby doll."

"Are you aware that your supposedly seductive chatter to that lady went out in the nineteen-eighties? I muttered, paying for the water and leaving the change in the tip container.

"Hey, if it's not broke, don't fix it. That's my motto," he replied, bouncing along beside me as if he were already playing his bass.

As we reached the back door of the theater, a clerk greeted us by jousting a FedEx package into my hands. Max looked to me and then at it. "The contract. From your agent? In Detroit?" I said, somehow keeping the angst from my voice. "Henry said it was going to come here. Do you remember? Do you even care, Max?"

"Oh yeah," Max replied. No one in the band was hurting for money; all had other jobs, but if one had a business, I always thought, one had to run a business. I had volunteered to look over the contracts, but I didn't think the rest of the band would ignore them, as they did. I pulled open the paper envelope. The cover letter said I had to get that form back to the company in Detroit, which was about to pay a huge amount of money for the rights to record the band's live performance. They would produce a new CD that would come out in stores the following year.

When I had arranged it all, it seemed simple. Get the guys to sign for the form and FedEx would personally see to it that the contract arrived on time. "But only if you can get it to me by six," explained the clerk at their office. It was nearly four-fifty now. I vowed at that moment, I was going to un-volunteer as Slam Dunk's under-appreciated and unpaid manager or get a power of attorney, so I could just sign all the forms myself. The proceeds from their events and the royalties from the CDs and DVDs went to the Slam Dunk Foundation, but honestly rounding up musicians was like organizing preschoolers on a sugar-induced Halloween trance.

I heaved a deep sigh. "Max, could you sign this? I know." I lifted my hand, palm out, to stop him from offering any stock market tips. "I'll go wait by the back door and catch the others as they come in."

In the next hour, my breathing returned from the aforementioned huff. I put the cookies I'd purchased while being stalked on a table near the stage entrance and like getting a reward, each of the guys signed their name and took a cookie. "Preschoolers." I chuckled.

"Whatever works," Henry said, coming up in back of me.

"I have to get this to FedEx by six, Henry, so—"

He patted my shoulder. "Would you mind, then, taking it over there? Just put in a bit of face time, and we'll muddle on without you. I'd feel a whole lot better than having one of these characters do it?"

"You are sure lucky, Henry, because I have a short errand I need to run near six, too, if that's okay."

"You're saving our bacon, Nica, you take your time."

The plan, which had been impossible to concoct earlier that day, was nearly forming. Details? I'd work them out once I stopped at FedEx and waited across the street from the entrance to Carlton Villas. I'd wait for Tina to leave, and then? Actually, I had a fancy idea of what I'd do except to talk with Tina, but after that? I didn't have that part worked out.

I sat fiddling with the piano's keys, replaying the chorus to their smash hit "He's Alive," and tried to make sense of the last few days. It was like a jigsaw puzzle with plenty of the pieces missing. It didn't help that guys were joking and telling what sounded like tall tales, even to my naïve ears.

"How many musicians does it take to screw in a light bulb?" Max cackled. In the next breath he blurted the answer, "As many as you've got and they all have their own twist on it."

One of the other guys shouted, "What's the difference between a rock musician and a large pizza? Don't know? The pizza can feed four people."

"Come on, boys and my niece, let's hit it. Let the music begin."

I was about to make my debut performance with the band and felt about as ready to do that as to swim the English Channel.

At five-thirty, Henry returned my nod. I snapped up my purse and grabbed the FedEx return envelope with the signed contract tucked safely inside, dropped it off without a hitch, and headed, eventually, to Carlton Villas. I concentrated only at getting safely into Quinn's office to read the files. Why? I was scared to think about performing with Slam Dunk. Practice was one thing, screaming fans, bright lights, me sweating buckets, was definitely another. Yes, I was in denial about the forthcoming ordeal.

I was pulling into the parking lot across the street from the assisted care home when my cell rang. Music blasted in the background as I answered that sounded strangely like Slam Dunk's hit "He's Alive" and I spotted a young man, dressed in a blue uniform with "Honolulu Security" printed on the back, lock a pristine inky black Chevy truck, so new it had no plates. He was the same guard who saved me when my heel caught on the doorstep my first visit to the facility.

The man slowly walked around the truck. Then he smiled like Publisher's Clearing House just gave him an oversized check and finally he looked around him and kissed the hood (could I kid you on this?). Finally he danced like he'd just caught a football and dashed to the end zone. "Guys and cars," I muttered and chuckled before concentrating on the call, from a number I didn't recognize.

"Nica, it's me, Max. Can you hear me?"

"Hi Max. I left fifteen minutes ago, can't you live without me?"

Max must have walked well away from the band because then I could hear him clear his throat. "Think you need to know something, Nica."

"Are you in some kind of trouble? With Angela from the ABC Store meeting?"

"No. Trouble's not exactly the word. It's more like a coincidence that I wasn't quite, well, clear about."

"Clear, you mean you have something to tell me that you didn't and because you didn't, it's a lie of omission?"

"You go straight for the soul, don't you, Consulting Agent Dobson. Or have you been hanging out with Pastor Jane too long?"

I waited, again allowing silence to encourage Max to talk about whatever he had on his mind. "When I flew into Honolulu yesterday, I met Diamond Dupris coming off her flight from Switzerland. That was before you saw me being chased around the Hilton by those voluptuous ladies. Diamond called me about a week ago. We talked a few times when she was in Europe."

"All kidding aside, Casanova, what do you think of her?"

"I felt for her. She's innocent of this crazy business. I met her at the airport. I needed to tell her I'd met her father and wanted her to know he was okay to me. Got a feeling she's going to hear some nasty stuff about Jimmy and maybe the fact that he treated a kid like me as if I was a human being could ease some pain. Don't know. Just had an inclination and since I knew you were coming here, I, well—"

"What did you say? Did you give her the same guarantee that Jane did? Did you promise that I'd find her father's killer, if in fact he was killed and not in hiding for the last thirty years?"

Yes, I did sound jaded. But the truth is: there were plenty of men like Max Robertson, in politics, in the Bureau, and behind bars. They were smooth and would promise anyone anything. These are great guys to have on your side when they're honorable, but not when they're not. But you already know that, right?

I waited for his next statement on the pathetic waif Diamond Dupris as I watched for Tina Yu to leave Carlton Villas.

"Find her father's killer, find out how Jimmy died, and where he's buried. Hope he is buried. Can't you check DNA or something if you dig up Jimmy?"

"No, not at all. DNA is nearly impossible to collect from a body that's been buried, especially one that's been dead for over thirty years, Max."

"But don't they do that in the movies?"

"Not the movies I watch, or maybe I don't watch *Castle* or *Bones* like you do. Even the chances of finding March after all these years are slim."

"But you still told Diamond you'd try, so that's good. You're a fine woman, Nica, and a Good Samaritan."

I cringed. "Geez, thanks for the pep talk."

Then I heard a booming voice in the background, "Hey, Max, my man. Henry's disappeared. You going to get sandwiches or not? You're going to have a mutiny on your hands in another five minutes if we don't get some food." Then Max said, "Gee, duty calls, Nica, I'm the sandwich kid again. Hey, please just remember, Di's a good kid."

"Hardly a kid," I mumbled. I turned off the phone, no good having it ring while I was alone in Quinn's office, if I could figure out a plan to get there.

I didn't budge from the car and was glad of that because right then Tina dashed down the steps of the building and into the arms of a medium-height man with a flashy diamond in his ears. "Well, now, that's interesting," I said out loud, still bothered by Tina's boyfriend definitely looking much like my afternoon's tail. They shared an R-rated kiss and then jumped into his black compact.

"Sweet Tina had not only sent a text to her tutu, but it seemed that she is somehow involved with a guy who looks a lot like my stalker. Wonder what else is fishy about her?" But this was not the time to ponder that problem. I messed up my hair to look somehow trendy or at least not as I looked previously in case anyone saw me, pulled at the neck of the t-shirt, squared my shoulders, and sauntered across the street. Yes, I did wait for their car move away from the curb.

Just as I anticipated, the truck kisser was at Tina's desk, iPad in hand, playing games. "Help you, ma'am?"

My acquaintance with Jesus had been a waving one for most of my life until a few months after I was inducted into the Angieski clan. Now, I accepted Him with joy, but Cousin Jane, the good-hearted buttinski she is, took time to accept that or else she just liked to preach to me. Henry says it's the latter. Yet, at that second,

I gave thanks, big time to Him because the previous "wing it" plan now as a bona fide and really good one. I smoothed my hands over the newly purchase and snug red t-shirt, smiled, made my voice go up an octave and hoped it would pass for a southern accent.

"Well, hello there, you dear, sweet thing," I drawled, and to my ears, it sounded like a high school performance of Blanche DuBois in *A Streetcar Named Desire.* "Why, aren't you just the sweetest man. I'm so silly. I was, well, visiting Ollie earlier today, and gosh, my earring came off." I showed him my left ear, but the truth was I never wore earrings.

"I don't see anything here on the desk, but if you want to call tomorrow, the receptionist might have locked it here in her desk," he said, pulling at the drawer, proving that he couldn't get it open.

"Oh, well, Grandma's little old three-carat diamond earring, I'm sure, is safe there." I smiled again and turned to leave. Stopped. Flipped around and said, "You wouldn't know, by chance, who owns a black Silverado truck way over there in the lot?"

The man looked like he'd just found out he was going to be a daddy. "I sure do. Just got that baby this afternoon. Why?"

"Oh my. It's probably nothing. I was going to have you tell the owner that a group of teenagers were all over it. I thought I saw one opening the hood while a second was under—"

Luckily, I'd stepped back. The security guard was out the door and I had the entrance to Oliver Quinn's office to myself. I keyed in his code, and shut the door behind me.

"Now what?" I whispered, but of course, I sat in his chair and moved the computer mouse to see the screen come to life. User name? Easy. First and last. Password? I sat there drumming my fingers. I'd only hacked into a few computers and wasn't skilled at that at all, just lucky because people typically use their pet's name (didn't know if people like Quinn were allowed to have pets), place of birth (no clue, but he looked more New York than Hawaiian), or car (I'd say he probably drove a Mercedes). I even tried "password" since that is still one of the most common one and easiest to hack, along with the other all-time favorite of 123456. "Crud," I hissed. *Mercedes* and all variations of that didn't work.

In the old days before medical leave, I would have gone through official channels to get the information. Now? I had nothing and unless I suddenly became psychic, I was not going to find out who was paying for Uncle Babes's care.

Just as I muttered something unprintable under my breath, there was a knock on the door. I froze and sweated and scurried from the leather chair.

I cackled and then again; like someone had just tickled my funny bone or something else. Then very slowly opened the door, just a crack. "Ollie, you naughty boy. What? You want to be left alone and no calls either. I'll tell the guard. Anything for you, honey bunch." Then I slipped out and firmly closed the door. "Ollie, I mean, Mr. Quinn—"

"Um, I just wanted Mr. Quinn to know I had to step away from the desk for a moment…um, an emergency, but I'm back," said the guard, who still looked rattled from my story about his truck being violated.

I forced yet another sensual giggle and repeated what the security man said. I didn't think guard noticed that I'd seen his eyes rolling. That was a good sign since it inferred he believed me in my cheesy acting role.

"What, Ollie Baby…? Okay, I'll tell him. Mr. Quinn doesn't want to be disturbed."

I was nearly out the door, still I couldn't help myself. I turned and said, "Now don't go telling anyone I was here. Okay?" This meant that as soon as I left, the guard would be announcing to anyone with an ear for gossip that Slick Mr. Quinn's had been entertaining in his inner sanctum. It was wrong, but it felt so splendid. Oh, don't tell me you've never done, or wanted to, something like that.

I called Henry before I left the parking lot to let him know I was on my way back. My perfectly perfect plan was a bust to review the financial statements on Babes, but at least I hadn't gotten arrested for breaking and entering.

Henry picked up my call and started talking even before I could tell him why I was running late. "Nica, honestly, you don't have to bother. We just need you on the keyboard tomorrow night. You don't have to practice with us."

"And like you promised, you won't have a mike anywhere near me?"

"You've got my word. You're strictly eye candy, so go back to the hotel and rest. Deal?"

So that was what I intended to do, except intentions don't always work in my world.

• • •

The penthouse was silent and the connected doors to the suites were open. Jane and Harmony and their little dog, too, either had retreated to their bedrooms or were off doing whatever they did, which I think included plenty of shopping on Jane's part.

Then I saw it. On the dining room table. Not just any little thing like a dozen daisies. Goodness, if it were any larger, it could have been used on a float for the parade in Pasadena. Blood red roses, great gobs of the long-stemmed variety.

Probably for Jane from her husband or maybe from her literary agent.

I walked closer. No. My name was on the tiny, ivory-colored envelope. "Now what did I do to deserve this?" I blinked.

I had trouble reading the card because my hand was shaking. Then it fell to the carpet. If words had power, these four jumped off the note and whacked me. "Now who is stupid enough to do this? Why, mystery solved. I'll just call the florist. Here it is.

Monarchs on King Street. We'll see who this wacko is, pulling a prank like this." The words came out in a puff which should have helped squelch that creepy feeling at my hairline.

It took seconds to be connected. Miraculously, someone was at the shop. I politely asked my question and longed to add that this was a federal investigation.

"Sorry, ma'am, we can't provide that information," came the response. "It's against our policy."

"You don't understand. There's no name on the card. How can I send a note of thanks?" I lowered my voice, fearing that my discomfort could be heard as tried to coax the truth from the florist. I even tried other methods, and then hit the "I'm fed-up" level. My mom always told me, "Don't take no from someone who can't say yes."

I put the card on the table. "It makes one's job complex when one must stand behind rules, doesn't it. Let me talk with your manager."

Whispers filtered through a hand over the receiver and then, "Ms. Dobson, hello. This is Jerry, and I'm the manager. Sorry about that 'policy' thing. Unfortunately, the order was placed in person, here in the shop."

"Did you take the order?"

There was the sound of rustling paper followed by muffled words before the manager came back. "The clerk you were first speaking with did. She just told me the gentleman was not one of our regulars. We *know* our clients. The card was already written and sealed when the clerk accepted the order."

"What name was on the credit card?"

"Let's see." Rustle, rustle, and a whisper.

As I learned early on in the bureau, follow the money, so I waited.

"Hmm, that's interesting. Why, the order was paid for with cash."

"Cash" was said as if it were a foreign term. "The clerk said it was busy in the shop and she can't describe the sender. We at Monarch's pride ourselves on being discrete and we hope you understand."

I wanted to yell, "Blah, blah, blah," but I politely replied, "Thanks," and clicked off. I flopped to the sofa and read the message, trying to make sense of it. "Jimmy March is dead." The note was written on plain stock, except the gold boarder, no way of knowing, unless one could fingerprint it, to find out from whom the message was sent.

I looked across the room. The roses seemed to be shouting a message that I could hear, but didn't understand. Who even knew I was looking into Jimmy's death? Okay, except my immediate family, Payton Yu and entire Yu grapevine, and the guy who was medium height with a flashy diamond in his ear, but he only tailed me from Carlton Villas. Jimmy's only odd connection was with sweet old Babes.

If this were a statement, then someone absolutely knew that Jimmy March was dead. If it was to frighten me, the sender didn't realize a bouquet of flowers wasn't likely to do that. Besides, why not send a letter and spell it out? Why the theatrics, if this actually was a threat?

Absently, I weaved the card through my fingers. Okay, I'm forgetting how Babes yelled when I talked about Jimmy. Others had heard everything that was said, but no one seemed especially interested.

"Wait," I muttered. What of Ollie, the ever-so-slick Oliver Quinn? Anyone and everyone in the band knew. Henry probably talked about Jimmy and according to Jane, all musicians were known to relish good gossip. I heard Max tell Henry that he'd visited the musician's union the day before, too. As chatty as Max seemed to be, by afternoon, probably half of Honolulu heard that I was asking for info about Jimmy March.

If I were just another camera-laden, overly suntanned tourist planning to eat my body weight in pineapple, I'd be thrilled with the flowers. But you and I know that you can't just turn off what you've been trained to do for ten years. That message was a warning. But was it a threat?

No one would really care if I threw up my hands and pretended to be the poor, little breast cancer survivor. Oh, too much for my chemo-addled brain to figure any of this out. That did cross my mind. But what if I was determined to find my birth parents or dig into my heritage? Could I not do the right thing and still face myself in the mirror? "Three dozen flowers can't scare me off," I said, grabbed the humongous arrangement, and placed it outside the suites with a sign that read, "Free."

Done. Over. Gone. Period.

Chapter 10

Have you ever tossed and turned all night long and then woke with a dread of a known origin? Yes, I said "known origin." Unless God brought the Rapture and I was one of the chosen, the dread shouted that I would be standing by a keyboard in front of five-hundred, charitable fans of Slam Dunk. I would be pretending panic wasn't clutching my heart. Could I keep up with the band? Now that's a silly question. Of course not. Could I not faint as I walked onstage with the band? No guarantees.

I threw open the curtain to the suite thinking how Henry had promised that as their "eye candy," nothing would be expected of me. I could act as if I knew what I was doing. More than a strong cup of coffee, I needed to have my head examined. I swallowed hard knowing it was much easier to face a terrorist with a homemade bomb than for me to walk on stage at the Hawaii Theatre Center.

I slipped on my bathrobe, headed for the kitchen, and wondered how I was going to keep my mind off the charity concert. Then I stopped short. Like out of some Stephen King novel, that colossal arrangement of blood red roses was back. It was right in the middle of the coffee table.

From her suite, Jane waddled into the room, yawned and gave me a hug. "You were asleep when Harmony and Tom got back from their snorkeling trip and I got back from the city council meeting and wow, those flowers were right outside the door." She'd switched to herbal tea with the announcement of her pregnancy, and still she was bouncing around. "They've got to be from my publisher. What a sweetie. Who'd thunk that my memoir would be number one on the *New York Times* bestseller list, other than me and God?"

"The publisher left a note?" I would not tell Jane my thoughts about the flowers being a treat. If I was wrong, she'd worry or stick her nose into it and I'd seen what happened when she did those things. If I was right about why I got the flowers, I knew how to handle the situation.

Jane laughed because Toughy, the Welsh terrier, jumped on the sofa squeaking a tiny soccer ball that had such a high pitch it could have cracked crystal. "Oh, no, but the arrangement is definitely for me. And you know what? Some joker put a 'free' sign on them."

Touching the bathrobe pocket, I felt the edges of that card that declared that Jimmy was gone. When my eyes flashed open at three in the morning, however, I attempted to convince myself the flowers were from Diamond. But at three-thirty, I knew she would have signed the card. At four, I tried to believe that maybe Payton had sent them because if I remembered correctly, and I did, he loved to pull pranks. At four-thirty, I threw out all the theories. The note was clearly a warning. But from whom? And why pay with cash? The arrangement must have cost more than three-hundred dollars I guessed.

I thought back and at about six, I wondered if someone, who wanted to simply wanted to be discrete or anonymous hand sent them in order to assure me that Diamond was Jimmy's daughter and he was dead. That is, someone who could afford to send this reassuring message with flowers when a text or maybe an email would have worked just as well.

As if on cue, my cell rang. It was Diamond and unlike her jumbled phone call from Switzerland, right then she was all business. "I've been here for two days and I am settling in at the

Dupris mansion," she said. "I made my mind up on the flight over that I'd talk with auntie the minute I got into Honolulu."

"Before losing your nerve?" Yes, like my Cousin Jane, I do speak my mind quite often and it has gotten me into more than one scrape even before I became a McAgent.

"She's so fragile, Nica, so tiny. I'd forgotten that she is fifteen years older than my mother. Auntie says she's jubilant I've come to her. She's so alone now that Mother's dead. She's begged me to stay with her."

Something in Diamond's words or her voice puzzled me. All these years and still Auntie is thrilled that dear little Diamond has returned to the nest? Why didn't she contact Lanie or Diamond long before this? Or it could be that Auntie was in the same room as Diamond as her voice, to my jaded ears, sounded hardly enthusiastic.

"I've explained everything to Auntie and she would love to meet you. Are you free for tea? At two?"

Wild horses, raging rivers, and the rain that threatened wouldn't have been able to stop me. "Thank you. I'd be delighted," I said, and copied the address on a pad in the kitchen.

I didn't budge from the penthouse until I put on that little black dress I wore for the reunion dinner, tied a scarf around my neck, and slipped on sandals. And then with the rain still coming in sheets, but with promises from the Weather Channel that it'd stop by late afternoon, I opted to take a taxi rather than navigate the drenched streets of Honolulu.

The mansion looked like one of those places you see in *Architectural Digest* and even though my husbands were wealthy, we simply hadn't lived in Monte Carlo opulence. The rain had stopped when the cab pulled to the curb. The porch circled the house and if Scarlett O'Hara lived in Hawaii, she'd choose the Dupris home.

As if the butler had been waiting for me, and he probably was, the heavy koa wood doors opened and he stood there like a sentry. I walked into the foyers. The place reeked of old money, old furniture I knew was worth a mint. Both of my late spouses had been wealthy, but theirs was new money. This was the old, stale kind that made you want to open a window if you wanted to breathe again.

Diamond rushed down a staircase. "Thank you so much for coming." She accompanied it with a hug. Now as a woman, I don't have problems hugging, but I truly had expected a warm handshake and not someone clinging to me as if for safety. "Now that you and Aunt are going to help me, I know I'll find really what happened to my father. I feel better already." She smiled and held my hand in a girlish way and then slipped her arm through mine as if we were chummy, like we were BFFs.

Diamond Dupris was taller than I expected, but still shorter than me. She was boney, in an unflattering, non-model way. Her skin was pale and if it weren't those dark rings beneath her gently almond shaped eyes and the quivering fingers she seemed to have to force to be still, she could have been attractive, I imagined.

As she led the way to a spacious library room, I once again noticed the accent. It had that softer misty sound of someone who spoke a blend of languages. I felt empathy for her. Whatever happened on this search for Jimmy March, Diamond was a fighter. I liked her. I liked her a lot.

"So this is the woman you have spoken about, Mrs. Monica Dobson," Victoria Dupris said after the proper introduction. She was wrinkled, ancient, and dressed in a black polyester pants suit straight from the eighties. She dragged out the word "so" and the way she said it, it felt to me that perhaps it wasn't to Diamond's best interest to have this stranger as a friend. "I have heard a lot about you. Sweet Diamond and I have just been having a nice, cozy chat and your name came up. We were just discussing little Diamond's plan." Her voice was husky, that raspy sound of a long addiction to nicotine. Frail fingers with blue, puffy veins studded with long, yellowed fingernails reached out to me. It was more of a finger touch than a handshake because as she withdrew her fingers, she placed a lacy hanky to her lips, admitting a shallow cough.

"Lovely to meet you, Miss Dupris. Dobson was my late husband's name, but I prefer Mrs. Monica Wainwright-Dobson." Two can play empress of the day. I forced a smile on my lips and kept my mouth closed.

She didn't get up to greet me; older, well-to-do women rarely do, but there was another reason. She was connected to a portable oxygen tank. *Emphysema*, I thought, and a teaspoon of empathy surfaced. She was suffering for her addiction.

Within seconds, a stout, silver-haired maid in a crisp black and white uniform brought in a dolly with a silver tea service. Her eyes were guarded and down, reminding me of a child who is constantly scolded. I'd seen that look before and knew it was her submissive way to survive in that household. Miss Dupris nodded and the maid poured. Accepting a cup of tea, I smiled and a flicker of acknowledgment shone in the woman's eyes.

"Humph. Ghastly service these days. If I have told you a hundred times, I cannot tolerate the way you hover, Inez. Will you ever learn how rude you are? Cannot you see you are once more annoying me and now our guest, too." The elder Miss Dupris spat out the words, and the maid's face became stoic as she retreated. Victoria Dupris grumbled a bit more, then turned to me and asked, "Cream or lemon?"

"Lemon. Thank you." And I waited to have either woman begin a conversation. But the moments stretched and the silence of the house made me think of a cheesy horror novel.

Diamond seemed hypnotized with the act of stirring her tea, watching the swirls of bland brown liquid and I wondered if she had been as shocked by the rudeness of her aunt's behavior to the maid as I was. But what was Diamond thinking, if she was thinking?

Then it dawned on me. Even if she felt disgraced by her aunt's comment, there was no way she'd protest, not in her position of being an outcast family member.

"I can assure you, Mrs. Wainwright-Dobson," the elder Miss Dupris began with a tone that would have kept shave ice from melting even in July, "I will do anything I can, yet it has been such a long time. You must realize even the best memory fades." She laughed quietly. "People come and go in life. Darling Diamond needs to be realistic. The things that happened in the past can be so difficult. She must be aware that not everyone feels that there is reason to expose details that have long been forgotten." Victoria Dupris sipped the tea, studied the cup, and then as if to punctuate whatever she was getting at, produced a tiny nod of recognition toward Darling Diamond, as I would now call her.

"I want her to find the truth." Another sip, another time to study the cup and then a nod and all this came about as if Darling Diamond were five years old or not in the same room, sitting on the very edge of that white, heavy brocade sofa as her elderly auntie.

Everything Victoria Dupris said felt like a lie and that's how her facial expressions read too, but since I became a practicing Christian, I have been striving to give even the most incredible declarations the benefit of the doubt. It could be that Victoria Dupris didn't know she was lying or it could be, flat out, that Victoria wasn't going to help her niece find out anything about Jimmy March or share whatever she knew to be true.

"The truth always has its way of surfacing," I replied, and after I sipped the tea, I studied the cup.

Sure, Diamond could be on a fool's quest, but if she didn't try, she knew the result. Besides Diamond's blues eyes silently pleaded with me for support and strength over the ninety-five pound domineering aunt. *Lord protect me*, I prayed because from the look in Diamond's eyes and the grunt from the spinster across the tea table, I was certainly going to need it.

The minutes stretched and the silence became even awkward. It was like she was daring me to start some insipid small talk. I wanted to scream, "Get me out of here."

As Victoria placed the plastic oxygen mask over her nose and face, drawing in a breath of oxygen, I swallowed the final drop of what I hoped was Earl Grey, but it was so weak your guess would be as good as mine.

I slipped the cup into the saucer. I'd had plenty. If Diamond wanted to discuss her efforts so far in finding information about her father, her aunt didn't bring up the subject. More so, if Diamond had any chutzpah I sure didn't see it. Hence, this topic was never discussed.

At the same instant as I stood, Victoria Dupris cleared her throat and frowned. I knew what that meant and I was ready to head for the door.

I nodded. "Thank you for the tea, Miss Dupris. I must run now. However, I've been wondering—" But the sentence did get any further because the butler was there to announce that Diamond's luggage, which had been delayed, had just arrived.

And that's how I found myself suddenly alone with the aunt. As Diamond closed the door, her aunt put the mask down and looked me dead in the eyes. Unlike Diamond, hers were the color of ebony and her look as sharp as a well-honed knife. The lines around her mouth were granite. I'd been surprised by how strong "frail" older people could be and I was glad to have the coffee table between us.

"I will not have you encouraging my niece, Mrs. Wainwright-Dobson, or whatever your real name is, since I have never heard of anyone with such a convoluted last name, especially in my social circles. If you are in this for the money, smarten up. That girl has nothing. Nothing. And besides all this will blow over. Unless people ask too many questions. People who should mind their own business. People like you. Once the questions stop, scandal dies. I have seen it before. Have I made myself clear? Or are you too much of a ninny to understand? Perhaps one of the servants can be called in and explain this to you in simpler terms."

I blinked. That was downright mean. "You're mistaken, Miss Dupris. I've not influenced Diamond in any way. She contacted me, not the other way around."

"So you say," came with a huff and a cough. "If I were you, madam, I would disavow all knowledge of that ghastly singer and so-called novelist Jimmy Whatever."

"March. His name was Jimmy March, ma'am."

"Whatever his name was, it is not your place to be involved in this. It is family business. Any supposed connection with my recently deceased sister, Elaine, will now stay with her. Your help is not needed nor is it wanted. Is that clear? You do not belong in our world. I am surprised you do not know your place."

For a moment, I actually feared Victoria Dupris was going to add, "Like that cheeky maid," or worse, and more graphic, but she even outdid my idea of an insult.

She picked up her cane, pointed it at me, and nearly spit the words, "Stay the hell out of our lives." She took a long dram on the oxygen, wheezed, and added, "If you know what is good for you. Or you will wish you had."

That whisper could have fast-frozen the entire Amazon river.

"Is that a threat?" Of course it was, but I didn't know what else to say. "Are you afraid there's proof of a liaison between Jimmy March and Lanie? Afraid of social disgrace?" I squared my shoulders and hopefully the chin came along with it. I certainly didn't want this ogre to see that inside I'd lost my unfaltering law enforcement edge. Besides, if this nut case attacked, I knew I could wrestle her to the Persian carpet or make it through the door. A tea table was, however, the only barrier between us and the flimsy antique wouldn't have stopped a lunatic for long. I wasn't going to guess how quickly the woman could move, even if she had a breathing disorder. Hatred makes people feel more powerful. I'd seen plenty of that in my old life.

Then she brandished the silver-handled cane. It all felt surreal. I was about to be attacked for asking a few questions by a nut job on oxygen for trying to be a good person.

As all this was bouncing in my brain, Victoria Dupris clutched the cane, gasped, coughed a bit more and placed the mask on again, drawing a shallow breath. She tossed the apparatus onto the sofa. "Her name was Elaine and I will thank you to use it correctly if we should ever meet again, which I sincerely hope we do not. Or you will not know what hit you, you, you, hussy." Then her face turned benign. The woman lips made the frown turn slightly upward.

I swallowed back a laugh. "A hussy? Are you attempting to threaten me, ma'am?" A grating snort came from her wrinkled face. "Excuse me, Mrs. Wainwright-Dobson. Would you repeat that? Did you say 'threat' or 'treat'? Unfortunately my hearing is not as it should be. The ravages of old age." She coughed, to make a point of how truly in poor health she was, except the steely hatred didn't leave the old woman's eyes.

Miss Dupris was not only vicious, I realized, but more crazy than I'd imagined. Then it hit me. We were no longer alone. The thick carpet had muffled Diamond's returned, with the kind maid following her holding a silver tray with a fresh tea service.

"Thanks so much for the *treat*," I gathered my purse, knowing that as I reached the entryway; my raincoat would mysteriously appear in the butler's hands. Besides, if Diamond had to go out again and leave the two of us alone, the old woman really would assault me. I wasn't about to take that chance. Victoria Dupris whimpered and brought the plastic mask to her face, but the silver handled cane was right at her side. Her eyes never left me.

Miss Dupris didn't bid me goodbye, but her eyes followed me to the door. Diamond didn't try to stop me as I moved toward the foyer, but then she was there, putting a hand on my arm. "Have you found anything out? Will people tell you anything? May I telephone you later, perhaps when Auntie is taking a nap?" Diamond's hushed voice was barely audible.

I patted the woman's shoulder. Even through the expensive fuzziness of her rust colored sweater, I could feel bones. She bent forward, an air kiss to anyone watching, and whispered, "May I call you if I learn anything from Auntie?"

"I'm at the Hilton. And you have my cell number."

"Yes, I know. I'll walk you out." Diamond started for the door, but that didn't happen because like a dog on a leash, she was stopped in her tracks.

"Diamond, dear. Could you do your auntie a favor and get my sweater," came Victoria Dupris's cultured voice, which had lost all its delicate tones, and sounded like it had the power of a baseball umpire, stopped Diamond as if the niece had been slapped with a voodoo curse. "I want the black one. I believe it is folded in the closet. Or perhaps in the Chippendale chest of drawers. In my bedchamber. Upstairs."

I spoke in a whisper. "You be careful, girl," and added in a louder tone, "Might be best if you just hung out around here for a day or so." The cell-phone stalker, as I now silently referred to the man with the flashy earring, might not be as timid with Diamond as he'd been with me.

"Are you going to get the sweater or shall I ring for that lazy Inez to come in here then have her go all the way upstairs?"

In the distance, I could see a depraved curl of Miss Dupris's lips. It disturbed me and I'm not easily troubled.

Chapter 11

The butler did it.

Okay, I've always wanted to say that. Alright, the butler didn't do anything beyond looking shifty and he somehow had a taxi waiting when I walked down the mansion's marble steps.

I didn't turn around to look at the house. If either of the Misses Dupris were watching, I couldn't give the younger one false hope that I could help her and the older, nutty one? I refused to provide any hint that she'd troubled me. Even though she had.

If I were trying to keep my mind off the concert and my debut as the keyboard artist, and I was, the visit at the mansion provided plenty to keep my mind for the event that was looming closer with each second. I could have returned to the resort, tried to book that pedicure or soaked in some rays, but oh no, that didn't occur to me. Instead, I was determined to dig a bit deeper into the night that Jimmy March was last seen. These days, we pretend we can access anything on the trusty Internet, but some stuff requires a trip to the good old public library. You can gasp now, but it's true.

I Googled the address of the main branch and asked the cabbie to drop me at the library on King Street. It was a huge pillared building with walls so thick you just had to whisper. I found the reference librarian, told her my need, and she sent me straight to an intern and the archives.

Here's the condense accumulation of what I found that was reported in the newspaper after a disturbance at the Honolulu Theater in Chinatown on the night in question. Or the lack of information, I should say. From the microfiche pages of the

Honolulu Advertiser, I read: One, someone reported hearing a shot fired. No name was given for who called in the noise. Two, when the police arrived; no one knew anything about a gun being fired and the officers' names were not mentioned in the short clipping. Three, the theater management refunded the cost of the tickets for the next night's event that would have starred Jimmy March. Four, one Babes Waller, reported to have been part of the band, said to a reporter, "Jimmy's not available right now. He's fine. No, he never played with a gun. He needs time off for personal reasons." Personal? How about personally suffering a bullet hole to his chest? That's pretty personal in my opinion.

I continued to scan the microfiche. But the next mention of anything happening at the Honolulu Theater was a performance of *Swan Lake.* Nothing at all about Jimmy March's abrupt cancellation of the rock concert. To me? It all sounded exactly what was written on that tiny florist's card: Jimmy March was dead.

That's what I was contemplating as I got ready for my first, and God willing, last ever performance as part of a rock band.

Since I just told you the condensed version of what I found from hours of pouring over microfiche and dusty newspapers, here's the abbreviated one on my performance with Slam Dunk. I smiled and I played.

Okay, I know you want more details and it's not pretty. As agreed, the keyboard was not connected to the audio system. I tried to keep up with Henry, Max, and the others. I didn't and I couldn't. And I stunk. Not only did sweat pour out of every pore in my body, but my face was the color of an overripe tomato. My hands shook so badly that more than once they slipped from the keys. My knees felt like overcooked spaghetti, but I remained standing. Yes, that was a miracle.

Have you ever had root canal work? I would have chosen that over the hour-long performance.

I survived, but just barely. Especially when after two songs I got the nerve to look into the audience and right in the third row I saw him. On the aisle was Payton Yu (who waved to me like he was flagging a taxi and then blew kisses—would this guy ever grow up?), Mr. and Mrs. Yu (both smiling and totally embarrassed at their son's behavior, or so it seemed), various Yu family members I vaguely remembered meeting at the science club in high school, and even Tina, minus her snappy dressed boyfriend. Next to Payton but in the aisle sat Alana, gorgeous as ever, snug in a wheelchair and clapping like crazy.

The band had barely taken its final bow when I dashed from the stage, pledging to God that I would rather do a year of community service picking up trash on a gridlocked interstate or face an auditorium of pre-teens with a gadzillion questions about how people die by the hands of law enforcement and how much money I made, than be on any stage ever again. Some people think of hell as eternal burning. Public speaking and public performing are my personal version, hence, I was not going to stray from the straight and narrow after that glimpse into my choice for the future.

As I dashed, I ran once again straight into Payton Yu. Arms as wide as his smile, he said, "You were fabulous, Nikky, oh, I mean Nica, you were wonderful. I couldn't keep my eyes off you."

"Payton, put me down please," I said in the steely way I might have said, "It's best for you if you'll drop that gun to the floor." People really do obey me, but not my pal Playboy Payton. He swung me off the floor. Even with that extra width around his middle, he was strong.

"I've got to say, I just came tonight for Alana, but man, you were the icing on my cake of life, Nikky, oh, geez, sorry." He let me go with one hand and slipped another around my waist.

If I hadn't been exhausted, trust me, I would have pushed him into next Tuesday. But I was and I didn't, which apparently seemed like encouragement. Then I was circled by the band and even Mr. and Mrs. Yu came backstage with Alana glowing with joy and shaking hands with everyone.

Payton pulled me aside. "That's the happiest I've seen sis since the accident. She was bouncing up and down with music and I thought she was going to knock over her wheelchair. I swear, for a time, I thought she was going to get up and dance. The docs have been guardedly optimistic that she'll walk again with plenty of physical therapy, but it's been a nightmare for Alana and us. You and the band are an incredible blessing to my family, Nikky, and I won't forget this."

"Then stop calling me by that awful high school name, will you," I pleaded.

"That I can't do because I love it," he said and I swear if he hadn't been such a guy's guy, he would have slapped his face for letting that gooey statement out. But instead of being embarrassed as a normal human would be, he pulled me to a quiet corner near the deserted dressing rooms.

"Look me in the eyes, Nikky or Nica or Mrs. Wainwright-Dobson, or whatever you want me to call you," he demanded.

I looked down into his smooth, but craggy face which was weathered just enough to show he loved the outdoors. I watched his expressions soften and then his lashes flutter. As an inept profiler, these signs I believe meant he was an experienced liar (wait, Payton was a politician) or someone who was about to spill the beans and get totally mushy. Therefore, I tried to get away, but when he touched my face, my feet refused to budge.

"Just listen. I apologize for all the adolescent, hormone-driven behavior I put you through years ago. If I could go back in time, I would have stopped the gossip. I would have told the truth and stood up to the others like a man."

"Payton, it's okay. It's over," I tried to interrupt him.

"Stop. Listen to me, hear me out, Nikky. I have regretted my actions or realistically my stupid inactions every day since that incident, regretted my behavior for two decades. When that line backer Buck Flint, and yes, he is the baby brother to Miss Margaret Flint, pulled you down to the ground there under the bleachers where I knew you were hiding to get away from the taunting of the cheerleaders, including Courtney, I just wanted you to get away. I knew, we both knew, what he had in mind."

"So you stood up to him," I whispered, "and what he had in mind didn't happen."

"Wait. Something awful still did happen when old Buck spread the gossip that you and I were doing it after every evening practice. And that you'd have sex with anyone who got to know you. I knew it wasn't true, but it would have been my word against Buck's and by the time I got back to practice after helping you get cleaned up, he'd told the world, that was our high school, all those wretched lies. Who better to take revenge against me because I was selected to be the quarterback when he wanted it than to lie about you and me having sex beneath the bleachers." He gulped. "I honestly thought the talk would die overnight because everyone seemed to think I could get any girl on campus, but whether you want to believe it or not, and I'm hoping you believe me, I was as socially awkward as any other guy in our class. Sure, I knew kids in our school who were doing it, but I wasn't part of that. You have my word on it. My sin was that some part of insecure me wanted to believe that you found me attractive enough to, well, do what Buck said."

I placed my chin on his shoulder. "I didn't understand why you didn't tell the others what really had happened, but I was just thankful you happened to be there when you were."

"I was there because I'd seen Buck staring at you since the start of school. When I saw him follow you, I just acted."

As if I'd lost control of my arms, they circled Payton and I felt his arm come around my waist. "I know this is twenty years overdue, but thank you. If you hadn't stepped in, much of my life, I'm sure, would have been different. We probably wouldn't be here talking today."

He pulled away and looked into my eyes. "And you wouldn't have been dubbed the easiest girl at Kukui High for the next three years. Yeah, I really helped."

"Stop it. It's over."

"Can I call you Nikky because I love to?"

I punched his chest, softly. "Okay, but if you rhyme it with anything, anything, Payton Yu, I will have you arrested for harassment on some trumped up charge that will take you a month of Sundays to get out of."

"Scout's honor, ma'am, um, Nikky." He laughed and yanked me to his chest.

Truth be told, I was rather enjoying being where I was until I heard a round of not-so-subtle coughs and giggles behind me. Yes, the entire Yu family, Slam Dunk members, Jane, Tom, Harmony, and thank goodness, not the little dog, were right there.

"Any announcements to make, little brother?" Alana asked, unable to stop smiling.

"Yeah, Nikky has accepted my apology for being a jerk," he replied and kept an arm around my waist.

Alana grabbed my hand. "Honey, I believe that was the first time in my life I've ever heard my sibling apologize for anything. I don't know what magic you've created that has changed the guy, but keep it up." She pulled me down and we hugged.

"I second that," said tiny Mrs. Yu.

Henry jumped on a chair and waved his hands. "Listen up, everyone. You're all invited to the Glass Slipper, that restaurant, okay it's a dive, but friendly and it's right across from the Aloha

Tower. We're all going there for a late supper and it's all on Slam Dunk."

I've never seen so many musicians, lighting crews, stagehands and their families, because this was definitely a family affair, move so quickly. It felt like a gale force wind hit the place, and there I still stood. But I had the sense to let go of Payton. Before I got all mushy about his apology and announcement that he loved my name, I let the crowd move me out of the theater. Besides, I needed to think over what had just happened. And if it had anything to do with my heart beating out of my chest, or that was some chemical reaction, some hormones that had been in hiding for years or a result of the cancer treatments.

Finding love again in the future sounded okay, but there was no way on God's green earth I was going to let my heart get smacked around by the likes of Payton Yu unless I wanted to and he showed maturity to my wishes. Remember, my friend, I've been married twice and had to learn what "death do we part" meant. While Payton was younger than husbands number one and number two, there was so much I didn't know about him as a man, like his moral code, his personal statement of faith, and if he was someone I wanted to see the last thing at night and first thing in the morning for the rest of this lifetime and perhaps beyond. Plus, did he always travel around with two muscled bodyguards? Or was that just during elections?

So when he slipped an arm around my waist again as we headed toward the exit, I stepped away.

"Did my magic evaporate that quickly?"

"No, Payton, you've got charm oozing from every pore," I replied.

"Sounds disgusting," he said and waited by the stage door while I grabbed my shoulder bag. "Nikky, listen for a second. I came on awful hard just now. I've always stayed back when emotional decisions were to be made, waiting to see if my feelings would be safe. It could be my heritage, but after forty-five years, my parents still smooch. Except that's only when they think nobody sees them. It's weird, but Alana and I have just tried to accept them."

"What are you getting at?" I felt my forehead wrinkle.

Payton looked at the bodyguards, nodded, and they disappeared. "After Alana's accident, she told me from that hospital bed about how she had a near-death experience when she was on the operating table. Yeah, serious and rational Alana told me it happened while she was having surgery to stop the internal bleeding. Our grandmother, we called her the Chinese name Nai Nai, and she were walking on a beach, holding hands and talking. They reached a place with waterfalls and lush vegetation. Alana said it reminded her of Sacred Falls State Park, on the North Shore. Nai Nai told her there was more for her to do so she wasn't going to die. You know Alana. She argued with Nai Nai, but my grandmother wouldn't listen. Alana said, 'I was told to get back in my body, stop my whining, and do the work God planned for me.'

"Then she freaked me out. Alana said, 'Payton, Nai Nai wanted you to know that you must stop being afraid when love looks you in the eyes. She told me to tell you that when you dream of the woman you have loved for your entire life and you must find her.'"

Payton was not smiling. This wasn't a trick to get my attention. His face was pale. "I've never told anyone about this. Alana asked me not to. And she doesn't know what happened next. I stayed the night in the hospital, on a pullout bed they have for family of dying patients and that night I dreamed I was back at the Kukui High. There was Buck dragging you down in the mud, but this time I was me. I was thirty-eight-year-old Payton Yu. I grabbed the back of his football jersey and lectured the big oaf on how if he ever even thought of looking in your direction again, I would rearrange his brains and he'd wish he'd never been born. I also used language that would have turned my mom's hair even grayer."

"Me? You dreamed about me? After twenty years?" What would you have said to that revelation? Yeah, I was dumbstruck, too.

"When I woke up that next morning, Alana was actually sitting up in bed with ear buds on, listening to Slam Dunk on her iPod and tapping a tune with her index finger, the one finger that she could move back then." He swallowed. "So, when I bumped into you at the International Market, you think you were blown away? I nearly had a heart attack, and my heart's in fine working condition."

"I don't know what to say. Except, Payton, it was just a dream."

"Nikky, I thought so, but if you'll have me, I'd like to do something so old fashioned that it's probably going to become hip again. I'd like to court you."

I chuckled, the nice kind that sounds warm. "Is there an app for that? I could Google it, maybe, and see if I wanted all that it entails."

"As the hopeful next governor of the State of Hawaii and responsible for our people, our *'ohana'*—our family, I would be honored if you'd accompany me to the Glass Slipper and let me buy you dinner and maybe even ask you to take a walk later." He bowed.

I blinked and blinked again. If this was the new and mature version of Payton Yu, it was bizarre, but oddly comfortable. "I may live to regret this, but can we shake on the fact that we'll consider this courting thing?"

"I'd even do a blood pact, but you may remember, I faint at the sight of it." He chuckled and made a face.

"That's right. I remember the last football game of the season and you scrapped your leg. You stood in the end zone, and yes, I was hiding behind some silly sign. But I saw you look down at your shin, see the scrape and the blood, and topple over. Everyone thought it was an injury until the coach informed the crowd that you were fine. You just had a delicate stomach. However did you get over that?"

He took my hand and the car keys that were in my fingers. "Too much information already? I have to save some of my most embarrassing moments for our next courting session. Come on, the family will think we've deserted them and who knows what Henry will make of this. Alana? She can read me like a novel, like all those romance ones she gobbles up."

Chapter 12

When we arrived at the Glass Slipper, the music poured out the open doors. Henry was right. It was a tropical dive and complete with cheesy tiki torches and ten-foot tall Hawaiian masks.

"You been here before, right?" Payton asked.

"No, you? But according to Henry, the poo poo platter is to die for and you can stuff yourself on everything from poke to loco moco and hear the best old rock and roll on the island." I told Payton how the place only served tropical drinks sans any alcohol as the owner was a recovering alcoholic. "Besides, he told me, 'Old rockers don't get that way when they mix music and alcohol,'" I explained to Payton as we walked through the front doors.

Henry, Max, and a few guys I didn't recognize were jamming.

Payton nudged me. "You know you want to sit at the keyboard."

"You know no such thing," I snapped. What provoked my irritation was that I didn't like the guy reading my mind, thank you very much.

"Go on, you want to. I'll find us a table. I've got some connections, know a few people here. You have fun."

"I would greatly appreciate it, Mr. Yu, if you should ever again want to read my mind, don't cross the line and tell me want I want to do." But I was now smiling.

"Duly noted, Mrs. Wainwright-Dobson, my love." He smiled the words and turned to meet and greet some locals who probably were prospective voters. Payton waved to the body guards we'd left at the Hawaii Theatre who were sitting at a table near the entrance and having a great time.

Time slipped away and the club filled with more people. At nearly midnight, the group took another break and I had my first chance to find Payton. He was at the bar and introduced me to the club's manager, Reba Price.

When Payton pulled out a stool for me, I realized they were talking about Jimmy March.

Reba reminded me of a Hawaiian Jennifer Lopez, ultra-shapely and enjoying showing it off. Her handshake was firm and she got right back to business. "I've only been here for a few years. I've heard about the March Man, larger than life from some of those stories. If I've learned anything in this business, it's smart to believe about half of the stories—especially about rock and roll singers."

"I saw Babes Waller this afternoon. Doing well," I said and she nodded.

"Max told me about the old group. Have you seen Pinkie yet?" Reba asked quietly, as Payton started schmoozing with a passing customer.

"Did Pinkie know Jimmy as a musician or a writer?" I had no idea who Pinkie was, but it was a lead. I wasn't going to blow it by sounding like an outsider.

"No idea. I've never met him, just know the name. Seems to me, and I could be wrong, that he managed or maybe played with some of the groups back then. Never Slam Dunk, but the others that Jimmy played with before joining up with Henry and the guys," she said and motioned to Henry who was diving into a poo poo platter.

Reba plucked a golden hibiscus from the vase on the bar and put it behind her left ear, making the Merlot-color of her hair looked stunning. "Wait, my dad mentioned Pinkie a few days ago. That's right, Pinkie lives with his kids now—has to be pushing seventy, think it's north of Pearl City. Dad was talking with a customer about old times and like bartenders love to do and I was washing glasses. I remember them saying that when his band managing skills went south, he played backup. When the Navy closed some bases, the bars where service personnel closed and even the good musicians couldn't find gigs." Reba toyed with the Club soda and juice she was sipping. "Never Pinkie's last name, Nica. But the barista, I recall, is somehow related to someone who Pinkie knew and I'll just ask—" But a customer wedged between us and started talking to the manager.

I got up and said, "I need a refill of the mango juice. I'll find out." And weaved through the crowd to the middle bar where the bartender was working.

"I'll take a chance and just to be risky, add a twist of lime to that," I said when I was caught staring at the nose rings, all four and strung through his right nostril.

"Hot crowd tonight." He smiled. "And you're the best of them." He had braces on his teeth.

That was so way not true, and I wondered if he thought I was a cougar. "Been here long?" I wanted to check his driver's license and contact his mama about what he was doing. This guy looked about sixteen and yet I swear he was checking out my cleavage.

"Nope. Reba's somehow related to my mom and when she heard that Slam Dunk was going to come here after the concert, she put on extra staff. I have all of Slam Dunk's music. Most of us around here worship at Diamond Head Christian Center. That's how we met. If you know this town, you know it. It's just about six miles east of Honolulu, big building. Gotta come to the Saturday night service, I tell you, the music is the most excellent. Hey, I could take you."

"Sorry, I'm, well, see Payton Yu over there?"

"Yeah?"

"He has decided he's going to court me." I smiled.

"That some type of new video game, right?"

"Close, but I'll explain it later," I replied.

The kid stuck his hand across the bar. "I'm a genetic science major at HU and hope to finish my doctorate next year. My mom likes to tell people, 'Time some more Christians became scientists,' but she only started saying this years back when I scored the highest on my SATs in Hawaii's history and got that scholarship. I love anything that explodes, but I guess with genetics explosions aren't such a good idea. What do you think?"

"Have you thought of switching to decaf?"

He got the joke and filled my glass. Then I asked, "So if you're helping, who is the regular guy?"

"George Stratford. In the back. Said his feet hurt. Seems to know everyone here and then some. A little quite for a barista. The strangest thing is that the man doesn't drink coffee and won't touch juice. Imagine being a barista and not drinking this brew. No, me either. Hey, you sure you don't want an espresso? I make a mean one." He bounced up and down, taping his hand on the counter.

"I have had enough already." Once I got past the nose rings, the barista was too cute, funny, and charming and yes, too full of coffee for his own good. "Think George would mind if I took my break with him?"

"Hey—no problem. If you know Reba, you get the run of the place." He lifted the hinged divider and motioned me toward the tiny kitchen.

George was alone. His feet were propped on a chair. The *Honolulu Advertiser's* sports section was in his fingers and his glasses were perched on his nose. An apron covered a white silk shirt and dark slacks. Taken out of the present circumstances, a kitchen in back of a club and put into some Hollywood-style duds, he could be taken for a has-been actor, one that unlike fine wine didn't get better with age. I'd seen his type all over the world. There was a slippery essence about him like a film on black ice on the highway. Unseen, and menacing. I would have to choose words with care.

Seeing me at the door, George placed the paper on the table and stood as if meeting royalty. His perfect white teeth sparkled. "You probably don't remember me, Miss Ticky. But I knew your dad. We worked on base together. Years ago. Your dad and I carpooled and sometimes dropped you off at the high school when you went early for some club. Payton said you were here."

"Science club? You still remember me?" I focused for about three seconds, and bam. There was something familiar about him and the thought made me a tad icky, so I stopped thinking and listened.

"Why, you're bigger, and fine-looking, but you look the same." He bowed slightly and took just the tips of my right hand in his. I half expected a fingertip kiss like in the movies. A part of me felt relieved when he released it and it was a part I didn't want to ever be kissed by this man. I know that's not loving my neighbor, but from the look in his eyes, it didn't seem like a neighborly love that was the subject of his attention.

I pulled up a battered chair to the table and motioned him to sit. "You're so kind." I took a sip of the water I had carried in with me, cleared my throat and got down to it. "I'm trying to find out more about Jimmy March."

"Jimmy?"

"Yes, I understand you might have known him…"

He scratched his head. Probably to buy himself time, or at least that's what I thought. "Who? March? Oh, yeah."

Of course that was a stall. But why? "I'm collecting material. I think a book should be written about him." At that second, I wondered if it was true. I concentrated on George.

George scratched his grizzled head, producing an indolent smile. "The gal pal of Payton Yu and dazzling beauty," he winked, "and you are a writer?"

At least with his description of me, he didn't add that I was an advisor for the FBI or I would have wondered if the entire world knew of my personal history. "I haven't told anyone about this yet. If I don't have the knack, I don't want to be embarrassed." If I were to write a book on Jimmy's life, it definitely gave me reasons to ask questions.

"You're a sassy little gal. But this Jimmy you say you're writing about wasn't always good news. He got kicks by grabbing trouble by the tail. Some stuff is best left alone." The husky whisper jetted near my ear. George slowly folded the newspaper, re-creasing the natural lines and making some new ones, then smoothing the corners.

"Listen here, George. The public has a right to know about Jimmy, the legend, and how at one time he was more famous than McCartney." Okay that was a stretch even to my ears since few today had interest in the wannabes of eighties rock and roll, like Jimmy March.

I pulled a hundred out of the pocket of my jeans. And waited. We both stared at the crisp bill. George smiled, but didn't move. I slipped another on the battered table, but held the corner tightly, my eyes not wavering from the hooded ones that now met mine straight on.

"Money can't buy happiness, but somehow it's more comfortable to cry in a Porsche than a Kia," he snickered and then said, "I'll tell you this right off, but you don't go around repeating that George Stratford, the best bartender this side of Atlantic City said so. Jimmy was mixed up with an evil bunch of thugs."

"Old news." I attempted to yank on the money and felt like I was in a bad Humphrey Bogart movie, but George didn't give an inch, refusing to let go of the bill.

"It was the underworld. Gangsters and gambling. Maybe big-time bookmakers from mainland China. Rumor had it at one time they had some politicians on their payroll, too. Rumor had it Jimmy was into it all. Didn't do nothing like those squirts who run high stakes poker. It was deeper. I don't know why a writer with the skill in music like Jim had did it. Maybe the adrenaline rush. Hear you can get addicted that that. Still doesn't make sense. You'd do well not to find out anything further." He extracted the bill from my fingers and slipped it into the chest pocket of his silky shirt, smooth as a pro.

"And Pinkie?" I didn't know Pinkie, but from the look that flickered in George's eyes for the briefest instant, I had scored. I'd struck a nerve. "Where does he fit into this?"

"Pinkie?" George's voice blasted over the rattle of pans as a cook cleaned a counter. I saw the woman cock her head toward us, blatantly eavesdropping as she slipped a pot into the sink. "He and Jimmy were pals. Let me amend that. Pinkie followed Jimmy around like a puppy dog. Pinkie was there the night we saw Jimmy, you know."

"Reba said Pinkie lives with his kids. North of Honolulu. Pearl City, I think. I won't be in town long. Love to interview him, too. Do you have the address or know how I can find him?" I tried not to be obvious as I fished in my jeans for the last bill. If it took more, I was going to have to hit up Payton for it. Bribery is like bluffing at poker and I was never good at either.

George palmed the money with another smooth move and spouted off Pinkie's phone number like it was one he called it regularly. "Son's name is Ringley, call him Ring. Imagine a kid growing up with that claim to fame."

I shook my head. Whatever this joke was, I didn't get it.

George let out a snort of laughter. "Get it? Last name's Finger. Pinkie Finger. Ring Finger. Wonder if he named the other kids Index and Middle? Can you believe that Pinkie was that cruel or it could be he was just as stupid as I always thought."

My brain, formerly clouded with chemo, made a connection and it had zip to do with inappropriate ways to name one's children.

Connections and numbers. George Stratford had something to do with numbers. The numbers racket. Jail. He was sent to prison.

How could I have been so dense? How could I have pushed it out of my memory? In a second, it all came back. I'd never seen so much violence and anger from a man as I had from George Stratford.

I thought to that night. It was the summer between my junior and senior year in high school and the memories flooded back. It was warm and Dad and George were in our garage bent over the hood of a battered pickup that George brought to our house. It was a clunker, but Dad was amazing with cars and George needed it fixed. I was there in the garage sitting on a stool doing advanced calculus, practicing for my SATs, and asking Dad for help now and then. Once in a while I'd take a peek at George. Back then, he did look like a movie star, or so I had thought.

Suddenly, a half dozen cop cars pulled up to the house, lights flashing and sirens screaming. One cruiser drove over Dad's manicured front lawn. Dad grabbed me and pulled me to the floor. "We'll be okay. You're okay. Just don't move, baby."

George nearly stepped on us as he ran through the house and out the back door.

I knew George couldn't get away. I'd watched enough *Hawaii Five-0* with Jack Lord to know that the cops would surround the house. What I didn't know, until I read the newspaper the next day, was that George had been arrested for the attempted murder of someone in a bar fight. Dad never offered any details, but he was just as shocked as me and Mom. Yet, now? I could definitely find out and had the resources to do so.

"Remember me to Pinkie, would you?" George shoved the chair near the stack in the corner and chuckled, seemingly to himself as he swaggered through the swinging kitchen door.

Would this three-hundred dollar investment be worth the introduction to one Pinkie Finger? "I've spent more money on less," I whispered and made plans to intrude on another life hurt by Jimmy March. I pulled my cell from my pocket. It was late,

Diamond was ill, her aunt was passive-aggressive, and the whole investigation, as I was now calling it, was a big fat muddle. I knew a lot of history about March, and from everything I'd read in college and from talking with Babes and George, it seemed like the writer and rocker was cursed. A black cloud of things that could go wrong went in that direction.

The Jimmy March curse? Had everything that man touched gone sour? A prominent debutant from a rich Hawaiian family was forced to become a recluse, their child was ostracized from her heritage or even Jimmy's biological family, and now the woman chronically ill. The few people I talked with seemed to freak when Jimmy's name was mentioned, or if not, stopped and considered their words they changed. And then there was the stalker. Was I any closer to knowing what happened to Jimmy's body if it were true and he lost at Russian roulette? Or after he'd been murdered like Diamond asserted?

Nope. But that didn't stop me.

Chapter 13

The day dawned, as days do, even in paradise. Instead of knowing I could dash outside and run in the waves, the image of creepy George Stratford was the first thing that came to mind. I couldn't shrug it off. I started the coffee and then noticed a flashing light on the house phone. That meant a message. It was straight to the point, in a guttural monotone: "I've left something for you downstairs."

"Of course, Ms. Dobson," said the operator when I called the front desk to have whatever it was delivered to the penthouse. I rather doubted it would be a brown-paper box with ticking inside, yet I felt nervous just waiting for the knock at the door and whatever it was to be delivered.

Moments later, after tipping the delivery woman, I fingered a sealed envelope. The stationery was familiar. The note was written on the same paper as the one that had come with the roses.

"You are not paying attention. Jimmy March is dead." And just to get my attention, this time that last sentence was underlined. Twice.

So it didn't take a rocket scientist to understand that dear, little Diamond Dupris was not to be thanked for the flowers and also that somebody out there didn't like an on-leave confidential consultant for the FBI meddling in private business. Yet, now I knew the truth was close. Perhaps, I thought, steering through mid-morning traffic, Pinkie could shed some light on the happenings of Jimmy's final day. "It can't hurt to ask," I said and then wondered if whoever sent the card and the flowers was trailing me as I drove west, toward the suburbs and Ewa Beach and an interview with Pinkie.

I exited Interstate Highway 1 and checked the GPS to head toward Pohakupuna Road. The neighborhood was a jumble of styles, from a trash-laden house with screen doors knocked off their hinges and a rusty truck nearly sitting on the front porch to a darling, pristine cottage straight out of the pages of *Coastal Living* magazine. In between these two homes, Pinkie and his wife lived in a duplex, probably built in the nineteen-fifties. Newspapers still in plastic bags, bikes, and toys littered the scruffy front lawn with stout oleander bushes framing the front door, sprinkling their spent blooms like a carpet of red, orange, and white.

Half dozen kids were playing baseball in the street, even though I could see Ewa Beach Park down the road. I edged to the side of the road after a girl pulled home plate halfway down the block, unperturbed that I'd just infringed on the game. I watched them for a moment, remembering how I'd grown up in a neighborhood much like this with kids running from home to home. There had been a feeling to trust, of love in the families and freedom to be children.

I thought of how these days, armed guards patrolled school buildings and parents worried if their kids were on a perverted website, at least the kids in the families I knew on the mainland.

"Maybe here in Hawaii those feelings of freedom to be a child weren't totally destroyed," I said. Had I ever been as carefree as those kids? Would I ever be again?

Even before I knocked, I smelled rich bean soup with Portuguese sausage, a staple of the islands and from recipes brought over by Portuguese immigrants who came to work in the fields. If I hadn't been there to ask questions about a long-ago murder, I would have asked to stay for lunch.

My knock produced a ramrod straight, gaunt apron-clad woman in her late sixties, possibly older, with a tot yanking at the hem of her skirt. "Ms. Dawson?" A baby wailed in the background and the woman frowned more deeply. "I'm Pinkie's wife." She opened the door and stepped back into the living room. "I don't think we've met, but then when Pinkie used to be on the road, I didn't go, even to the shows. Somebody had to stay with the babies and now I've got the grandkids to handle. So here I am staying home again." The statement was gruff and practiced, as if she enjoyed appearing trod upon.

I nodded and would have shaken her hand, but she turned and lifted another baby from the playpen, motioning me farther into the house. I stepped over red, yellow, and blue plastic locking blocks, a stuffed bear with one ear hanging loose, muddy socks, and a baby's bottle half filled with something pink and thick, like papaya juice.

Some homes can be shabby and ooze with love. This one did not. It looked like too many people were squeezed into it. Yet, here and there were expensive pieces of electronic equipment, like a huge plasma television and an enormous stereo system.

"To be truthful, Mrs. Finger…" I knew when all else failed, the truth was about the best solution around.

"You just call me Mildred, or Mil. Most folks do."

"Thanks. I've only heard about Pinkie and the old days, from my uncle, Henry Angieski, and the others. I've come to ask some questions about those times. That's why I'm here."

Mildred nodded, crinkled the lines in her forehead and buttoned the top of her lavender-colored sweater. "Cool even for us in Hawaii. I've heard the locals call it a two-layer day but then again the locals are always calling things stuff that doesn't make sense."

I had no explanation why she didn't want to be considered a local and frankly when she gestured me toward the back of the house and the kitchen, ducked her torso outside, and hollered, "Pinkie, dearest," I didn't care. The soup might smell like heaven in a bowl, but the woman's sour face made me wonder who the cook of the family was. Surely she could not have made it.

I sat at the kitchen table as Mil stood at the back door and yelled for her husband. Then yelled again, "Pinkie, you put that shovel down. Didn't you hear me call? What's wrong with you, man? It's that woman who is writing the book. She's here, Pinkie. The author is here. And you wipe those feet this time. Whoever you're talking to on your cell can wait. We got company." Mil's complaints sounded like to fingernails on an old fashioned blackboard, but when she turned a smile was plastered on her lips. "Enough mud gets tracked into this house in just one day to plant his precious vegetable garden right here in the kitchen. Land sakes that man never even notices the filth and he's as happy as a clown," she snorted. "Too happy most of the time." She stepped away from the door.

From my place at the kitchen table, I could see him. Pinkie shrugged out of a soiled work shirt to unveil a sweat drenched t-shirt. He removed the Boston White Sox baseball cap and ran his hand over a shiny hairless head and shoved his cell into the back pocket of his muddy jeans.

He was of middle height, no distinguishing tattoos or scars, and there seemed to be nothing but average about him. Pinkie Finger was an older guy, who at one time probably had been a muscular man, except now those muscles sagged. He and the misses certainly weren't living in the style that Babes Waller did, minus the electronic stuff in the cramped living room. Yet, when he saw a grandchild run toward him, the smile made his crinkled face glow. He snatched up the child, twirled her around, and plunked her down, never missing a step as he walked to the back door. I clarified my thoughts. Pinkie Finger was a rich man.

At the doorstep, Pinkie put the child down and slipped off the muddy boots. He wiped loamy dirt off his fingers. Mil stood near the sink and cluck-clucked, grumbling. I could see he was ignoring her in a practiced way.

Mil muttered another complaint and disregarded a little one bawling and begging to be picked up. Instead, she leaned against the refrigerator and watched as Pinkie scrubbed off the dirt. Then he said, "I'm afraid I don't have much memory for details about the old days, Ms. Dawson."

By the length of time it took Pinkie to clean his hands, he wasn't in a rush to divulge just what he knew either. I sat still, I found the courage to put the coffee cup Mil had placed in front of me to my lips, but I wasn't going to open them.

After washing up, he snatched the fussing tot from his wife's arms and sat directly across from me. He kissed the plump tike, nuzzled her soft cherry-red cheeks and she immediately cuddled into her grandfather's embrace. He also avoided my eyes when he spoke. "Now, what specifically can I help you with, miss?"

"George Stratford at the Glass Slipper said you knew Jimmy March, knew him well back in the old days. Those are the times I want to know about." Then I did it. I sipped the bitter brew, and vowed to keep my face from the cringe I knew would appear. But shock of shock, it wasn't bad. "Anything you can tell me would be helpful. Just bits and pieces. They don't have to make sense and from your time together here on Oahu."

"Bits and pieces, okay, well, I remember Jimmy. He was working at one of the posh spots in Honolulu, as a waiter, maybe. I was a doorman waiting to get a music gig. Jimmy said he was a writer, always spouting ideas for a book he was going to write. We'd take breaks together and sit on the loading dock to smoke. He had grand ideas, that Jimmy March. Then one day, he quit because he was going to join a band. Remember, this was in the seventies and eighties. These were disco joints. So, you just want to know about here in Honolulu? Not before?"

I'd nearly dropped the steno notebook I bought to make me look like a real writer when he said, "So you just want to know about Jimmy here in Honolulu? Not before?"

I wanted to shout, "Well, duh," and I was a dud for never thinking to ask this question. I finally managed, "You knew Jimmy before Honolulu?" Why had I assumed? Honestly? Because I either suffered from chemo brain, a now acknowledged medical condition, or I was total dud and a dolt. I'll take the former.

Pinkie looked off in space, shook his head, and chuckled. "Yeah, way back. Hung out in Memphis when we were just out of high school. Tough neighborhood, tough times, but back then everything seemed possible." He bounced the baby on his knee and gently placed her on the floor where she immediately crawled toward a pile of toys. He closed his eyes, and when they flicked open he added, "I tried to tell him he was wasting his time on music, that man. The guy could tell stories, better when he was sober, but he was always spouting stuff about Freud and Jung all the way to Confucius and Karl Marx, then he'd ramble off books of the Bible, that Jimmy, quoting chapter and verse like he was a preacher's son. He never went anywhere without a book. No matter what you've heard, miss, Jimmy was a good guy. Sure, he was foolish. When you grow up with nothing and nobody to count on, that happens. And don't let anyone tell you he wasn't a fine friend."

Mil huffed.

I tuned her out.

So did her husband.

Pinkie was lost in memories.

I waited, pretending to review imaginary notes on the steno pad. I hoped he'd share whatever he was thinking.

He shuttered slightly, got up, and poured a glass of water. Took time drinking it and then asked, "Anything else?"

"If you wouldn't mind, I have some of the background information, but could you tell me more of what happened those final days, before, well, before." I couldn't say Jimmy's death because in fact I could only say that if I knew where his body was? Or if he was actually killed that night? But was I the only one troubled by that discrepancy?

"Let's see, where to start? It happened when we were playing in Chinatown. College kids barged in to the club. I remember looking at the other guys in the band and we knew they'd be trouble. Back them days, college kids stayed close to the university, unless they wanted action. You know what I mean."

I nodded, not wanting to discuss whatever he thought I knew what he meant or something like that.

"At the bars close to Pearl Harbor, IDs would be checked. But in Chinatown, bartenders and bouncers looked the other way, especially since these rich kids had plenty of dough. And that's what they were with their good clothes, straight teeth, and gold watches, and that's when Jimmy got it into his head that he'd be the next big super star."

Pinkie rinsed the glass and nodded his head. "Jimmy was one cool dude. Don't know what William; he's my grandson and we've got him studying medicine at Harvard, or Corrie; she's our oldest granddaughter and at Vassar, would call it today, but if anyone needed a definition of cool, man, it would be Jimmy March."

Pinkie puffed his chest at the mention of the grands. Since everybody knows that Harvard and Vassar aren't economical, I looked around the kitchen with the tattered wallpaper and sagging screen door and wondered where the tuition came from. Rich parents? Didn't seem impossible, just unlikely.

Pinkie's arthritic fingers touched my hand and said, "You heard his music, miss?"

I scribbled what he said about the club and nodded. "I know his writing, his novels, and some of his poems. And his music."

I made more notes; writers did that. "What about the gig at the Hawaii Theatre? Did you see Jimmy before, well, before it happened? Before the accident? Like a few days before? Was anything bothering him? Anyone troubling him?"

Pinkie scratched his bald plate and screwed his eyes shut. The bottom jaw extended in and out. Then for the first time, he really looked at me. He may have already put me in the same category with the rich kids he played to in the seventies, yes, nice clothes and gold watch. I stopped smiling, so at least he couldn't see my straight teeth.

Pinkie's eyes flashed to the ceiling. It was obvious if he wanted to lie, I would have no way of knowing.

The baby sat in the middle of the well-worn linoleum tile, drooled, shoved a fist in her mouth and then fussed. In one smooth move, he plucked her up, grabbed the bottle she'd refused before, and offered it again. "Yeah, saw him a lot that fall and early winter. Knew he had been back and forth to the mainland, heard he was in Washington, D.C. Came to Honolulu a dozen times, before that night, the night when he…well, told me his ship had come in, his luck had changed. He was dressing well, new shoes, my goodness, those slick suits with the wide lapels, John Travolta had those kind. I figured that he must have a sweet little deal going on. Maybe a record deal. You remember records, don't you, Ms. Dawson? When I asked him about it, I had five kids at home and Mil was working as a maid for one of those families that drip with money. We were barely keeping food on the table and me always looking for work. Tough being a veteran and living here in the Islands. But no, this time, he clammed up. Like he was too good for old Pinkie."

"Did he usually brag? You probably knew him better than anyone. Was this like him?"

I decided in that instant either he was an exceptionally good liar or some part of what the man was saying was the truth because he pursed his lips, looked straight at me, and nodded.

"All the guys bragged. Still do."

"Why didn't he want to tell you more? Was it like him to withhold information or even places where you could get a gig? From what I've heard, he was generous to a fault."

Pinkie didn't answer, but went on as if I hadn't spoken. "I knew that if the club where Jimmy was playing liked his singing, they'd be crazy for me. But every time I approached the March Man to ask about it, he put me off. Finally, after the band I'd been playing with folded, I cornered him. I had no jobs lined up and Mil was pregnant. Again. I asked him about it in front of the boys. Anyhow, he pulled away from me like I had leprosy and then he shoved me. Got hostile. Not like Jimmy. He was a cool dude, like I said. Nobody could ruffle that man's feathers, but there he was hot as a skillet on Sunday. He acted like he had the world on a string, but I'd known him a long time, and something wasn't right."

"Think he wanted to keep the gig to himself? Or what? Did he have other problems?"

"I've thought about this for years and that's probably more years than you've probably been on the earth, and it still don't figure up right. Jimmy was generous. He had a smile that could charm the soul of the devil, if the devil has a soul. Don't remember his exact words—it was years ago—but he said something like, 'You don't want none of this stuff, Pinkie. You got babies. You got a good woman at home.' I'm a smart man and could tell he was in over his head. And he really had to keep the business secret."

"Had to? Did you find out any more? Did he tell you the secret?"

Pinkie played "This little piggy goes to market" with the baby's bare toes, he nibbled at a cookie she tried to feed him and avoided looking at me.

I fiddled with the second cup of sludge and shook my head when Mil offered more coffee. I had forgotten she was standing in back of me. "Did you see Jimmy the night he died?" I cut to the chase. Pinkie didn't even blink when I said that Jimmy had died. So did that make it true?

"What about those men you saw talking to Jimmy?" Mil asked turning from the sink where she'd been scrubbing the same pot for the last ten minutes.

"All those ancient memories make my shiny head tired, Mil. Don't remember. But, goodness me, if I told you back then that there were people talking to Jimmy…" He exhaled and turned to me. "My Mil has a steel-trap memory. Yep, if I said there were people talking to March, then it had to be true." Pinkie balanced the baby as he replaced a tire on the toy fire truck produced by yet another whining child. The kid immediately snuggled under Pinkie's right arm and looked at me with enormous brown eyes.

Pinkie shook his head and shrugged.

His body language said, "The interview is over," but I had other plans. "Did you know the men? What did they look like? Musicians? Henry Angieski says that folks in the business can always tell other musicians." I readied the pencil and stayed tight to that kitchen chair.

"Listen, miss, I'd like to help you with whatever you're writing, but it has been years ago. They were men," he replied. He handed the baby to his wife and the child started wailing. He nodded and started to walk to the door without turning back.

He knew a whole lot more and I knew it as sure as I knew I wasn't a writer. Pinkie was selectively forgetting. On a sheet of paper, I scribbled my cell's number and the phone number at the hotel and the number of the room where we were staying, ripped it out of the spiral notepad, and put it in the middle of the kitchen table, then said, "If you or Pinkie should remember anything else. Anything might help put the pieces together. And if it's a matter of money or you need…"

"Don't need your money," Mil snapped, but she took the paper and slipped it into her grease-stained apron. She followed me to the front door, held the screen door for me and whispered, "I think you'd better leave now. I got stuff to tend to and babies to feed. Besides, Jimmy March is dead."

I turned to ask, "How do you know?" but the door slammed in my face.

The dead bolt kicked and I got the message. I'd reached a dead end attempting to get information from Pinkie or Mil.

Realistically, someone had to know something. And someone certainly did—as I was about to find out in a dangerously up close and personal way.

Chapter 14

At the car, I looked toward the house. Everything was still, until the lacy curtains moved and I could see, yes, it was Pinkie's baseball cap in the window. Then I saw him on a cell, making sure I was leaving. Rather than dash for a quick getaway, I sat at the curb, watched the wind ruffle with the palm trees and the kids playing ball. What was Pinkie's real recollection of that last night that anyone saw Jimmy March alive?

Based on Diamond's version of the story, Jimmy and Lanie were lovers and about to go off to find their thrills on Blueberry Hill or whatever was popular in the eighties. According to the rumors and what Diamond said, someone came right into the dressing room and shot Jimmy. Lanie was terrorized, and after making sure that Jimmy was alive, was taken away by someone in the band. Babes Waller was there. Who else? Apparently Pinkie Finger. And his complicated spouse Mil? It wouldn't have surprised me.

For old time's sake, I drove the surface streets back to Waikiki and thought through my list of suspects who knew more than they were saying about that night. There was Babes Waller, a good musician, but never a clever man when it came to money as I'd been told. Except for the catch that the guy was living in the lap of institutional opulence. Sleazy bartender George Stratford revealed tidbits when money changed hands, my money, and reminded me of the Cheshire Cat. What of Pinkie? I found it hard to fathom that he was nervous of me asking questions, so who else had ruffled his feathers? Could it be that his finger was on Jimmy's pistol?

"Then there's dear little auntie," I said out loud, slowly running my fingers over the steering wheel and pulling into the hotel's parking structure. If I were writing a murder mystery, a character like Victoria Dupris would seem hackneyed and an editor would probably send a rejection letter saying, "You've been watching too much TV. Write a character that hasn't been done to death." Nonetheless, Victoria Dupris was real and with a viciousness that disturbed me for Diamond's sake. Yet, she'd invited Diamond back into the clan.

"What about those mysterious people? Who were they—the authorities or some serious-looking guys Mil had mentioned? Where did they come into it? Or was this just her way of diverting my attention, a ploy to throw me off? The plot is so thick you could stand a fork up in it," I muttered, turning off the car. "All I have now, after spending an hour with Pinkie and his grating wife, are more questions and the desire never to drink another cup of coffee in my life." I slipped out from behind the wheel, slammed the car door way too hard, swung my purse over my shoulder, and pulled out the notebook before heading toward the elevator. It was mid-day, but inky in the garage. I was frustrated and hot. I longed to sit on the lanai and sip something cold for about a month.

Later I would say, "I heard an engine revving. I never even looked in the direction the sound was coming from. But then that huge black car turned on its high beams and aimed at me. It happened and then it was gone."

I fussed, but Jane wouldn't take no to yet two more bitterly strong cups of coffee as I kept repeating the meager details of my brush with metal, or worse. When Jane left for a meeting, Henry took over, called the police, looked at the lump on my knee, and created a makeshift ice pack from a plastic zipper bag.

By the time an officer arrived, my breath was back to normal when I told her, "There wasn't even time for my entire life to flash in front of me. All I could visualize was shrimp bisque—I was going to look like gooey pink soup splattered from one end of the parking garage to the other." I bit my bottom lip and moved the cold pack from the left to the right side of my knee, which was bumped on a minivan as I dodged for my life. "I kept thinking, 'This isn't really happening.' But it was. It felt like one of those bad dreams you get from eating pizza after midnight."

"What else?" Henry grilled, as if the police officer wasn't about to ask that same question. "Didn't you look at the license plate? If a car were coming straight at me, you could be sure I'd see that. Are you keeping anything from me? Child, this isn't a joke, and forgiving someone seven times seventy doesn't apply when they're attempting to kill you. How about the driver? Anything? There's a nut out there hurting people, tried to kill my grandniece right out in public. He's got to be put away." Henry circled the room, clenching his fists tighter with each lap. At the bay window of the hotel suite, his body shook as if he was shaking off snow or if he were a dog after a bath. He turned toward me.

I saw him wipe away a tear. That hurt more than my bumps and bruises.

The police officer realized the scare didn't affect my intelligence level and suggested I get some rest, leaving her business card. "In case you remember more details. I'll call you again in the morning, ma'am. I need to run this through the computer and see if there have been other incidents. HPD takes reckless driving seriously. I've all the info here to file it. We'll need your signature on it. I contact you tomorrow or the next day."

When the officer left, Henry started on me. Again.

"You just try recalling numbers when a huge black car wants to mow you down," I said. "No, Henry, I didn't see anything except the headlights and knew unless I threw my body straight onto that Honda, I was going to be history. You'd put a nice piece in the paper, wouldn't you? Would you write an obituary that said what a good person I have been and would have been?"

"Don't you sweet talk me, Nica. You were nearly killed," he yelled, as if I hadn't caught the drift of that concept from the welts and blackening bruises now beginning to show on my knees and forearms, not to mention a pounding in my skull.

I rubbed my knee, felt the lump. But as I did, I offered prayers of thanks for protection, good timing, and the fact that I took yoga classes and walked lot of miles in the attempt to keep tabs on the size of my tush. If I had been slower or less fit, I might have spent the next few days in a Honolulu hospital. Or worse.

It was the "or worse" that made me sigh, close my eyes, and realize it was past time to tell Henry the whole story. He had to see the notes and know about my interrogation tactics. The other "coincidences" could have been just that. But this attempt wasn't just to frighten me. Someone wanted me dead. Now that was a sobering thought. But for what?

Time to spill the beans, cleanse my soul, put on my big girl panties, and act like a grown up. Time to ask for Henry's forgiveness about not being forthcoming with the nasty little details. Afterward, I felt better but Henry didn't and that was obvious by how quiet he was. By the time I'd finished, the sky was a perfect pink dusk, the dim lighting made it easier for me to confess.

The only sounds in the room were Henry swirling Pepsi and ice cubes and his breathing. For at least twenty minutes, he hadn't even grunted as I told of my escapades. Then he got up and began to inhale and exhale deeply.

"Now calm down, Henry. Even in this light I can see it. You're getting pale. All that huffing can't be good for your blood pressure. Sit down. Please, let's talk." I patted the sofa next to me, used a cooing voice, but the pacing and muffled whispered words continued.

"You know my blood pressure is perfect and my heart is strong as an ox's. That's the bunch of baloney Jane uses when she wants me to cool down. Doesn't work for her and it won't work now. Listen here, you're an adult. You worked for the FBI. You know how dangerous the world can be."

"But I was just asking questions…"

"Don't interrupt. Get serious, woman." There was dead silence as we both seemed to muster our energy, and our anger for the situation.

I broke first. "Yes, Uncle Henry."

"Okay, I admit it was scary. I will admit I'm livid. No, that doesn't say it. I'm fuming, big time. Why didn't you tell me about the flowers and that note? What about the nutty aunt or the guy with the cell phone? Baby, this isn't some situation where you have a dozen trained FBI agents watching your back. This is the real world where we mortals live and where happy endings aren't guaranteed."

I watched his cheeks puff in and out. "It's probably just a freaky coincidence." Yeah, and pigs fly and chocolate has no calories and I could fit into a size six. I didn't need to see Henry's frown deepen to know that this line of reasoning was dangerous and stupid.

"You sit still, miss. What about the notes? The flowers? What were they, Nica? Little tokens of endearment, kissy, kissy, or filled with hate and meant to scare the pants off you? What are your theories behind them? Don't you get it, baby girl? Far as I can see this is treacherous business." He heaved himself out of the easy chair that he'd briefly landed in. He looked old and worn, like sneakers that you keep long after you've gotten a new pair.

I didn't like the old part or the worn. It had been just a year since I'd found him, but he and Jane were the only relatives who cared about me.

Then he started pacing again. "Somebody really doesn't like the way you're messing in their business. You've been told to butt out. That's what I'm getting from the notes and the calls and the flowers. Now what are you going to do about it?" He turned and stopped directly in front of me.

I looked up from yanking at the shreds of my formerly favorite linen slacks to assure him I'd mind my own business. I wanted to say that I would spend a day or two shopping, looking for some knickknacks to take back home. I really wanted to. That's want I would have said if I were any other person, other than FBI confidential informant and consultant Nica Dobson. That would have been the smart, safe plan. And it was okay, for about five seconds; after that the guilt would have come back, because it wasn't true. For five, maybe six seconds, I convinced myself that the right thing to do would be to butt out. In fact if I'd said any of those things, they would have been big fat lies. I'd just asked for Henry's forgiveness. How could I lie? On the other hand, I wasn't going to let the vision of me as shrimp bisque change that. "What it says to me is that Jimmy March was murdered. For goodness sake, look at the evidence."

Henry flopped into an easy chair. Somehow he didn't look that surprised and that surprised me.

"Evidence? Proof? Who are you getting this proof from? Think about it, child. You've talked with a bunch of old geezers who like to fabricate anything that sounds more intriguing than what was on *Access Hollywood* or an afternoon soap that day. Sure, they're like brothers, brothers who try to constantly outdo each other. They can tell a good story, some of which wouldn't think twice to tell tales that would make even you blush. Well, it's my opinion that you've stuck your nose in family business and family scandal. You're a buttinski, Nica, just like your Cousin Jane. Normally, that's a trait to be admired. But this time, the message is loud and clear: Buttinskis get their keesters kicked."

I didn't have a rejoinder because he was right. A maniac pointed a two-ton weapon at me and used it. I was blessed I was sitting there, bumps and shredded slacks and all. I realized with my nosiness I was swimming with sharks of an especially deadly species. And the ocean was bloody already. With Jimmy's blood. And these sharks were invisible.

What if the situation were different? What if something terrible had happened to my adoptive parents? I knew that I had to continue to sift through the questions. Someplace there were answers. As for asking those who seemed to know what happened, perhaps I could be more subtle, then, say instead of charging in on Pinkie and demanding the scoop.

In case you met Cousin Jane at one of the book events she's always invited to in order to publicize her memoir, *Games of the Heart,* and heard her talk about me, it's probably all true: I'm not a subtle person. Maybe the idea of finding the truth about this long ago death wasn't rational to Henry, yet it worked for me.

I moved the ice bag off my knee as Jane whooshed in. Even in the late stages of pregnancy, she made it all look beautiful in a glowing, motherly way. I bucked up again and gave her the *Reader's Digest* condensed version of what had happened just an hour before and for the last few days. Unlike Henry, Jane asked more questions, questions without answers, including, "So how does your lover boy Payton Yu fit into all this?"

"What are you talking about?" And it did come out as a snap. "Lover boy?"

"He'd like to be. That's obvious. I cannot believe you wouldn't. If Tom wasn't in the picture, honey, I'd arm wrestle you for the hunk. So, what's your answer?" Jane asked, frowning as she sipped herbal tea. "It's times like this when I need coffee. I am going on a coffee bender as soon as Baby Morales decides to enter the world."

"Payton? For the record, he's not my lover boy. Really, Jane, I plain do not trust him."

"Nica, I hear your words, but I know people. I know love. Your body is saying something way different. Besides, when you were being stalked, you allowed him to put a big, strong arm around you, right?"

I refilled the ice bag, grabbed some guava juice from the fridge and said, "You know, I want to believe that Payton is everything he says, all squeaky clean, but I still remember him from Kukui High. He was always working an angle."

She leaned closer, making sure Henry was still out on the lanai. "Do you think that Payton, fair-haired descendent of island royalty, is hiding something from you about Jimmy's death and the disappearance of his body?"

"You've got the facts now, Jane. He's got the contacts. His family and Diamond's have been connected since before statehood, and what if, well, what if one of Payton's relatives was involved in getting rid of Jimmy's body in order to protect someone else? It's history, but not that long ago."

"Honey, have you thought of confronting him? You were trained in profiling, right?"

"And if I find out that he's not disclosing information about a murder, then what happens to Payton, even though he was just a kid when that murder took place?"

"You'll do the right thing," Jane said, picking up my long empty coffee cup and smelling it, "For old time's sake...I am sooooo going on drink sooooo much coffee after this baby is born." She patted her bump and laughed. She crinkled her forehead and watching her do that made my head pulsate more. "You said that Babes Waller seemed more cognizant at times. What if you talk with him again?"

"Will he remember me? What would I say?"

"You're asking me. I'm that nosey preacher from Vegas who made your life a living hell, remember?"

"And Jane, if you were me, what would you do?" Yes, I'd come to that. My training had evaporated. When it came to dealing with these emotions, I was useless.

She hugged me hard. Well, as hard as a nine-month pregnant woman can. "Take Babes his favorite treat…which is probably donuts. Musicians and donuts were made for each other. And sit and listen. Stop asking questions. Definitely don't do as I do and jump to conclusions."

"Sure. What then?"

"Then try to piece together what he's not saying from what he's said about the night Jimmy was last seen, killed himself or was shot."

"I can do that," I replied, suddenly finding a smidge of comfort zone.

"Then go back to Diamond and the Auntie Evil and do the same. When there's silence, don't interrupt it."

"Okay." I stood up, gingerly testing my knee and wobbled, willing tears not to sprout from my eyes.

Jane grabbed my hand. "Tomorrow. Do this tomorrow. By the way, did anyone suggest that you need to go to the hospital to see that everything is in working order?"

"I'd know if it weren't, Jane. I'm going to take a couple of aspirin and sit here."

"Gramps and I have to meet with the press; I'm taking him along for arm candy, actually. Figure if I have Doctor Daddy from Slam Dunk there, the press will lose interest quickly in what the vocal minority has rallied to hassle our homeless population. Besides, honey, you're in no condition to go. Stay here, we'll be back in a few hours."

I nodded, but as soon as they waved their goodbyes, I slipped into my bedroom, pulled off the messy slacks and soiled shirt, and crawled between the covers. And the second my head hit the pillow, I was out—that is until my phone woke me at three. "Hello?" It wasn't a number I knew.

"What in God's name happened to you, Nica?"

"Who is this?" I might have been the hit in hit and run, but everyone I cared about was fast asleep in the adjacent suite.

"Payton."

"Payton?"

"Are you in the hospital? Are you delusional?" His voice was rough and came in spurts, higher than normal.

"Oh, Payton. Whatever are you talking about? I'm fine, but with a whopping headache, so if you'll let me get back to sleep I'd appreciate it."

"No way. Are you crazy? If you've had a concussion you shouldn't go to sleep. Didn't the doctors at Queen's Hospital tell you that?" he snapped.

"I'm fine, I'm just going to sleep for a while…" And I clicked off the phone.

I don't know long it was, but the dreamless sleep was suddenly interrupted by hands on my shoulders, shaking me.

"Nica? Nica, wake up. You can't sleep. What harebrained idea have you gotten about sleeping after a head injury?" Payton was sitting on the edge of my bed, glowering over me. His dark eyes sparked and his forehead was filled with wrinkles.

I rubbed my eyes. "It seemed like the logical thing to do."

"Only logical to an idiot," he barked, pulling out my pillow, plumping it up and shoving it again the headboard. "Now sit up. I'm getting some coffee for you." He stopped, stepped back, and grabbed a robe from the closet. "As delicious as you look in just panties and bra, I'm more concerned with what could be scrambled in your brain right now. Put that on."

"How did you get into the penthouse?" Like it mattered, but it seemed important then.

"Cousin Freddy's the night manager here."

I would have shaken my head about the Yu connection, but it hurt way too much.

Two awful cups of coffee later, Payton seemed satisfied that the Sandman would never get his clutches on me. I tried to explain the full and real explanation from the sleuthing at Carlton Villas, to the visit with Pinkie and Mil Finger, to the creepy George Stratford. And the shrimp bisque episode.

"Just because this place feels like paradise, Nica, doesn't make it so. You grew up here, you know that."

"But why me as a target?"

"Why not?" he replied, pulling two more pillows out of the closet, placing them against the headboard, and crawling over me to stretch out. "I could get used to this."

"What? Seeing the aftermath of me nearly colliding with a car?" We stared at each other. Sure, I knew what he meant, and you do too. Rather than enter that zone of no return, I looked at the ceiling instead of meeting his eyes.

"No, this." He pulled my hand to his chest. "Like an old married couple, lying here talking and knowing that no matter what happens in the world, we have each other."

"Can I trust you?" I asked in a far smaller voice that was supposed to happen.

He ran a finger down my cheek and turned my face to his. "In your bed? In your heart? Or with your head?"

Chapter 15

I picked up my aching head and placed it on his shoulder. It was hard and firm. It felt right. "All of those things."

Payton gently lifted me off of him and turned to look at me. "Nica Dobson, I would gladly take care of you forever, but you're not the type of woman who readily lets a guy do that, and we both know that's the truth."

His big brown eyes were the only things in my world and I felt like a stupid, infatuated teenager again when he saved my virtue that terrible November afternoon underneath the bleachers. I pulled away. "Yes, no, you're right, Payton." I slipped off the bed and turned my back on him.

"Okay, it's crazy. You're a confidential consultant with the FBI. You shoot people if you need to. You appear before Congressional hearings. You wear a badge. I'm an island boy, surfing and planning, already, to retire someday to a ranch on the Big Island."

I flipped around and nearly lost my balance. Payton grabbed me, inches close again. "What about this gig as the governor? Is this your goal or that of your parents?"

"Parents? No, in case you didn't notice, I'm a grown-up man now. It's complicated, but I'm thinking of withdrawing from the race."

I shoved him away. "Withdraw? If you don't stay and win, Governor Margaret Flint will have nuclear power plants dotting the islands and probably sell off state land for pennies on the dollar. Why by the time Tom and Jane's baby goes to college the coral reefs will be dead and so will the aloha spirit."

"Wow, I didn't know you felt this way. But it seems logical to stop now…"

I nearly spit and sat straight up. "Logical? For whom? What are you hiding, Payton?"

"You." He turned, walked through the living room, flung back the drapes, and stepped out on the lanai. Immediately the trade winds circled inside the suite.

"Me? Whatever do I have to do with this?" I demanded, but there was no anger in my voice now, only confusion.

He looked toward the city and where Diamondhead was, even though in the black of night, a faint image could be seen. "I've talked with my advisors. They want me to stay as far away from you as possible. It isn't even this Jimmy March thing. Even if it's just the mud ruthless Miss Margaret needs to stir up and plaster me with. And—"

I didn't wait for the next excuse. "And if I find, somehow, that your family was involved with the cover up of how Jimmy March was killed then your entire family will lose face. That's it, isn't it?"

"You really did hit your head. Listen up, woman. I wasn't going to tell you this, but I can't and won't lie to you. My campaign committee believes it'd be the kiss of death for my career if I marry a woman whose first two husbands died under questionable circumstances."

"I have no questions on how they died, Payton. I killed them both with my bare hands. No need to ask anyone. Oh," I exhaled, "No. I am just lashing out. But what you have to do is just tell me to get lost. And I will," I snapped.

He didn't turn but said, "I'm not about to lose you a second time."

Okay, since you already know after my treatments I became a marshmallow, hence why I really cannot return to the Bureau, I'll just skip this part about my silly tears. And the kisses and the handholding and the talking that continued through until daybreak and when the sun finally peeked over Diamondhead.

We kissed goodbye just as Henry opened the door of his suite. "Oh, hi, kids. Um, just off for a run." The man lifted an eyebrow and said, "Guess you two are old enough to know what you're doing." Then jogged to the elevator.

Did we? Did anyone? I pondered those thoughts watching Payton disappear down the stairs, saying he needed the exercise. I thought some more about "us" straight through a long, hot shower, a bowl of pink papaya, and an oatmeal muffin and out toward my car. Yes, I am pleased to say I didn't even flinch as I walked near the scene of my almost demise in the dreaded parking garage.

Quite honestly, after burying two husbands, I was shy about a commitment of any kind. My heart felt something for Payton, but as an adult, and you know what I mean, lust and love can feel much the same at the beginning of any relationship. There was no way I would ruin Payton's chance to be elected Hawaii's governor and stop the exploitation of Hawaii's natural resources to satisfy my needs and desires. I was made of better stuff. I didn't need Payton or another man to complete me that was certain. But what of want? Yes, I wanted him.

It had to be my subconscious protecting me because while I wrestled with wants and needs, where Payton was concerned, I was suddenly and unknowingly standing at my BMW. I unlocked it, crawled inside, and went through the plan I'd created while eating the fruit and muffin.

Babes Waller, if he were in right mind, held some secrets that would reveal the truth, at least *his* truth. But there was one stop I needed to make before I drove toward my visit with Babes and that was at the Dupris mansion. I left the car in a parking spot just away from the front door, but by the time I climbed the white marble steps to the plantation style porch, the butler was there. *"I wonder if he spends his day peeking out the side windows,"* I thought.

The morning was already in the high seventies, but his "Good day, madam" could have frozen boiling water. This time, the faces on Mount Rushmore were more animated than his.

I tried to step inside, but he blocked the foyer. "The Misses Dupris are unavailable." The faux-English accent was even more cultured. It was a big put on because I'd overheard him scolding Inez on my last visit, and the accent was more Brooklyn than British. He walked toward me and darned it all; I backed up, only to find myself on the porch.

I jumped and stuck a foot in the opening. "Not in? Or unwilling to see me?" I asked, feeling the hair on the back of my neck prickle as an idea struck.

"Although it is not necessary to explain their whereabouts, they are not at home. The Madam and Miss Dupris drove to the ranch on the North Shore," he grunted and then looked liked he let the cat out of the bag, seemingly regretting that his ire had disclosed too much.

"Oh, how silly," I started and focused on my wealthy socializing matron personal which sounded like bad acting to my ears. "I am sorry. I didn't ask your name?"

"It is Everett."

"Mr. Everett, forgive me, I didn't explain. It's Inez I want to speak with."

"But Inez is the maid. She does not receive visitors in this home."

I put on my best "queen of the manor" look and stared at him. "Actually, it's a private matter, but I'm certain we know some of the same people." Well, I wasn't lying, was I? We both knew that Everett person, and the Dupris women. I smiled, hoping he couldn't tell I was now pulling at straws.

He looked me up and down, focused on the five-carat diamond that I had kept to impress people and it worked. He snorted again, but motioned me into the grand foyer. "I believe she was about to leave for the day." He glanced at his watch and trotted off in a direction, I assumed, that housed the kitchen quarters.

I could see from his face that he was confused. I was certain he'd grill Inez at the first opportunity, too. In his world, upper and lower classes didn't mix in his book and I'd stepped over the line, from the huffing I'd heard after the snort.

I studied the Gauguin prominently featured on a foyer wall and then the kindly gray-haired woman appeared. A dark cotton raincoat covered her uniform, and the middle buttons holding on for dear life as they strained across her plump bosom.

"Mr. Everett said you'd like to see me?" she asked in that same tiny, non-intrusive voice I'd had heard during my first visit to the mansion.

"May I walk you to your car? I'm harmless, really," I asked and handed her a business card from the Bureau.

She looked at the card and then at me. She nodded, so we walked through the huge industrialized kitchen to the back of the home. It was sprinkling and in the distance clouds grew darker, intending to dump plenty of rain. "The bus will be here in five minutes. I usually leave in the evenings, about nine, but I came in early today. Mr. Everett gave me time off since there's a housekeeper who can serve tea and the madam will be out until this evening." She sighed and then smiled. "My oldest boy is coming home on a military leave and it's his birthday tomorrow." I'd seen it, that sweetness, on other moms and it was something I knew would never be mine.

Yes, we all have our private spots where unfulfilled dreams are stuffed. That was one of mine that I hid from the world, and most of the time from myself. But it was there.

"I still have a present to buy." There was a nervous rambling in her flowing Latin-accented voice, then she stopped smiling and turned to me. I think this time she really saw me. "Excuse me, but do you know me?"

The sky crackled. In with distance thunder vibrated and the palms trees shivered. I had heard heavy rains were heading toward the city and it was weird weather for spring in Honolulu, everyone said, including the gal on the Weather Channel.

I took a few more steps toward the street, sensed that Inez was following. There was no doubt in my mind that she would be discrete. Mr. Everett, I was sure was watching from a window and would interrogate Inez the next day. If I was wrong about Inez keeping mum on what I was about to discuss, so be it.

"I was here for tea with Miss Victoria and Miss Diamond Dupris. My car is just over here," I motioned. "I'll take you home," I offered and was met with a skeptical glance. "Really, I don't mind. I'm trying to help Diamond find out about her parentage. I'd like to talk with you and it doesn't make sense for us both to stand on that corner in rain that's headed this way. I'm afraid I don't know your last name, Ms.—"

"Gonzales. Mrs. Inez Gonzales, but everyone just calls me Inez. I don't mind waiting for the bus."

"Please, let me drive you home, Inez."

She looked at my business card again. "Okay, yes, Miss Diamond told me about you and what you are trying to do. She's sweet, and I loved her mama; even with that wild streak in her, she had a good heart. Frightful business for Miss Diamond. Miss Victoria asked me specifically not to talk about the past, so I've kept my distance. Every time I see Miss Diamond, I see her mama's eyes shining through, hopeful and alive and giving. I've tried not to say anything that could upset the family. Miss Victoria isn't well, you know." Inez whispered as if the palms might report back to the Madam that she'd been conversing with me. Or perhaps, I was just imaging it. Nope, I definitely felt like the palm trees heard our conversation. Maybe the bump on the head did do some damage.

"Please. My car is this way." Inez looked in the direction that I pointed and when we got to the car the first sprinkles plummeted to the windshield.

As we left the mansion's grounds, Inez sat taller and even looked younger. She became more animated, chuckling about the weather, the cake she'd made for her son. "A captain in the Navy, my little boy is now a captain, a child who never learned his right from his left. Oh la la, but he's a big man now. He tells me so all the time." It didn't take a psychotherapist or trained profiler, even of my low standard, to see Inez was relieved to leave the restrictions of the Dupris estate.

"When did you come to work for the Dupris family?"

"So long ago. I've been with the family since I was a girl. I was tiny when my parents and I escaped from Cuba on a boat. It was a terrible time for my country, but America welcomed us. There were no jobs in Miami back then, so Mama and I came here to Hawaii to live with a cousin. She was in the Navy, but she's gone now many years. She had children at home and I took care of the babies and stayed. When the children no longer needed me, I started to work."

"Always with the Dupris?"

"My life is full. My children are grown. All college graduates. My oldest Pedro, a pediatrician, works at the free clinic in San Francisco. Deanna is a congresswoman. She lives in Kapalua and travels to Washington all the time. Gordon, well you know about him, the big captain man. And then there's my baby Rosa, grown up now, of course. She was a surprise baby. My husband and I were finished with babies, but God had better ideas. I was too old to be a mama again, but she is a true gift. She's a news reporter, but working other jobs too. All have their father's features and his hair. He was a handsome man. Yes, all are smart, too smart to be servants."

What was it with me and traffic? The sea of gridlock seemed to stretch for a zillion miles. It was slow-go through the cushy neighborhoods that surrounded the Dupris mansion, but it gave me time to keep Inez kept talking. This was the way it was done in the mysteries I'd read and in the ones shown on TV. Besides I was safe in the car and there was a witness, too, should I have needed one if that black Suburban was out to get me again.

At the longest traffic signal on the planet, I asked, "So you've seen lots of changes in the family?"

She chuckled and there was something in her laugh that made me miss my adopted mama. "When old Mr. Dupris was alive, he set up a trust fund for me and the others so that after the first of the year, when I retire, I will have plenty of money to travel and visit all my children whenever I want. Of course, I can't go in softball season."

"You play softball?" She was fit, but softball?

"Everyone played back in Cuba, so even when we were in Miami my brothers insisted I play, too. I've loved it since I was a girl. Still play a bit, but mostly I coach at the Honolulu Boys and Girls Club. Got a cracker-jack team this year."

"Hmm." The signal was still red, and I doubled the thanks knowing that He had everything to do with this, since Inez was chatting away. "Did you get on well with Mr. Dupris?"

"Oh, yes. Mr. Dupris taught me how to make investments and offered the staff shares in his company, as well as our salary. Most of the staff shunned his offers. I have always been a good listener. Mr. Dupris had old-fashioned ideas about woman's work and the place women should have in society, but I was a maid, and he believed in hard work, so he treated me well.

"My girls, oh they hate it when I talk about how I was treated when I was just a kitchen girl, but Mr. Dupris was never mean, never spiteful like some rich men are."

It didn't take the IQ of a Mensa member to read between those lines, as if what had not been said was printed in bold. Victoria

Dupris was mean and spiteful, I thought turning on the car's headlights. The thick layers of fat black clouds made everything feel gray and cold but the sprinkles weren't any heavier than when we left the house. The light turned green, and we got caught at the next intersection.

I turned to Inez. "I know it happened a long time ago, but could you possibly think back to when Lanie was a girl, before Diamond was born. Did Lanie ever sneak out of the house, runaway, get strange packages? Have odd visitors? Was she, um, wild?"

"I only remember once when Miss Lanie didn't come home for two days. The first afternoon, everyone in the kitchen said she was at the beach with the gardener, a young man from the mainland who watched her every move. I caught him watching through a window once. Mr. Everett stopped that. But when he showed up for work the next morning and didn't know a thing about Miss Lanie, rumors took other directions."

"What was the man's name?"

"It's been a long time. Staff comes and goes. Does it matter? He was full of mischief, that man, and quite the flirt." Inez laughed, remembering another time, and the smooth-Latin sound was good to hear.

"Go on. Do you know more? About Lanie?"

"Her disappearance was foolish, but sure did get the family in a tizzy. Seems she had taken the bus out to the family ranch and was alone there with the housekeepers." She looked at me, the light was still red, and then continued. "The Dupris owned several ranches; this one was on the North Shore, near Turtle Bay. When the rumors started the day she disappeared, I thought at first they were talking about someone else. I thought she'd run off with the man who delivered the milk and cream. You're too young, but at one time and to the rich folks, dairy products were delivered to the back door of everyone's home. Our Lanie was sweet on him, too, when she was a child—we all liked him—he would sit down with the girls, Miss Victoria and Lanie, on the running board of the milk truck and tell them grand stories. He was a husky man from Chicago, strong and sang as he dropped off the milk each day. Sang old Gospel music. He flirted with me, too, and said that in World War II, he'd been around the globe on a merchant marine ship. That man could spin some tales. Lanie loved to hear them especially the stories of Europe. After he left for the day, Lanie would run to the kitchen and tell me everything."

"Were there other men or boys you suspected when she disappeared?" The light finally changed but the traffic was so congested I didn't move more than five feet. There must have been an accident or construction ahead, or He wanted to give me more time to talk with Inez.

"Then Lanie fell in love with one of the men working on the marble porch around the house. He was a white man this time. Had a southern drawl and mud under his fingernails. She was sixteen and in love. I'm no expert like Dr. Phil, Miss, but I think she was seeking affection because she didn't have it at home. From a mother. Mrs. Dupris died just after Lanie was born. It happened in those days. Mrs. Dupris was a traditional Hawaiian woman, but something went wrong. I didn't ask for details. It wouldn't have been my place," Inez said and continued. "After the thing with the marble cutter and another episode with a boy the family had known through the country club, Mr. Dupris sent Lanie to a boarding school on the mainland. It was all the way to Tennessee, a fancy finishing school in Memphis.

"I saw Mr. Dupris cry, oh, how he loved that girl. He slammed the door to his study after he put her in the car for the airport and didn't come out for hours. She had argued that she would do what she wanted and see whomever she decided to see. She yelled that she didn't need her father's blessing."

We inched in the traffic. "Any problems at school?"

"The girl had a tutor. She never attended public or private schools. I'm sure there were problems, but I never heard about them. I was just a kitchen girl. But when she left and wrote to me from the boarding school everything seemed fine."

"She wrote to you, from Memphis?"

Inez nodded. "The following Christmas, she came home for holiday break; she was quieter and took long walks. She kept cosmetics and dime store jewelry beneath her bed. She had lacy underthings, too. Please don't tell Miss Dupris this. She's more difficult now that I'm about to leave. Oh, please be careful, please don't say anything." She grabbed my forearm. "I am certain she would find a way to take away my retirement. She's always looking for loopholes and never forgets anything anyone says or does, especially when she's upset. Most things upset her these days."

"You have my word." We looked at each other and her eyes accepted my promise. "Tell me, Inez, do you remember if the man who came with the work crew to build the porch was named Jimmy?"

She stared straight ahead. "Had I known, I would have warned her. My own husband thought he should be in show business. He was an actor; not a good one but with a certain flair. Before he escaped from Cuba, he'd had some success there. I know what that life can be with folks in the entertainment world. I have known people like that man Lanie was in love with. My husband came home one night, packed a suitcase, and told me he was going to be a star. Going to Hollywood to make it big, he said. We never saw him again." She opened the car door, but held the handle even as the sprinkles dotted the shoulders of her serviceable coat. "Yes, Miss Lanie's beau was named Jimmy. Jimmy March." She watched my face and I've never been good a poker, so you know she could tell I'd just gotten the answer I was fishing for. "Yes, I know he's that same musician I read about that just suddenly disappeared."

"Anything you can remember about them as a couple could help Diamond." I turned off the motor and waited.

She took a ring of keys from of her purse. "A week or so before I read how the performance had to be cancelled, I had seen a picture of her Jimmy. I remember one day Lanie dashing through the kitchen door, saying she was going out for a long walk. She always came to tell me and knew I worried. Her father hated how she paraded around in the baggy clothes, but she refused to wear maternity things. Or stay in the house."

"You knew she was pregnant?"

Inez nodded and looked at her lap. "Mr. Dupris thought if no one said anything and she stayed home and didn't go to parties and so on, it would all go away. Like an unplanned pregnancy would just go away. Oh, he was old fashioned."

As if she were torn with telling me the truth or rushing away to escape, she looked toward her condo and then me. Finally, she got back into my car and closed the door. Her cheeks sagged and she fiddled for a tissue from her pocket, she touched the corners of her eyes, and sighed. Deeply.

"I saw her. I should have run after her. I could have stopped her somehow before she got into that car. This Jimmy was driving. I've carried this burden too long. I should have stopped her." She inhaled and straightened her spine. "I hope whatever I've said can help you. I hope that Miss Diamond can gather courage and live a better life than her mother. We can't change people. We can only change our attitudes. Bless you for taking time to listen. *Vaya con Dios.*"

"*Vaya con Dios, mi amiga,*" I replied. Praying that God would be with her always.

The woman's smile felt sad as she gently shut the car door and headed for the condos. Everyone knew of the pregnancy and connection with Jimmy March, including her rich and powerful father. Then why wouldn't Victoria Dupris help Diamond find out the truth? What in the world could she be hiding? Why in the world was she being so darned mean?

Chapter 16

The rain had stopped by the time I pulled into a parking spot at the Ala Moana Shopping Center and it had turned into a Chamber of Commerce day. The temps were in the low seventies and the ocean glittered with silver waves as far as the eye could see. I stood for the longest time looking out at the ocean, feeling the trade winds caress my soul, the winds I didn't even know how much I had yearned for while working in Washington and then Las Vegas. I'd been so caught up in overachieving and pushing myself for some unattainable perfection, I didn't see I was unhappy inside.

Standing there, I felt closer to God than at any other time in my life, closer to Him than in the churches and holy places I'd visited around the world. I whispered a prayer for forgiveness, "Oh, Father. Thank you for loving me when I couldn't love myself. I see now how I tried to be better than everyone at everything and still down deep believing I was worthless. I didn't need to prove myself. You've loved me all this time." I held the railing, breathed in my words. A calm came over me and for the first time in my nutty, hyper-motivated and super-charged emotional and intellectual life, I felt at peace. I whispered a string of thank yous. Maybe this serenity happens to the Christians who have been in the church forever. But as a neophyte, I floundered and worried and fretted. I also knew more than ever that only I could help Diamond Dupris find the truth.

I walked into the mall, sat at a café, and ordered passion fruit ice tea. I sipped it and thought of the revelations of the last hour.

What did I know? Lanie Dupris was a willful teenager. Even in my sheltered, geeky teenage world, I'd heard rumors of bad little rich girls and their escapades. I took out my notebook and wrote: *Lanie was sent to boarding school in Memphis—the hometown of her lover, possibly why she didn't protest too much.*

Did it really matter that Lanie had kept makeup, bright flashy stuff, and lacy underwear hidden away? When Lanie was sent off to boarding school, did she and Jimmy reunite there in Tennessee? And was it Jimmy in the car with Lanie just before his death, like Inez said? There was no doubt now that Lanie and Jimmy were romantically involved. Even if no one saw them doing anything more intimate than sharing the same front seat of a car. Also Lanie was pregnant and from what she'd told Diamond, she was certain that Jimmy March was her father. So did Jimmy just drop off the planet, fall into a black hole, or run for the hills? If so, why? Lanie had money and position and that's how he probably got the new duds that Pinkie had told me about. Or was he shot to death in the theater that night? Or even more of a conundrum, did he lose at Russian roulette? Or, was he even dead? Were any of those sightings that Payton told me about true?

Diamond had a right to the royalties from her father's estate. Yet, there was no true evidence. Even if Victoria Dupris and Inez were subpoenaed into court, and told the truth, which was doubtful in my mind on the part of Auntie Evil, I just didn't think that would be enough.

If this were *Castle* or *Hawaii Five-0,* everything would be snugly tied up in less an hour. Like magic, and a twist from Hollywood, Jimmy's body would suddenly turn up. Diamond would be able to prove he was her biological father. Wacky Auntie Victoria would turn all sweetness and light or somehow be eradicated and in the end of the episode, Becket and Richard Castle would make goo-goo eyes. Or more.

I thought about Babes again. I was weary of having people like Pinkie Finger and George Stratford evading the truth and Victoria Dupris threatening me. People stalking me. People in big cars attempt to squish me like a bug. It was one thing when I was working for the Bureau to have scrapes and near-misses happen, but totally a different story when I was merely asking questions for a friend, a friend who I didn't know well at all. And that's not all.

There was Payton Yu. Yes, the aforementioned hunk who dashed to my rescue and kept me from falling asleep last night, whether or not I did have a concussion. Sometime between waving goodbye to Inez and pulling into the parking lot of Carlton Villas, it dawned on dunce-me: How did Payton know to call me after the near-miss, scrape with death?

I had allowed myself to be vulnerable, allowed him into my bed (actually, on top of it and nothing happened, but not because I wouldn't have wanted it to). But Henry and Jane didn't call him. I certainly didn't. Could he be playing some perverted game with me again, just like in high school when I never knew if he'd speak to me or make fun of me depending on the crowd he was with?

Confused? Yeah, me too, and especially so as I tried to make sense of what could be Payton's motives. Suddenly there was George Stratford, the bribe-hungry bartender, strutting out of the nursing home doors. He stood and looked at the sun, preened his fingernails, adjusted his shinny jacket and slipped his fingers around the waistband of his slacks and waited. Then a black Lincoln pulled up to the curb, not twenty feet from where I was sitting.

I held my breath, watching him leer in my direction. I knew what a goldfish felt like until I become conscious he wasn't looking at this goldfish, but a statuesque Asian woman in the shortest, reddest leather mini I'd ever seen.

I shielded my face with my purse, but George was too glued to the young woman. He called something to her. She sniffed the air as if there was a bad smell and then teetered down the street on five-inch scarlet stilettos. Even behind my purse, I could see the employee lot and Quinn's Mercedes wasn't there. Sometimes, the best plans of action come from spur-of-the-moment ideas. That's what I've heard. But for me, right then, I just knew I needed information and knew who could give to me. Right—there was no plan.

I walked straight into Carlton Villas. Tina Yu seemed more bored than ever and brightened when she saw me.

"Oh, you're back. Babes asked for you, Ms. Dobson. We were playing the piano together and he was remembering so much. I can't get over it. We talked about you and he said he liked how you smelled."

"How's he feeling today?" I asked, more to be polite. So we talked about Babes's health until the conversation slowed and I popped the reason for the visit. "Tina, I need help. You're the only one I can ask."

"Sure, if I can," she replied, twisting a ringlet of hair around her index finger.

"Before I leave the island…"

"You're leaving? Payton said—"

"Um, well whenever I decide to fly back to the mainland, just temporarily—" I began, shocked that the Yu Family Communication System was so thorough and quick. "I want to make sure that the payments for his care here will continue."

"Do you need me to show you the statements, Nica?" she offered.

I grabbed the edge of the faux walnut desk and tried to take normal, natural breaths even if my heart was going to wild, with this wild dream come true. "Yes, that's what I need."

"Sure thing. Come around this side of the counter. Or I can print them out?"

I was there in a nanosecond. "Both. Both is good."

That's when I saw it. Tina did too. We said at the same time: "The Yu Trust." And then again in unison, we said, "What?"

"Tina, did you know this?"

"Know that Babes's care was being paid for by someone in my family? No way. That's like totally weird. But you knew about it, right?"

"I did, of course," I lied. If I seemed surprised, I knew, she'd be on the phone or texting someone in the Yu family before my feet met the sidewalk.

Instead, I took the printouts from Tina's hand, folded them, and slipped them into my purse. I steadied myself, thanked her, and said goodbye.

Like a zombie, I walked to the car. I crawled in and sat. Shocked. So Payton knew about Babes and was connected to all of this. Ergo, he had to have information about Jimmy March and the man's death. I'd been right about old island moneyed families functioning by a totally different set of rules than us lower-class folks.

"You just never learn, do you, Nica?" I demanded of myself.

The caution of "You are too trusting" came too often from my FBI supervisor's mouth and at least dozen times on performance reports, which were like black strikes against me. When I got involved with Jane and her now husband Tom Morales in Las Vegas, and with the human trafficking crimes, I had just wanted to help stop the sale of babies, bring to an end of the mess, but instead nearly got Jane killed.

Now? Because of being too darned trusting, I ruined any chance of Diamond getting the life-saving treatments she must have and yes, I'd once more broken my heart. I hated to admit it, but I had fallen for Payton. Again.

"Stupid, stupid, stupid," I yelled and banged the steering wheel in frustration.

There was only one stinking reason that the Yu Family Trust would be footing the bills for that premier facility. That hit me like a punch in the belly. They wanted to keep him under their thumbs, out of anything that could link one of the Yu family, those influential Hawaiian movers and shakers to a messy murder years before. Especially since Babes could no longer understand how to keep a secret and if I wanted to have anyone throw skepticism on Babes's credibility, what a perfect scheme. Carlton Villas was made to order. If he ever ranted about who killed Jimmy March, well, who would believe a guy who thought poker chips were silver dollars? For all I knew, Babes and even Payton's dad could have taken part in dumping Jimmy's body from a boat miles off the Honolulu coast or taken it to Maona Falls and thrown him over or maybe just drove to some sandy beach on the North Shore, dug a big hole and unloaded Jimmy's body there. Visitors see Honolulu as a busy touristy city. Yet, if you have a chance to drive the Kamehameha Highway around the island there are hundreds of deserted spots, places to dispose of dangerously damaged cargo, like Jimmy March.

I would prefer to say at this point I pulled out the New Testament that I always carry in my purse to study how Jesus would behave in a situation like this. I'd like to say I drove to Ala Moana Beach Park, took out a blanket, and sat under one of those enormous banyan trees.

Some women would pray and wait for the answers. I didn't even think of doing that. I drove straight to Payton's campaign headquarters. There on the street was Payton's black Suburban and so I pulled up so close that I hoped he'd never be able to get his car out. Then I slammed the car door hard enough to get the attention of a crowd of supporters who were milling around in front of the building. Next I charged right into office and, like Moses and the Red Sea, people parted so I wouldn't trample them.

Even Payton's local bodyguards stepped back. Maybe they knew if they hadn't, I would have slugged them with my purse.

I don't think I've ever been so blazing angry. It was one thing to fool me, he'd done that with my heart in high school, but to con the voters and cheat them out of an honest governor was immoral and wicked.

To say I was steaming when I pushed open the door to Payton's glass-enclosed office would have been an understatement. Thinking back, I remembered what the psychologist at the bureau told me about possibly having uncontrolled emotions. But frankly, I didn't give a fig. I was screaming, but I can't exactly remember the words, except they included being involved in a huge cover up of an old murder, causing a defenseless woman to die because she couldn't afford treatments and to campaign for the highest public office in the state while lying about everything in his life. Or reasonably along that line.

Payton stood up from his desk and you'd expect with me going ballistic his face might have shown alarm. Nope. He didn't look troubled and definitely not afraid. He just stood there smirking, like a Hawaiian business tycoon and beach boy, wearing cream and white patterned Aloha shirt as crisp and calm as his face.

I took a deep breath, about to spout more accusations and in an even louder voice when I realized we were alone. But I couldn't stop. "I will see that this entire conspiracy to hide what happened to Jimmy March and the Yu family involvement is spread across the pages of the newspapers here in Honolulu, throughout the islands and the entire the country, Payton." I took a breath an added, "Enough lies," I said and my voice now sounded deadly calm.

"Cousin Tina called me," he replied.

"So you could be prepared when I came to tell the press the truth?"

"Nica, you might want to sit down. This could take a bit."

"I do not want to sit, and actually I don't want to be with you for another second," I barked.

"Wait. Wait for a moment at least because just maybe I saved your life last night. It would have been awful if you'd fallen asleep with a concussion," he said, walking around toward me, but not within touching distance.

"How can you be sure I even had a concussion, Payton? You're not a doctor now, are you? How did you even hear I'd been hurt? Besides, how do I know that it wasn't your big, old black car and one of your goons who tried to run me down? How do I know it wasn't you or one of your people who got to Pinkie Finger to stop him from telling me anything? How do I know—"

"Because, Nica, you know me."

"No, I don't. I thought I did, but you're—"

"You know me. I'm the same dolt I was in high school. I get myself in all sorts of jams because I can't say no. I'm that same guy now. Look at me."

I did. I stopped and looked, and before I could thrust the next accusation at him, he said, "Tina didn't know anything about my family's business providing care for Babes." He held up a hand, stopping me again. "Sure, I knew. But I knew the real reason. Do you want to hear it or are you going to storm out of here like you came in? I wouldn't blame you.

"Okay. The honest truth? Babes Waller and my dad go back to old army days and the war in Vietnam. I've heard the story at least a hundred times. Dad always says, 'I was caught in an ambush of gunfire. The other guys in my platoon ran for their lives which is what I should have done or they were dead. Babes must have seen some movement in my body, because he ran back in to the clearing and dragged me into the jungle.' When telling the story, Dad always reminds everyone that both he and Babes were a lot trimmer in those days."

"Babes saved your father's life?" I plopped into a chair.

"Yeah, and that was the first of three other times during the war. Either Babes was awfully lucky or the guy was my father's guardian angel. When Babes started becoming disoriented, my father was the first to notice since Babes ran errands for the company and was Dad's driver for years. Sure, the trust is paying for his care. There was never any discussion that we would not."

Okay, do you want to know my pithy reply? "Oh."

"See, Nica, hold on. If you'd just informed me whom you were visiting at Carlton Villas, I'd have told you all of this. You just said you were looking for answers about Jimmy March, and honestly, I don't know anything about that."

"Oh?"

"I'm so sorry. Now you can't trust me and it's my fault." He sat on the edge of the desk, looked down, and ran a hand through his thinning hair.

I stood and put my arms around him. "I'm the one who's sorry. If jumping to conclusions were an Olympic sport, I'd get a gold medal. But just for sanity's sake, how did you hear about my near miss with death?"

He looked up and placed his cheek on mine, then whispered. "Do you remember the officer who came to take your report and statement? Susanna is engaged to my cousin Andy, who is Tina's older brother. Your accident was new on the Yu grapevine. Here's where I want to say: Let's start over. But I don't want to start over, honey. I want to pick up where we could have left off last night. You cannot imagine how I long to do just that. However, if you didn't have a possible concussion and I didn't have all of Hawaii putting my every move under a microscope and to be displayed on the news at five, I would." He pulled back and it was only then that I realized the entire office staff had stopped work and were standing facing the glassed-in office and watching us like we were in a fish bowl.

"Oh. Ohhh, I have to stop saying that. I am so very sorry, Payton, I am," I said, stepping out of the embrace and moving back three feet, but our eyes were locked.

"Not me." He laughed. "I need to have a righteous partner in the governor's mansion, a spouse who tells me when she thinks I'm wrong. You seem to have no trouble doing that, Nica."

"Oh…wait, what? We hardly know each other."

"Think again. I have known you since you were sixteen years old, Nikky Wikiwiki Ticky. And you hold more secrets about P. Yu than the world needs to know. So as soon as we can have some time alone, I'm going to prove that to you by—"

The pounding on the office door stopped him, but the deed was done, as they say in old novels. I knew we were a couple and as for that being problematic to his election, there were no doubts of the heart, we'd figure the answers in time.

The door pushed open and three of his staff rushed in, one carrying a jacket and white dress shirt with a red and blue flowered tie and two with folders brimming with notes. "Ms. Dobson—we have to get the next governor to the debate. Payton, you're going to be late. You cannot be late—the press will rip you to shreds."

Another staffer wrung her hands. "Be late and Miss Margaret will have a field day on how irresponsible you are."

"Gotta go, boss."

"Car's waiting, Payton."

And he was gone. And I also knew what I had to do and it wasn't attending a political debate. I had a niggling feeling of dread, something that rarely happened to me, but chalked it up to not having time to eat…or perhaps it was the clunk on my head from the previous day. But I knew what I needed to do, and I needed to do it right then. Babes's name was on the top of my list, if I had a list, that is.

Chapter 17

It was also way past time to talk with Diamond. Alone. I'd heard her story twice, but each time it felt as if she were holding something back. And it had to do with the aunt.

Auntie Evil might be old and angry, but my gut said she was armpit deep in this. That gut feeling shouted that somehow they had a good idea of what happened to the infamous Jimmy March. Could it be that one of them knew where he was living, if he were alive? Or could they know where he'd been buried? Or it could be, as the psychologist told me while being debriefed before my medical leave, "Sometimes after a life-changing event and after time away from the Bureau, our people find they visualize mysteries, conspiracies, and complicated plots where there are none." Okay, if that were not enough, she also said, "And don't be shocked if you have huge swings in your emotions. You've been through a lot. You might go from being the ultra-smart consulting agent with nerves of steel to what you think is a fretting teenager with PMS."

"Oh, goody," I had replied.

Was I that way? Had I done that about this investigation? Why had finding out about Jimmy become an obsession, so much so that I started to see evil even in Payton? When does obsession turn to paranoia? No, actually, I didn't have any answers, but I was saved by the ring of my cell.

It was Cousin Jane, and even without caffeine, she sounded wired. "Nica, listen to me. Listen this time," she ordered like I was family. Wait. I was. "Hey, girl, I can tell when you're not listening."

"Sorry, Jane. I was just thinking."

"You think way too much. You have got to act more and think less," she reprimanded me.

"Yeah, like you and that debacle in Vegas?"

"Which, as you'll remember," she corrected me, "I was able to turn into a book and according to an email I got from my agent, rumor has it that Reese Witherspoon might play me in the movie."

I shook my head and sat down in the car. Only Jane could turn a near-fatal disaster into a pot of caviar. "So what am I supposed to be listening to?"

"Gramps just called from Carlton Villa. He's there visiting Babes. You will never guess what has happened. Come on, honey, guess."

"Jane, oh, hold on, I've got another call." I put her on hold, but didn't catch the other in time. The message was from Mr. Everett. He said, "Miss Dupris would like to see you as soon as possible."

I clicked back to Jane. "That was a call from the Dupris' stuffy butler and Diamond needs me. Could you let Henry know that I'll call him right after my meeting at the mansion and if he's still with Babes, I'll drive over there at afterward?"

"Sure, sure, finish with Diamond. Gramps said he'd be with Babes for a while. Nica, be careful. I've got a weird feeling about the things that go on with that family."

"Me, too."

At the mansion, I left the car right in front of the grand entrance. Of course, Mr. Everett instantly opened the door.

"I got your message," I said. "Is she in the library again?" In my wedge sandals, I'm close to six foot, but just to make myself a bigger presence, I puffed out what was left after the surgery of my breasts and extended my elbow from my torso.

It must have worked as he stepped aside while saying, "Yes, madam, she is in the library. And then he dashed in the opposite direction.

I threw open the heavy koa wood doors and there she sat. Waiting. Frowning. If a Category Five hurricane had a face, then it would look just like Auntie Evil. Yes, then it dawned on me that she was the Miss Dupris who had summoned me. I scanned the chilly, dark room half expecting to see Diamond sitting next to the window like a penniless relation straight from a Jane Austin novel, terrified to speak for fear she'd be thrown out on the moors.

"Good, you're here, too," I said, loud enough for Auntie to gasp, but that could have been the sound of her oxygen hose. "Where is your niece?"

"I do not want you to bother, Diamond. She said she needed to rest and let me make myself perfectly clear because apparently you are too dense to have understood my previous warning. You will not speak with her or disturb her now or ever again. I thought, looking at you, that you understood English. Apparently, that is not the case. I told you not to poke your nose in family issues, not to interfere." Her scratchy voice throbbed with anger. It wasn't the choking back kind that you see when people are passionately violent, but more of the disturbing, deadly version from someone who is considering committing a horrendous act.

Victoria snapped her hand and pointed a quivering index finger at me. "Oh, sit and be quiet. I have quite few more things to tell you, you interfering and intrusive young woman."

I sat on the matching white brocade sofa, straightened my spine, to give me more confidence and then said, "I need some answers, Miss Dupris, from you and your niece."

She wheezed, reaching for the oxygen mask that lay on the sofa next to her. "Do not interrupt me, you impertinent busybody. Now listen because I do not plan to repeat myself. Ever."

My instinct told me to run like the wind. But I couldn't. I had to know what she was about to tell me. So I folded my hands in my lap and crossed my ankles, although I knew I could spring up and get out if I needed to.

"You have interfered in business, family business, which does not concern you. You are a meddlesome, prying troublemaker."

"And a friend to your niece," I added.

"A friend? Oh my goodness. That is ridiculous. Diamond has no qualities that could be considered friendly. She is ineffectual and worthless. She is devoid of personality and dull-witted. But you know that, is that not true, Mrs. Wainwright-Dobson?"

I'd already been called a busybody, meddlesome, prying, and impertinent. Now she was telling me I wasn't qualified to be a friend. I had a sneaky suspicion the elderly woman could come up with some adjectives about my inquisitive personality that would have made me blush.

I'd learned, and apparently retained the information, how when someone is ruthlessly angry, if we can sit back and appear relaxed, the combatant will sometimes spill whatever beans needed to be brought out in the open. *Oh, geez,* I thought, *I'm rambling like Cousin Jane.* Nonetheless, I willed my breath to slow and plastered a calm smile on my lips.

Auntie Evil's voice got louder. "If Diamond was smart enough to have friends, she would not be associated with someone who lies to get entry into a secure nursing home and pretend she is the niece of Babes Waller." She shivered. "Oh, even thinking of him and this conniving ways curdles my stomach."

"I liked him a lot, Miss Dupris," I snapped. Although the guy was out to lunch in a far more benign way than Auntie Evil, I preferred Babes hands down.

"It is time you knew the truth about Mr. Waller, missy. That man tried to extort money from me, saying he'd smear our family name from here to New York City. Blackmail me? Well, you can be certain that I stopped that." Her mouth screwed up as if she was going to spit. "And you say you are a friend of Diamond's, but I also know how you frequent nightclubs filled with musicians and criminals."

"Have you been following me?" Well, duh, of course she had or she wouldn't have this information.

"My employee George reported it all," she snapped and then the flicker in her eyes revealed she'd played a trump card.

"Ah, I get it. So that's how you knew about where I was going and what I was doing. George Stratford? On your payroll?"

"Why, you hussy. How dare you demand answers and question me about my staff." She sucked in a long breath of oxygen, but this time rather than helping, she swayed a bit and coughed deeply, a mucus-filled one that made me turn my head away.

And while Auntie Evil was sucking on the mask and coughing, it all came together. George delivered the flowers with that ugly note which of course had been dictated by Miss Dupris. He probably drove the black car with orders to stop me from being a busybody. And when I saw him outside Carlton Villas? Sure, he was there on behalf of Victoria to make sure that Babes wasn't in a position to tell me anything. Would George have killed Babes if he was lucid? Victoria was certainly used to getting her way, regardless of the circumstances, but thank heavens, I knew that Babes was still okay, since he was chatting it up with Henry.

As I finished putting two and two together, I realized she was still lecturing my wanton behavior. Then she barked, "Those bars are filled with hoodlums and now you, you call yourself a friend? Oh, please. As for Diamond? She does not have the sense she was born with and will turn out just like her mother. A woman without scruples. I am not surprised. The rotten apple does not fall far from the tree. I thought Elaine had learned a lesson with all the sorrow she brought on the family. Shame that is what she caused. She shamed us and I'm still attempting to live that shame down."

"I think perhaps if you answer a few questions, I can help," I interrupted. Yes, like call the EMTs and place the fruitcake into a psych lockdown ward for a few days, under heavy meds and have her evaluated by a team of psychiatrists who study sociopaths.

"Be quiet. Here is her illegitimate daughter following in her disgusting footsteps. Like mother like daughter." Victoria inhaled even more deeply as if she couldn't get enough oxygen. She fixed her dark eyes on me and the whistle of the machine echoed in the cavernous room. Suddenly, she sprung up and dropped the apparatus to the tea table between us. Clunk.

I flinched.

The cane that had been resting on her knee was now pointed at me. "Stop fidgeting. I have not finished with you yet." She punctuated that sentence with thrusting the cane over the tea table and at me.

Did I really need yet more proof that Auntie Evil was off her rocker?

Just let her loathing run its course, though I quickly amended my first silent comment with, *She's got a lot of years of disgust saved up.* I leaned against the stark white brocade sofa and faced the deranged lady. From the depths of my purse, my phone ring. There was no way I was going to reach for it, not with the hold Victoria Dupris had on that silver tipped cane and the fact that she was standing over me whipping her cane through the air.

"I've warned you at our last meeting. You do not belong in this world. You have, however, dragged my dim-witted niece into your filthy, depraved cesspool of rock and roll, honky-tonk singers, taverns, and musicians. What is next? Will she start carousing with novelists and writers? Humph. All degenerate and loathsome people. They only want one thing—"

I might still be, according to my doctors, a bit tired from the treatments, but right then, adrenaline was my champion and in that split second I knew everything. "Why did you kill Jimmy March? Tell me."

Much later, I would wonder where that thought had come from and how I had the courage to ask it, but the words tumbled out of my mouth of their own volition. I'm a baby Christian as far as Christians go, but it had to be the Holy Spirit talking through me. I was surprised, let me tell you, when that came out.

"Humph, so what do you know? And for how long?" She swayed slightly, but looked stronger than before. Her face showed I'd hit on the truth. Instead of making her angrier, she actually smiled, if a twist of her pinched lips was a smile.

Directly in back of Victoria Dupris, a cabinet filled with dozens of fussy little statues was the answer. It was there all along in a gilded, nineteenth century oval picture frame. It was a photo of a beautiful, softly plump young woman, round and full of smiles. She looked like she was giggling. Encircled in her arm was a dour figure, a tiny, dark haired woman whose deep frown matched a much-younger Victoria Dupris. Sibling rivalry gone very much astray. "You envied her and her relationship with Jimmy," I said.

"Relationship? Don't even make it sound like love. It was sex, sex, and even more sex. She had no heart. One must have a heart to give it to another in a so-called relationship," she spat the words. "One must be able to love to feel that way. Elaine could never experience real love, I will have you know. She was too shallow for that. She had to be the star. Had to steal whatever glory might come to me. She murdered our mother. You knew that, is that not correct?"

"What?"

"If she had not been a huge baby, our mother would have survived childbirth. I know that to be true. I was with the midwife and the doctor when Elaine was delivered. There was so much screaming and blood, but I refused to leave Mother to those strangers. Elaine killed Mama."

"Terrible things happen in childbirth," I started to say, but Victoria Dupris was way past being able to connect with logic.

"Then? Our father turned his back on me. He ignored me. He showered her with everything she ever even hinted that she wanted. She was exquisite and smart and with curly hair and oh, so very clever to get what she wanted from anyone she wanted. I was wise to her. I hated how she used her voluptuous body to twist any man around her finger, including our brainless father." Victoria reached in her pocket and pulled out a lace-edge hanky. I expected her blot to the spittle that had formed on her mouth. Instead she ripped the edge right off it. We both watched as the lace dropped to the carpet and she stomped it with her orthopedic loafer, grinding and grinding it into the pile.

"You were tired of seeing her happy?" Okay, I'm a glutton for punishment, but I wanted the whole story.

With a plunk, she dropped the cane on the table. "You are laughable in your stupidity." She fumbled again into the pocket, but this time no hanky appeared. Instead she held a tiny silver-handled gun. It looked like a toy, but the way Victoria Dupris cradled it, it was meant to frighten or kill me. She turned it around in her hands, and for a long moment, studied the barrel like an appraiser on *Antiques Road Show*.

If it were in a museum display, I might have admired the inlay of pearl and the delicacy of the silver-scroll work, but since it was currently pointing at me, it was tough to enjoy its workmanship.

"I have made a decision. I am going to kill you. Therefore it cannot hurt to tell you the truth. I am sick and tired of you, Mrs. Wainwright-Dobson. If it is true that you worked with the Federal Bureau of Investigation, which I find unfathomable, you will discover my reasoning to be sound and intelligent. Elaine not only killed our mother, but she murdered my only reason for living when she stole the one man I ever loved and who truly loved me. He told me we were going to be married and the baby that Elaine swore was his? It certainly was not. I was the only woman he was romantically and sexually connected with. He told me so. Elaine was a tramp, he told me. How would she know who impregnated her? He loved me."

I laughed. It was crazy and the timing was awful, but I did it. "You're going to kill me? I've done nothing." Could I make it to the door? The old woman was frail, on oxygen, and used a cane. I inched to the edge of the sofa, ready to spring. My cell rang again. At least it was on, which would make it easier when I dialed nine-one-one. Of course, I could only call the police if I was alive.

"Yes, because when you are dead, the secrets will die with you. Diamond has the intelligence of a gnat, so she will not go against my word. I will tell people you came here to rob me." She swept her hand around the room, indicating the priceless antiques. "I am old, some say senile. They will say I did not know what I was doing. Insanity? Perhaps, but those of us with breeding will never be incarcerated."

She looked down at the oxygen mask. If she went for it, I'd go for her gun. But she didn't.

The words can out in a pant. "Now I suppose Mil Finger will need even more money. She and that lout she married." Her hand shook and the gun sagged.

"Mil Finger? And Pinkie, too?" I couldn't move if I wanted to.

"Mildred was my personal maid. She came to work here just before Elaine caused Jimmy's death. That overbearing fool is an expensive tool."

The barrel of the gun dropped an inch. Now I would be shot in the stomach rather than the face, if she pulled the trigger. Oh, joy. "I can understand having your heart broken, Miss Dupris. But why Jimmy? Why did you kill him?"

The gun snapped back and Victoria's hand became steady as the barrel pointed once more at my eyes. There was a time the Old Me would have dashed over the table, wrestled the old gal to the ground, and come out with a commendation from my supervisor. But now, the New Me could not stir from the sofa. I was afraid and I knew I was afraid, which made it worse.

"You are one of those know-it-alls. You cannot even imagine what I had been through before Jimmy and I became a couple. You are beautiful. You are elegant. I have always been plain and born with this stupid limp. I never measured up to anyone's idea of a debutant. Then my little sister took Jimmy away from me and turned up pregnant, swearing she was carrying my own lover's child. She murdered our mother, turned our father against me, and took every good thing in life that I valued away. Once she was dead, Jimmy and I would be free. I went to the theater that night to kill her."

"You wanted to kill Lanie?"

"You stupid woman. Must I continue to repeat myself? Yes, I had always thought of killing her, always planned it, even when we were children, so that Daddy would pay attention to me, to know I existed. You do not know what it is like to have to put up with a Daddy's girl who got everything. I had always planned to kill my sister."

I've heard about siblings not getting along, but if you're blinking now with the hatred Victoria Dupris had against her sister, join the club. I was too.

"I followed her to the theater. Jimmy was about to go on stage. But she waltzed right into his dressing room. I calmly told her why I had to kill her. Jimmy was there and nodded, at least I think he did. I had it planned. I had my own money. We would disappear and people in our social set would never know that Jimmy and I were living in Brazil. Then that idiot Babes burst in to the room. He tripped and knocked my hand just as I pulled the trigger."

Her face became harder, if that were possible as she said, "I killed Jimmy March. I killed him." She gasped, flopped down on the sofa, but somehow her hand remained steady. "I saw him on the floor with blood all over his shirt and the hole near his heart. There was blood everywhere and on me, too."

Her eyes closed for a second, as if remembering that day. "Do you know what Lanie did then? Answer me, you impertinent hussy," she ordered.

"Ah, she cried?"

Victoria snickered and coughed. "She laughed at me. She did not even bend down toward her lover. She looked at me and laughed." The words came in labored puffs, but she continued, "I swore right then that I would never forgive her. Now she is dead and I am dying and I have discovered that I cannot carry the hatred I felt for her on to Diamond. I do feel sorry, I want you to know. For myself. Now, when I am gone, Diamond will get everything. My own lover's child, yes, I have come to realize that Elaine did tell the truth on that one thing. Diamond does look like Jimmy if you really need to know. She will inherit my fortune."

She started sobbing but managed to get to her feet. Then looked at me with eyes of steel and asked, "What will people think?"

The gun was now at eye level and I could actually see straight into the barrel. "Wait, Miss Dupris, think this through. Don't you want to tell Diamond all this yourself? Would you like to tell Diamond how you feel before you fire that gun? You didn't mean to kill Jimmy. Everybody will agree to that. The authorities understand things like this. They always understand the truth. It was just an accident, a horrible accident."

"I have thought about options. What you cannot understand, I am certain, is that this is a question of breeding. If Jimmy and I had left Hawaii, perhaps I would not have been troubled by the scandal of someone of my status marrying a ner-do-well. However, that was not the case. I could not tell Diamond and the authorities that I was in love with Jimmy March, because what would people in our circle think? Consequently, you must die."

Chapter 18

Have you ever thought of where you'd like to be when your earthy life ends? I hadn't either and yet there I was in the library of a grand mansion in Honolulu and as they say in detective fiction, "staring in the barrel of a loaded gun," thanks to Victoria "the fruitcake" Dupris. Whatever courage I had had as a consultant with the bureau was gone. I tasted fear in my mouth and it was bitter.

Her arm quivered but then straightened. I knew without a doubt that the toy gun could pop a hole straight through me. Of that I was sure. Death could either be painful as I quickly lost blood all over the ancient Persian carpet or quick. *If I have a choice, God please, make it fast,* I prayed and squeezed my eyes shut.

Then there was a clunking sound. Trust me, it was not a bullet because I felt no hot pain. I was not dead because my eyes flew open as Victoria Dupris hissed, "Inez, how dare you interfere with what I am doing—you are hired help." She gasped, teetered, and tried to reach for the oxygen tank.

"You are not going to kill anyone, Miss Dupris. This is wrong." Inez's voice thundered through the sitting room and if I had not been paralyzed with fear, I would have hurdled myself over the back of the sofa to hug the maid because somehow that toy gun was no longer in Auntie Evil's claw.

"Get out. You are fired. Get out right now. I have always disliked you. Father forever praised you, said you were bright and I was the dull witted one. He said I was not even half as intelligent as a stupid maid right off the boat from Cuba." Victoria screeched and it all came out in a child's voice, as if she'd regressed sixty or seventy years.

Inez walked over toward Victoria and picked up the gun. Then she grabbed the softball off the floorthat she had pitched straight at the gun, and that saved my life. She tossed the ball in to the air, smiled at me, and placed it into a pocket of her denim work apron. She was not only a baseball coach. Apparently, true to her words when we'd talked, she still had a mean pitch.

Inez pulled a cell phone from her crisp white apron pocked, pressed some numbers, spoke calmly to the operator and asked for the police and paramedics to come to the house. Then she commanded to her mistress, "Sit down and inhale on the mask, ma'am. Come now, here's your oxygen. Breathe in. It's right here." She sounded like she was speaking to a child who is spent from a tantrum.

Finally, Inez looked at me. My legs felt like over-cooked pasta and I flopped against the back of the sofa.

• • •

Looking back on that afternoon and my near-death experience, I contribute the wobbling legs, so different than before the cancer, to just that. Before the cancer, like lots of women, I thought I could handle anything. I was woman, hear me roar. The cancer made me mortal, and honestly that wasn't so bad.

I have bossy Cousin Jane to actually thank for my near miss. She told me she had a frightening feeling, hearing I'd been commanded to come to the Dupris' mansion, and do-gooder that she is? She barged into Payton's debate with the incumbent governor. Jane pulled a microphone away from some citizen who was asking a question of Governor Flint, so she could use it. The governor, true to her base instincts, used a string of four-letter words before attempting to have security grab Jane. As they were dragging her out of the debate, she screamed at Payton, telling him where I was. She told me later, "I let him know that Victoria Dupris was dangerous, a nut job, and if he loved you even half as much as those gooey eyes indicated, he'd better get his backside over there to help you. I never saw a man move so fast, especially Payton, who at least on TV always pretended to be Mr. Joe Cool. The guy loves you, Nica." Payton called the mansion on his way there, and Inez took the call. Hence, I am alive.

Back at the mansion? Payton arrived with the Honolulu fire department and he raced to me. We held each other tightly as Miss Dupris was strapped onto a stretcher. From the grim faces of the EMTs, my guess was that she'd expended too much energy attempting to murder me. Later, I would learn that was right.

Moments after the ambulance pulled out, Diamond dashed in the front doors and Inez held her as she learned everything that happened. "Oh, oh, Nica, I am so very sorry." She rubbed my arm up and down and cried. "I took the car and drove to Carlton Villas. Oh, had I only been here…"

"Sweetie, if you'd been here, who knows what would have happened. It was Inez and her killer curve ball that saved the day." We hugged and then I pulled away. "Why did you visit Babes?"

"You said Mr. Waller was a friend of my father's. Your uncle Henry told me so, too." Diamond stopped for a moment, inhaling deeply, and said, "We must sit in the garden. It's lovely outside and this room is too stuffy. It stinks of lying and death. I need sunshine." She threw open the patio doors, which creaked from little use and we followed her to the lanai.

That's when I saw something in her that hadn't been there previously. There was determination. Yes, she was a Dupris.

Inez, Payton, Diamond, and I sat on the terrace, the Pacific glowing blue in the distance, and Diamond said, "The trust, thanks to Mr. Yu's family, has had Mr. Waller on a new drug, Seniella. It has been used for years for sufferers of migraines, and now there's a drug trial to study if it can assist those with dementia."

"And Babes is one? He's on this medication?"

Payton put his arm around my waist. "Nikky, yes, like I told you, Babes saved Dad's life. We've been trying to help him. When we heard about the success of the drug in Europe, I sought out information and we got him into the initial testing."

Diamond smiled and nodded. "He's starting to remember things from the past. Not just way back, but that too. He told me about the night Jimmy died. He saw the gun in Victoria's hand, saw Jimmy slump over, saw the blood. He knows, because he told me, that my father pushed my mother aside. He saved her life. And in that instant, the bullet hit him in the chest. Mr. Waller and a Mr. George Stratford loaded Jimmy's body into the back of a van. Victoria was with them and they drove to the Dupris ranch on the north shore. Daddy's buried in a grave in the family cemetery there. It's where Grandfather and Grandmother and aunts and uncles are. I brought Mama ashes with me, and I hope you'll come with me, Nica and Inez and Payton, when I place her ashes next to Jimmy's." She swallowed hard, but there were no tears. She walked to the edge of the patio, put her slender face into a cluster of yellow plumeria as Inez silently went to answer the phone.

I could see Inez talking and then she came back to us. She walked close to Diamond and held her hand. "I'm sorry, Miss Diamond, but the paramedics did everything they could. She had a heart attack they believe and, and…she's been released from all her anger and pain." Inez hugged Diamond.

"It's better for her. The world has changed so much and Auntie hated change. It was hard for her," Diamond whispered and then turned to Inez. "You won't leave me? Please, don't leave me now that Auntie is gone. I don't know what I would do without you, Miss Inez."

"Oh, baby, I would never do that." She hugged the woman again. "I never really wanted to retire, but Miss Victoria made it clear that she didn't want me here anymore."

"You're going to be fine, Diamond," Payton said in his practical, grown-up voice. "My trust attorney also handled the trust for your aunt. I asked some questions, nothing personal, and everything is set to come to you, from this house to the family estate where your father is buried."

I was about to console Diamond, although like Payton said, she would be okay surrounded by good people, especially Inez, when my cell rang. Jane's photo came up and I knew it wouldn't do to ignore her. It never did.

"Hi Jane, it's over and I'll tell you about it when—"

It was Gramps. "We're at Queen's Hospital, Nica. Jane's delivering a baby boy right now. Tom's with her. I am way too old fashioned to be there, but how about that. Me a greater-than-ever-Gramps. Come over when you can and bring that boyfriend of yours. Since it looks like it going to be permanent with you two, he may as well get used to Jane, Tom, and me."

After we'd seen Henry Angieski Morales, all of two hours old and the spitting image of his daddy and the loud mouth of his mama (don't tell her I said that), Payton and I found the hospital café and sat.

We didn't talk for the longest time and then suddenly questions burned for answers. I swallowed a long drink of ice tea and asked, "Did you know Victoria was in back of the threats, the attempt on my life, getting George Stratford to check in on Babes, and even drive the black car that nearly killed me? Did you know Victoria had Pinkie and Mil Finger on her payroll of evil, too?"

His hands slid to my face. "I want to hear everything, Nikky, but right now, I have to tell you that I am not going to let you get away from me ever again."

Then the guy actually took my breath away. "Nikky Wikiwiki Ticky Wainwright-Dobson." He got down on one knee and a crowd of doctors, nurses, technicians, and visitors who by now had recognized Payton formed a circle around us. "Would you do me the great honor of becoming my wife? Will you marry me? At once? Now, before the election?"

"Yes. But? Before the election, Payton? But what if Governor Margaret Flint stirs up a scandal? Remember the dead husbands?" I tried to pull him up, but the guy was more stubborn than me and became more so as the crowd cheered.

"Let her. Nikky, precious, this is Hawaii. Scandals and dirt are in every family. These are the islands. You either learn to man up to scandal or you move to the mainland." He laughed and kissed me. "And there are even a few skeletons in the Yu family, but we'll talk about that on our twentieth wedding anniversary *if* I wasn't dreaming and you actually said yes."

"I actually said yes. Nikky Wikiwiki Ticky and P. Yu are officially engaged."

So we became engaged. For three days. And we did, marry that is. Payton won the election with a significant victory. Even now, when people meet him on the street or at events or walking along Waikiki, they laugh at him and rib him for taking twenty years to ask his high school sweetheart for a date and then marrying her in just two weeks.

Baby Henry is too young to understand, but he's going to have twin cousins once we return from the orphanage in Beijing with our own babies. And every member, even the extended aunties and uncles and cousins plus more than I can keep track of, have been celebrating our merger, um, marriage. The Yu and Angieski clans couldn't be happier. Especially me.

More from This Author

(From *Games of the Heart*)

Place the blame where it should go: On chocolate.

I opened the front door of my Vegas condo. And nearly slammed it, except the man I faced handed me a golden, foiled-wrapped container with the unmistakable Godiva label. Then he took a step back. He'd baited a hook, and I was caught.

I grabbed the box. If it hadn't been for that lure of dark chocolate, I'd have stayed happily ignorant about sex slaves, black-market babies, cheatin' preachers, and an assortment of lowlifes that intruded on my cluttered, fluttered and frazzled life.

If I'd slammed the door, I'd would never have been rejected, arrested and nearly exterminated. Wait, like always, I'm getting ahead of the story and how it all happened.

You see, at the stroke of another hot summer midnight, I found myself feeling the breeze on my backside and sniffing the corners of a chocolate snare. I ripped open the box, placed a sensually scrumptious chocolate into my mouth, slurped and swirled the wickedly decadent cocoa around on my tongue, and eyed what the devil had dumped on my doorstep. Medical studies have proven it's a bad idea to let woman with PMS eat a pound of Godiva at one time, or some news report said, I think. Trust me. It's an even *worse* idea to try to take chocolate away from a woman, with PMS or not.

The guy didn't know my cycle, but he certainly knew women. So he didn't come closer until I'd gobbled up three more. In a row. Then I handed back the empty box.

Forget what you're thinking. This man was not a hunka hunka burnin' love, but seemed to be my pudgy grandfather. Or a doppelganger dressed collar to cuffs with glitter galore, gold and gosh-awful fake-e-o alligator-esque cowboy boots, with spurs in the shape of skulls. They clanked when he backed up, reverberating like cymbals.

He squinted in the porch light as his chin dragged low. He grumbled, muttered, and withdrew his left hand from behind him, producing yet another box with the chocolatier's signature label. I salivated, snatched it, and stepped back. You see, I'm not addicted to the stuff, I'm chocolate-enriched. I am not officially plump, I'm just short for my body weight.

Okay, that brings you the abbreviated version of why five minutes later my disgruntled relative was huddled on the beige sofa in the sterile Las Vegas condo I got with my current job and why I was stomping in front of him. See, I am usually the one who solves problems, being that I'm a minister and all.

Yes, you heard it right. I might not look like one as I am rounded on all the right edges and with a propensity for wearing clothes showing a smidge of cleavage and it's true if you've heard that I have Victoria's Secret's site as my homepage. Like it or not, that's me, Pastor Jane Angieski. I'm fully licensed, fully educated, and fully confused most of the time.

You're not the first, you know, to wonder how a flashy woman like me got into the ministry business. Most folks do not come straight out and ask if I am a preacher because they're so dumbfounded to find out I know the Good News backward, forward and well done in the middle. My response? "You see, they have quotas. Recall affirmative action? Needed more women who had some curves and padding in the ranks, and that's me," I say.

The one who asks gets a glazed look and nods. Honestly? Hold on to something sturdy because here it comes:

During college, I worked in retail (see above Victoria's Secret reference), at a mortuary where I applied make-up to the dearly departed, gave out contraceptives and condoms at a free clinic in Watts, and did time asking, "Want fries with that?" Along the way, I made enough so I could head to UCLA for a master's in psychology because I'm outrageously curious about people. Honestly, a few days before graduation I went to a program on campus, because the A/C in my apartment was broken and I knew there would be cake and coffee. The program was to recruit grad students into the ministry. I signed on the dotted line right then, attended seminary, graduated with honors, accepted an assistant minister gig straight out the door, and got kicked out because I worked with the cops in tracking down hoods in the hood where I was the pastor for this ghetto church. The church council didn't mind that I nabbed the bad guys looking like a lady of the evening who could do it all through the night. What they didn't like was that I appeared on the front of the *L.A. Times* in a hot pink leather miniskirt, strappy sandals that only enhanced the look, and a blouse leaving little to the imagination of your Great Aunt Tillie. The story hit the national news, and wham, bam, thank you, ma'am, little old me was seen and talked about on *60 Minutes*, MSNBC, Twitter, YouTube, and it then went viral. *Time* begged for an interview but better judgment snapped in. I declined—well, only because my denomination's district council put the brakes on that one. Besides, I don't always want to stay second fiddle in church hierarchy. I do have pride. I'd like to be known, someday, as an important minister, but not the television evangelist kind with those flapping eyelashes and hair like Marge Simpson. No offense, Marge, but it's not a good look for either of us.

The happy ending to the above knuckle-rapping was that the jerks who were dealing, drugging, and pimping went to a "helping" place in California, clogging an overstuffed prison system even more, and I got thanked by getting my backside booted to Vegas. I wasn't exactly demoted, but I'm no longer a full pastor. These days, if I should burp without saying, "*Pardonnez-moi,*" the council knows. Hence the youth minister I'm filling in for left exact instructions so I wouldn't lead the teens on a slope that has flashing orange signs reading, "Beware: Point of No Return."

Back to the man of the midnight hour—the grumbling continued, and like waiting out a storm, I sat down next to that huddled mass of manhood, Henry J. Angieski, Ph.D., my grandfather. In all my thirty-five years, I'd never seen him defeated.

Quick footnote on my family: He and Gram couldn't have children, and knew it before they married. Gramps always says it like this: "Uncle Sam really needed me and thought a tropical Asian trip might help me to understand humanity better." That meant he was unemployed after grad school, was drafted and sent to Vietnam. About Dad? Gramps says, "I found the son of my heart there, always hanging around the barracks. He had red hair, like your Gram, and the most intense almond-shaped eyes I'd ever seen. When I was accepted into the doctorate program, your Uncle Sam let me come home with the things I found there, from the bullet wound in my knee to a ten-year-old kid." Gramps and Gram made it official— adoption was different then. They couldn't trace Dad's biological parents; the country was in shambles and of course had already been invaded by the French, English and Russians before the US stepped into the mess. Then Gram died, a painful battle with cancer, and a couple months later I came into the picture. When my parents decided that parenthood didn't shake, rattle, or roll on their personal Richter scale, Gramps once more manned up. Story goes that they piled their macrobiotic rice, pine nut smoothies, ceremonial drums, unfiltered carrot juice and love beads inside a rusting, purple VW van dotted with painted daisies, dumped pint-size me on Gramps' doorstep, and went in search of their bliss. I believe they were ten years past the real hippies. Last I heard, when I was sixteen, they were in Sedona, finding and selling therapy rocks to tourists. I'm happy for them, really, but getting a rock in the mail for your birthday stinks. That's enough of me, at least for a minute, as it was the grunting, grumbler grandfather on the ghastly sofa that this is all about.

He sighed from the pointy toes of his red boots. Then grunted. I would have sworn he swore, but I knew better.

"Call me Onesimus." The statement ended in a pheewee.

"What-a-muss?"

"Get a clue, you're a preacher. You should know this stuff, always spouting it off as you do all Bible belting and never letting a man swear without raising those eyebrows. Oh, don't give me that look, girl. Won't do you any good this time. I'm immune. Been looking at myself to long one of your freeze-frame frowns frazzle me. You know I'm talking the truth."

My mouth flapped, "Old or New Testament?" If only someone had videoed my mouth gaping and eyes blinking, I would have been a shoe-in for *America's Funniest Home Videos*. "Onesimus, Pastor." He spoke as if I were a dolt, which I felt like. And a stranger, which I certainly wasn't.

He never calls me Pastor. Never before had he even raised his voice to me. "Who are you and what did you do with my grandfather? My gramps is happily living in Carlsbad, California. That's right along the Pacific and north of San Diego. My gramps is in bed right now, not in Vegas, baby."

We stared at each other, and then a two-watt light bulb my brain flickered. "Do you mean Onesimus, as in the slave the Apostle Paul writes about?"

"Bing-a-ding ding, girl. Listen, Jane, I'm having a crisis, one that's, well, personal, as personal and private as it can get for a man."

From the dancing rhinestones on his denim shirt, past the belt buckle, which was the size of Rhode Island, to the candy-apple red Mustang convertible, which I noticed since it was in the middle of my driveway, the man was either auditioning for a low-budget movie or had lost his senses. Besides, my grandfather never needed help. Never wore cowboy clothes, either, for that matter. He was dependable, taught music at the university, and played with an aging boomer band who'd just found out they were hip. The man had style, grace, out of *GQ*. Okay, there were some fifty- and sixty-something women circling like ravenous seagulls chasing a fishing boat, but he always chose right from wrong when it came to women. Then again, I never had a conversation about the birds and bees with him.

"Ohhhhhhh, personal and private," I muttered, regretting my decision to have the second Lean Cuisine dinner, even if it was diet food because I absolutely, positively didn't want to discuss my grandfather's sexual inadequacies or performance.

Heck-o, I never intended or wanted this talk. But I blurted in more than a squeak than a pastoral voice, "Crisis? Men your age are past that. For Pete's sake, don't tell me you're here in Vegas to marry an eighteen-year-old half-dressed dancer who wears pink feathers that glow in the dark with matching pasties that barely cover her nipples. Or that she's employed in a strip club as a stripper."

A giggle came from me, a grunt came from him.

"Say any of that is true, and I'm kicking your knickers back to Carlsbad." I yanked his sleeve, being careful not to dislodge one of the three million rhinestones on that part of his shirt. He either didn't get my little joke or…Wait, this couldn't be.

"She's not some chorus babe, Jane. She has to be, well, I'd say, eighteen or nineteen. But she could be sixteen. I've never asked."

"Whoa, hold the phone. Not a chorus girl? Who is she?" I could no longer hide in the kitchen.

"She's got nothing to do with this. I'm like a package of ham that's been shoved to the back of the refrigerator. The whole world is out to get me, although Switzerland stays neutral. Lately I wake up in the morning and wish my parents hadn't met."

"Get out of here." Mr. Rhinestone started to get up and I grabbed him. "I'm kidding, Gramps. You're better at telling jokes than Jerry Seinfeld."

"Humor is another way to be serious, Miss Pastor Lady. My problem is the damn-blasted stroke."

"The stroke happened, you didn't cause it, Gramps, and the physical therapist said you'd be okay. What changed?" I could feel the corners of my mouth head south. I looked around the room for his Bertha, his ever-present guitar. He was alone, and that troubled me enough, until it finally sunk in that he hadn't reputed that she might be a chorus girl. For once in my life I was speechless, at least for five seconds. "Are you huffy like this to the folks you preach to? Wonder that they let you get in back of a pulpit." He planted his boots in the middle of the "it comes furnished" living room.

I stuck out my arm, because I could sense he was about to bolt. "This isn't about me, Mister. When were you going to tell me about this girl? Have you, um, married an adolescent? If you're sure she's at least eighteen, um, should I be relieved? Wait. What's happening to my orderly world?" I held my head and rocked it back and forth.

"Stop your yammering, Jane, for sanity's sake. It's not like she'd have me," he said and waved a hand in the air, raked it through his abundant steel-gray hair, and frowned. Deeply. He pushed past me and limped to the front window, stretched back the tan drapes. I followed, and we looked at the convertible.

I had to grab the above-mentioned drape for support when it hit me. Ton of bricks to the noggin. He was doing it with a teenager. I slapped my mouth. I tried to take a long, cleansing breath. In and out, yoga style. I sputtered, "Are you, well, cohabitating?"

He didn't even look my way. He wasn't using the cane, so that should have been a good sign until he said, "I'm old, feeble. I'm useless. I'm disabled." He retreated to the sofa, slumped over, blending in with the beige fabric so much that if it weren't for rhinestones I could have convinced myself this was a nightmare and the result of the diet cupcakes I had for dessert.I stared. Was that a yes or a no to my question on lusting after a teenager? His face turned to pea soup with undertones of eggplant and I winced as he slid the knee-high cowboy boots off his feet. He rubbed his toes and then let his head flop back. With his eyes closed, his face was a street map of wrinkles.

When could this all have happened? We talked every other day at least, emailed, and this was the first I'd heard of any setback or a, um, teenage romantic interest. Or his extreme lifestyle makeover to a rhinestone cowboy.

Do you think about ministers as uptight, buttoned down, repressed and sometimes clueless? Heaven help me, I'm not like that and I never get speechless. I like talking, but right then I was without a comeback, snappy or otherwise. As an itinerant pastor, actually, which means I fill in for ministers when they're on sabbatical or away from their flock, I need a stock of flip answers because most of the time I'm cross-examined about my credentials. That was definitely the case in point when I arrived six weeks ago at Mega Church, USA, technically known as Desert Hills Community Church. Don't know what they were expecting. What they got was a slightly less busty version of a young Dolly Parton, just slightly, without the good lookin' makeup. It wasn't what they'd ordered in a new youth pastor. Honestly, that's what I heard when I was quietly taking care of business in the ladies' room as two of the office staff were chatting about me. It wasn't the Dolly comment that hurt, mind you—I love her—it was the dig about my inability to apply cosmetics.

Yes, being a Chatty Cathy helped in most of the scrapes in which I've found myself, but right then, I opened and closed my mouth and still nothing came forth.

With my history of relatives abandoning me (note to self: check the Internet to see if parents have been incarcerated again lately), I was floundering big time with Gramps, who was the color of rotten grapes and breathing unevenly on my sofa. My finger fluttered to my robe's pocket and my cell, ready to punch 911.

You see, he wasn't just my grandfather and a professor, he'd become a heartthrob. With his band, Slam Dunk, he created classic rock hits that you can't stop humming and did it time and again. Sort of a Paul McCartney-esque guy, and maybe I'm a bit partial, but I think he's better looking, in a grandfatherly way, than Sir Paul. He had friends, recording sessions, folks he knew at church and even an on-again, off-again romance with my good friend U.S. Senator Geraldine English.

While looking after Gramps as he recovered from the stroke, I licked my wounds from being sacked along with the serious reprimand from the council and spent quality time nagging him. That kind of stuff. Home was Carlsbad, California, and if you think about golf and tennis at La Costa, locking-block kid heaven of Legoland and a chi-chi beachy town just north of San Diego's city limits, you've got a snapshot of where Gramps calls home, and sometimes me, too. If you're singing a Beach Boys song or something from the Mamas and the Papas, you're a bit younger than Gramps, but you probably know the kind of surf city where I grew up.

So after his stroke, I was Nurse Nancy. I needed a time-out, still store from the above-mentioned butt-kicking. When he refused all coddling, I accepted this temporary position at Desert

Hills, which came with a pint-size furnished condo that had no charm or style. Somehow it suited me; I didn't want to care. I was a temp. I would be out of the job in six months, so it would have been nuts to drag anything personal to the desert. I'm to the point when a man asks me out, I tell him to step back and think it over. How was I going to counsel Gramps with this track record? Wait, don't answer that.

"Did you have a setback?" I swallowed fear, and it tasted just like the second boxed chicken Alfredo.

Mumble, mumble. "Yes."

"When?"

"Not another stroke?"

I have no idea why, but I moved to the door and walked out on the porch. Okay, he'd driven here. He could control a car. That had to be a good sign, or had I been hallucinating about the car in the driveway? Even in the streetlamp's meager glow, that Mustang was red. I closed the door. "Gramps, why aren't you driving your Tundra truck?"

"Wanted to breathe new-car smell again before I died."

"So you rented it, good. When did you arrive?" Call it a premonition, but I was glad I was near the sofa when he said, "Three weeks ago."

Now it was my turn to collapse into one of the two nondescript loveseats in my beige and glass living room. "Excuse me?" I clucked. "You've been in Vegas for three entire weeks and you are just now coming over here to see me?"

He tilted forward, lacing his hands, resting his forehand on his fingers and, silly me, I assumed he was praying until he said, "Trying to figure myself out. All I discovered was I am a limp, broken and empty shell. Crumpled. Look at me, really look, Jane. There's no man left. I know I'm not the first to seek refuge in the bright lights of Sin City. Yeah, all I found were bright lights and an old, big city." He studied the cream-colored Berber carpet as if the answer to the meaning of life were in the weave.

I checked it out, too. I didn't find any help so I said, "What you did wasn't that unusual." I was walking a long, thin line, like the one in the middle of a highway, with two semis heading straight at me. "Lots of men find they want a playmate." I added, "Like your very, very, very young one." It was grunted under my breath. It was snide. It felt good. I'm a preacher, but I'm human.

Gramps ignored me, which was just as well, and talked to the carpet, holding his head in his hands. "I'm on the run. From the world, friends, co-workers—heck, even strangers. And especially God. The body you see is as good as it's going to get, but honestly, Jane, I'm hurting. I am angry, angrier than when your grandmother died, a heck of a lot angrier than when your folks decided parenting wasn't their thing. Didn't know I could get so stinking mad. I'm stinking angry at myself for getting old. I'm a worn-out geezer, a windbag, a codger."

I circled him with my arms. He was small. When did he shrink? "Oh, Gramps. I love you. Why did you wait so long? Why didn't you tell me? You're not alone." I squeezed his shoulders, and then it hit me. I pulled my arms back, stiffened my back. "Wait one confounded second. I have called you. I emailed, just today, I sent you a joke. The one about Las Vegas. Remember it? Americans spend three hundred billion dollars every year on gaming in Vegas, and that doesn't even include weddings and elections? You wrote back, 'Ha Ha,' and said everything was fine."

"Cell phones don't care where you are. With the laptop you'll find in the trunk of that car, I was connected with you and the college."

"The college? Classes aren't over. It's not the end of summer session. Did you quit?" It didn't seem that illogical that he'd quit a career spanning three decades since he was driving a hot convertible and living with an underage floozy.

"They let me go."

"The chancellor fired you? The best music professor in the entire University of California system?"

"Might just as well have. Retirement. There, I said it."

I felt the air slide from my lungs. We both knew it would happen sometime, but my grandfather always looked and felt young, at least that's what he said and what I wanted to see. "Retirement." It was the F-word for people who never planned to grow up or slow down. I sounded disgustingly chipper as I said, "This is great. Why, you can create some new music, you can travel, you can have hobbies, you can—"

"Stop your preaching. Jane, look at me. I'm not some coot who lives in the past, who sits around whittling apples and bananas out of wood or solving the world's problems with the other coots at a local watering hole. I'm a musician who had a stroke and now finds even walking a pain in the—well, and a royal pain it is. I can't play because these fingers can't even manage to find the frets." He stared at his hands and balled them into fists. "As for traveling, just getting to Vegas last month was all I could do. This kid, who turned out to be the pilot and was barely shaving, asked me if I wanted a wheelchair to get off the stinking airplane. For Pete's sake, they had me board with the mommies and the babies."

"Gosh, Gramps, I'm coming with you next time."

"Jane. The geezers board first."

"Ah, do you want to tell me what you've done here in Las Vegas?" I asked, and it was a roundabout way to learn if he was doing the horizontal snuggly-buggly with the underage hoochie-coochie strip club dancer.

"Nothing."

"You sure?" Okay, I really didn't ask that because I really didn't want to know. I just nodded.

He loosened the leather and silver braided bolo tie from his neck, slipping it out of a clasp that looked like the great state of

Texas. Unbuttoning the shirt's top buttons, he rubbed his throat and said, "Sitting in a hotel room overlooking the Strip, watching the fireworks go off at Treasure Island, that hotel with the pirate theme, ordering room service and watching Nick at Nite, reruns of *Andy Griffith* and old movies. That's what I've been doing. Most of the time, I was having my own, what do you call it, pity party, like you did after Colin's death."

I moved the ten feet to the kitchen and grabbed bottles of water. "But you're here now. We're a pair when it comes to pity parties." I pretended to wipe something off the stove, squeezing my eyes shut. But bringing up Colin's name made an image flash into my mind. For the millionth time I could see me in the stands as Colin's F-15 explode into a fireball right over the airfield. The air show crowd gasped. I remembered falling forward into the crowd with my chin hitting the bleacher in front and then everything in my world went black. Now each day as I brushed my teeth or dried my hair, I saw the scar on my chin from my fall. It was a constant, daily reminder, if I needed one. Pilot error, the final report had said. Not enough left to bury him.

I blinked back tears. "Remember you dragged me back home? I recall you stormed my quarters on the air force base and snapped Ben & Jerry from my quaking fingers. You growled, 'Get that caboose of yours off the sofa and put on some clothes, girly. You're coming home.'"

Gramps laughed. It was hollow with a raspy cough, too, but it was a start.

"Yes, and then you stopped at Denny's, forced me to eat something other than ice cream, and took me to a jam session with Slam Dunk. As I remember it, soda spewed from your nose when I tried to play some of your music."

He laughed a bit more, less shallow.

"Was it root beer or Pepsi?" I asked.

"You were so pathetic."

"Yeah, runs in the family. Look at you. Let's get you an omelet or a peanut butter sandwich. Then you can tell me your plans." And for a second I regretted that word "plans," because a seventy-year-old midnight cowboy driving a brand-new scarlet-colored Mustang might not have the wherewithal to formulate good plans. There was also the matter of the lady with the pasties on her feminine places. She was hanging in the air, at least in the air I was breathing.

"Jane, girl. There's more." By that time, he'd finished the makeshift midnight meal. "The crisis is more than just this failing body, this bundle of bones. God's let me down. I'm not a Christian anymore. Maybe it's me who has let Him down, don't know the answer on that."

"Um, oh." You've probably made notes right now that if you ever need counseling, I'll be the last to be asked. I don't blame you. I wasn't too keen on myself at that second. But you have to understand that this was the man who had taken me to church and introduced me to the congregation three days after I was born. This was the man who had given me away when I married, been there just five months later when the jet exploded, and Gramps arranged Collin's funeral. He had cheered me on when the District Council of my denomination granted my pastoral papers and held my hand when the same District Council threatened to withdraw them.

Jumping from one sure-thing conclusion to the next, exceeding the legal limit, what would I have said to any other man or woman if I heard this? I racked my overly educated counselor's brain and came up with zilch. When the loss of faith comes straight from the mouth of the man you've idolized for your entire life, the earth opens and swallows your most patented advice. Big help I was. I stood there mute.

"I'm a slave to this body. And before you start quoting scripture with all the verses and lines and all that other stuff, which you're good at, it's not like Job and the thorn in his side. There are no earthly reasons why I should continue to live as I have."

Standing at the sink, hot water spewing, I couldn't seem to get my mind to order my fingers to twist the knobs to shut off the flow. When I did find my voice, my hands matched the color of the car in my driveway. "Have you talked with Him?" I picked up the sponge. I scrubbed and scrubbed the plate in my hands, long after the gooey remains of cheese and egg came off. I poured out the last cold cup from the coffeemaker and drank it in one deep swallow. I wiped up imaginary spills on the counter, and I was about to organize the refrigerator and take out the trash, after mopping the floor, when finally Gramps spoke again.

"I've yelled a lot."

"You look pretty calm now." I slammed the refrigerator once I'd placed the maraschino cherries in heavy syrup next to the mayonnaise and close to the Tabasco sauce. I'd alphabetized everything while I was waiting.

"As I was hiding, I realized I was a wretched waste of humanity, actually. You don't need to blink—I saw that—I didn't do anything you'd find disgraceful for a man of my age. Now I think I've worked out a solution, of sorts."

"Men your age still do a lot," I interrupted because I didn't want to putter down the pathway of anything remotely connected with Gramps' young chick, but a gal's got to be tough. "I still don't get it." For the tenth time I washed out the coffee pot that didn't need another rinse.

Gramps stifled a yawn. "Hey, stop grumbling. You're not boring me, but I'm fading fast."

"Cut to the chase, Gramps."

"It's dancing."

"You're going to become a professional dancer, you who refused to dance at my wedding because you have feet of clay or something like that? Positive thinking is groovy, but dancing isn't something you jump into, especially competition dance like those shows on TV. Um, how will this help you?"

"Honey, how can someone with your over-educated brain be so lacking in common sense? I'm old and disgusting, but I've got an ace up my sleeve, and you're going to help me. We're going dancing."

"You've seen me dance, Gramps, and it's almost as disgusting as my playing the rock music you and Slam Dunk perform. Besides, I inherited your left feet."

"How often, Janey, do you miss this point?"

"It's two in the morning. How's that for a reason? If you want to go out dancing tonight, you've got the wrong granddaughter, even if I am your only granddaughter. Besides you've got more explaining to do, especially the part about the little lady who has been making you happy. Wait. Where are you going?"

"Let's settle this tomorrow. This is a wagering town, and my best bet is that the guest room is straight down the hall, and knowing you, Jane, there will be fresh sheets on the bed, a bathrobe in the closet, and plenty of toiletries in the bathroom, still in flowered wrappers. If you want to talk more, you're about to have the bathroom door closed in your pretty little face. The rest can wait until tomorrow, and you can come down a bit off your high preachin' horse." He turned and muttered in a loud voice, "Have you always been this bossy? I'd forgotten."

I was sputtering as he limped out of sight. I really and truly wanted a strong cup of coffee, but at two A.M., that's madness, although I've been nuts before. What I did was to take deep cleansings breaths of the coffee beans, flicked off the light and headed to bed.

I crawled between the sheets, pulled them to my neck and tried to focus on happy thoughts. Where was my happy place? The sandman and I wrestled. Like clockwork, I checked the clock at regular intervals from two to six, when the alarm turned on the radio to those ghastly chipper voices of early morning talk show hosts, announcing another hot, but dry "reallllly fabulous day in Vegas, baby." I slapped the thing to the floor. It bounced, and the sound hurt my head. In my quest to get to my happy place, I'd neglected to shut my blinds before those four hours of tossing and turning not to be thought of as sleep, and now the sizzle had begun to heat the room. It was going to be a scorcher, for sure.

Then from the living room, I heard elevator music. I don't even have an elevator. It was from *West Side Story*. The normal Gramps, before he became a rootin'-tootin' cowboy, would have listened to the Rolling Stones, rap, or hip-hop. This was bad, I thought, as I pulled myself up to sit on the edge of the bed. Now some preachers get on their knees, and trust me, I've got the calluses to prove I do this, but right then God and I needed to look at each other. "I know you never give us more than we can handle, but Lord, I am just not that good. If you want my help, give me a clue." I shrugged into my robe, dove under the bed for my scuffs and headed to the living room as I mumbled, "Help me because I may just do something I regret."

Miracles were real. "Thank you, Jesus," I yelled and waved my hands above my head just like an old-fashion revival meeting.

He was gone. As anyone who knows me will gladly tell you, I have a fertile imagination, so I could nearly believe that he'd left or been Raptured, but the crispy bacon calling my name from the stove told the truth and nothing but it. Plus the table was set for two. At one place were chocolate chip waffles and tall OJ. The coffee smelled strong; the mug was steaming. The newspaper was folded to the comics.

What's a girl to do? I dove in to the feast. If I was wrong and I had been Raptured, I was thrilled to see that the food was yummo.

As I pierced the last forkful, using it to wipe up a puddle of Log Cabin syrup, Gramps limped through the front door with a plastic grocery sack in his hands.

"So, they were edible?"

"I should have waited." My mind raced to the "situation," as I'd named this catastrophe sometime between 3:15 A.M. and 4:30 A.M.

"No way, Janey girl. I figured coffee would get you up. I'm not sleeping well and been up for hours." He poured a mug of coffee, took the carton from the bag, and added enough milk to make this java junkie cringe. "Before you start haranguing an old handicapped geezer about how I don't need milk in coffee because it just takes away the real coffee taste and blah blah blah, you'll want to know the church secretary, Vera, has been calling you every fifteen minutes since the crack of early." He lifted the coffee mug and said, *na zdrowie,* which as everyone of Polish descent knows is the right toast for any drink.

"Forget the 'to your health.' I want to know why you didn't holler for me when I got the calls."

"I've been around a few churches and found that the preachers need their sleep as much as their flock needs to talk with them. Besides, she said it wasn't *that* urgent. Isn't Desert Hills like the rest of them, and if someone stubs their toe they're popped on the prayer chain, or is it more a gossip mill?"

I wasn't going to fuss, although the stubbed toe crack clipped a nick too close to the quick. The prayer chain at Desert Hills did spread the word about illnesses, deaths, and various folks entering rehab. That said, I sometimes thought people didn't pray, but preyed off the info. I'd noticed whispering during the hospitality time and how people quieted when I walked by. Hey, maybe they had me on the prayer chain for God only knew what. A bad hair day? I chalked it up to an ugly part of human nature, and that some folks are uglier than others.

I dialed the church's number and reached Vera. She cracked a "Good morning, honey," and then said, "First off, the District Council is visiting next Friday and requested an appointment with you, but that's not why I've been calling. Pastor Bob says he has a surprise for you and the youth group." I could tell by the tone that her eyes were rolling and her head was making circles. Vera had been the secretary for Desert Hills Community Church for decades, seen other preachers come and go, and little except Pastor Bob's "surprises" fazed her.

There was more to Vera than met the eye, which was plenty considering she looked about as much like a church secretary as sixty-ish Sarah Jessica Parker if she stumbled into Desert Hills, forgot any fashion sense, and plunked her keister behind a computer. The only secretary-like item was cat's eye glasses that perched on her nose. She smelled as if she were marinated in Smuckers jam, which wasn't appealing when mixed with the essence of Marlboro on her breath.

"Any idea what it is?" Did I need a surprise with my beloved grandfather on the lam from God, taken up with an adolescent deviant, and the District Council waiting to slip my neck through a noose? Not.

"You're not going to like it, Pastor Jane. But heck, it's a crapshoot around here. Might be something you can add on to what you're already doing. Hold on, Jane."

I could hear her cooing to someone standing in her office about, "You are so sweet," and then she was on the line with, "Put on your big girl panties and make up your own mind. I gave up mind reading years ago when I quit traveling with the circus."

The line went dead and my appetite with it, which says a lot. Pastor Bob Normal, whom I had begun to secretly and in various muttering times call Ab, apparently was taking over my life in ways that are abnormally annoying even for him.

It took me twenty-five minutes flat to jump into tan slacks and a blazing pink cotton T from the last Victoria's Secret sale and drive to church, just two miles north of the condo. I like to think I'm hip but I'm unhip about mega churches. Give me a steeple and a cross? I'm good. That said, when I drove up to Desert Hills a few weeks ago, I thought I'd stumbled into the Silicon Valley. The building humongous, all windows and sand-colored brick, stretching greenbelts and a flagpole plunked in the middle of it all. The cross? Good question. I asked, too. There isn't one outside, and that, I was told, goes along with the new trend to make the worship center more available to all people. Call me old-fashioned—wait, don't you dare. Yet, it's been my thinking that a church isn't a church without looking like a church. Since I didn't get a vote—and since I was only filling in for the youth pastor, I probably would never get one—on this issue I kept my lips sealed. I know that's a shock.

Faced with a crisis at home and one at church, I gingerly parked my scuffed SUV in the "staff" zone and slapped the sunscreen over the dashboard so that later, when I left for the day, I wouldn't scorch my bountiful backside, and straightened my spine. Like a courteous little soldier, I marched up the marble walk to face my fate. I had barely plastered on a tooth-brightener smile when the pastor met me as I whooshed through the automatic doors into the Foyer of Heavenly Conditioned Air.

"'Bout time you're here. Memo's on your desk. Questions? Vera's got it," said the senior minister, all this with the palm of his hand facing my face.

There was this thing about him that brought out a feeling of grease in me, like the kind that forms on the top of simmering spaghetti sauce when you use cheap hamburger.

He cocked his Elvis-impersonator head. "Yes?"

I was grateful the man wasn't psychic, but I refused to talk to the hand so I waited until he dropped it. "Good morning, Pastor. How are you today? Questions about what?"

"Board decided. Youth group. You. VBS. Great opportunity."

"Excuse me?" I shivered. "Repeat that, please."

"No can do. Off to a fundraiser breakfast. Think again, Pastor Jane, if you have any notions that this place—" He waved a hand around the cavern of the foyer and then swept it toward the marble floor. "—Well, if you think for one second the church is financed by prayer. Money talks, not just here, but everywhere. Vegas is no different. Never kid yourself about that."

Taking yet another cleansing breath, I touched the sleeve of his blue silk suit jacket. "Vacation Bible School starts Monday. And where did you leave that reality check? Today is Friday. You're saying that my youth group will handle it?"

"What don't you get, Pastor Jane?" It came out in a huff as he smoothed the sideburns that went out in the seventies.

Trust me, the man was not into retro. He'd just forgotten we were in the twenty-first century, and possibly women didn't always do what big old strong men ministers said to do.

The gauge on my internal combustion steam-ometer was shouting, "Danger, danger, run for your life." Alas, being low woman on the church totem pole didn't give me any wiggle room. Even if you were on my side, and even if I'd become Old Faithful and blown my cool, I would have been out the door and on the pavement before you could say, "Amen to that, sister."

I bit my tongue, really, clamped it so I didn't shout how he could have found other flunkies to do his bidding, because Ab was in a heated discussion on his cell.

"For golly goodness' sakes, hold it, will you?" he said to the phone. He pulled it away from his ear and turned to me, his eyebrows knit together. We were so close I could see stubble from a unibrow. I might be his flunkie of the month, but the unibrow produced wonderful waves of superiority in a deliciously perverted way.

"Now what is it? Jane, are you or are you not a minister? Then minister. For heaven's sake, do the job you're being paid to do, which if you'll check your business card, madam, it is to be a minister. Organize VBS."

"Yes, of course," I snapped. Flunkie or not, he was the boss, even if the last twelve hours had been rotten.

"Then why *are* we having this conversation? Get on it or get out." His cheeks became blotchy, and I believe I was about to get a royal chewing out when Vera's five-inch platform heels came clopping down the marble hall. We both nodded as she walked by and, not for the first time, I wondered what control the secretary had over the minister. Suddenly he was all milk and honey when he said, "Listen, Jane, you've come highly recommend, can do miracles and walk on water, that kind of stuff. We're excited to have you here at Desert Hills. You know what I'm talking about, even with your very public mishap, shall we call it, and I know you are capable. Besides, these are little children, not something like the hardcore hoodlums you personally arrested while preaching in Los Angeles, in that 'hood. I'll be praying for you. Hey, we'll get the entire prayer chain to jump on this. Works for me," he said. He patted me on the arm and began talking about market gains, and I knew that was the end of our meeting.

Then he topped the icing on the cake with, "We're praying for you." Who the "we" were I had no clue, but he beat all land records as he dashed to the silver Lexus parked next to my dusty SUV.

I've been a happy camper, a cranky one, and also ticked off big time. Right then I skidded to a halt in the third category, with black marks on the pavement of my mind. Let the cookies crumble where they may. Handling sixty puberty-crazed kids in a youth work program, preparing sermons, doing outreach at shelters and missions, keeping tabs on activities, and counseling kids and their parents was making my half-empty cup permanently slosh all over my good intentions. Vacation Bible School? Nietzsche said that which doesn't kill us will make us stronger. And when I get to heaven *if* Mr. N is there, I'm going to give him a tiny little bit of my mind. I give pieces of my mind out so often, you realize, that I can only spare a bit, but Nietzsche is going to get it.

Pastor Bob's comments about, "This place is not financed by prayer. Money talks in this city," irked me and made my breakfast lurch and become a fat belch.

My office is barely big enough for a woman with skinny thighs to move to the desk, but I made it anyhow. I poked *the* memo, moving it with one finger. I read it. I flopped in my typing chair. Then read it again.

I'll cut to the chase. The pastor and the board, with pressure from parents who had decided that they wanted VBS, but never got around to organizing one even though all the advertisements went out to the community over the last month, voted last night that the teens, who didn't work during the day, could run it. Of course, mind you, no teens had volunteered nor heard about this, and their youth minister, moi, didn't know nothing no how, either. Bottom line? Two hundred children would show up at Desert Hills at 9:00 A.M. Monday morning, and I was to give them a week of Godly training. Oh, me and whatever teenagers I could scrounge up in just over forty-eight hours.

You might wonder what happened to the children's ministry leader who should have been in charge of VBS. Me, too. Every workplace has skeletons, yet Desert Hills seems to be over its national average. "Oh, just taking some time off." "Guessing she needs a vacation, baby on the way and things." "Something like a sabbatical." Even Vera looked off into the distance and got a soft look on her drill-sergeant face, which was so nipped and tucked it was hard to tell if she was smiling or grimacing. Only thing she said was, "You'll need to talk to Pastor Bob about this, Jane." So I stopped asking because my first question about the children's ministry leader had to be to good old Ab Normal himself. Clashes happen, even in churches, and the District Council in its wisdom sometimes pulls ministers away from their flocks, such as me being yanked screaming and kicking from that inner-city church. Somebody was bound to spill the beans eventually. See, contrary to the word on the street, I can be patient.

A few minutes later Vera dropped her plentiful posterior in the straight-backed chair across the desk from me, plunked a cup of coffee in front of me, and rolled her big brown eyes. The need to know what happened to the previous children's minister was far, far away in another galaxy.

"Read it? Didn't have the heart to tell you over the phone."

"I know VBS is good for kids and great PR, but honestly, Vera, can I handle this?"

She tipped back the coffee mug, pursed her lips, coated deeply with layers of pink and lined with red, which perfectly matched the Hawaiian print of her form-fitting shirt. Vera wiggled her eyebrows up, squished her nose and said, "Beats the heck out of me."

"Thanks a bundle."

Holding the doorframe to the cubicle Vera said, "Harmony Miller is waiting to see you. She's got a nasty bruise on her arm. Thought you should be the one to ask about it." Then she lifted her eyebrows, and I saw a fleeting bit of grandmotherly emotion cross her eyes. "Want me to stay?" Again, as Vera reached for my now-empty cup, even her face, plasticized by surgery, softened.

"Is she in your office? She wasn't in the foyer when Pastor Bob and I had our chat."

"No, think she went to the kitchen to help prepare the lunch the women's group is taking to the rescue mission. The Daily Bread Team feeds about hundred each day and sometimes more on Fridays. But hey, you know that, since you're there often enough. Either you like what they're doing or you're going for the free lunch—just kidding."

Have you ever noticed when people say, "just kidding," they're really not kidding at all?

• • •

I saw the bruise before I focused on Harmony. It was fierce and covered much of her forearm, more purple than black. I'd always thought she looked like a very young Meg Ryan, but her vocabulary could have made a sailor squirm, until I reminded her that even this kitchen was part of the church. Lately it would only make a Marine squirm.

"What's on the menu for the Daily Bread today?" I flopped an arm on her shoulder and felt her stiffen before she wiggled out. I dropped the arm. She wouldn't have been the first kid, or adult, to show dislike for a pushy preacher. Second guess? More bruises under her scruffy T-shirt.

"Chicken or cheese sandwiches, pickles, chips, and fruit," she replied and moved out of my reach, rubbing her shoulder. "Always, coffee, water, soda, and milk, too. We'll leave the platters of veggies, hummus, and pita bread for the crowd that comes at night."

"Sounds better than the stuff I have at home. Harmony, you wanted to see me?" I asked in a light, hopefully non-threatening way. I stayed close, but didn't touch.

"No," she snapped in response.

Harmony wasn't like the whiney kids in the youth group. This was the first I'd seen she had a temper and honestly? It made me feel a micron better because all the fight hadn't been kicked out of her like some of the kids that I'd known who had been tossed from one foster home to another.

We both stared at her feet in dusty, ragged, high-top basketball shoes and then, I hope without her knowing, I allowed my gaze to travel to her face, noting she could be the Goth poster girl since black was the only color of her wardrobe. As I looked into her blue eyes, I could see a frightened little girl in there. I continued, "Vera said you asked for me. I have time now. Want to come to my office with me or when you finish?"

She turned away. I wondered if she was willing her eyes in another direction, then she turned quickly, only to turn away again before saying, "I didn't want to talk to you. Vera said I should."

"We're finished here for now," said one of the women, placing the sack lunches in a box. "Thanks, Harmony. See you at the mission? You can get a ride over with me in about an hour if you're going to help serve again today." I waved to the ladies and then whispered to Harmony, "Want to head out of here and get something cold and slushy at Starbucks?"

Harmony looked at me for the briefest second. We walked into the hall and toward my office and then she finally said, "I gotta' find a better place to live."

I would have closed the door, but there wasn't one. Taking a breath, I vowed to respond in my quiet voice, even if I were shocked, which I knew I'd be. "Are you hurt? Were you assaulted? Did someone touch you inappropriately? Molest you?"

Also Available

In the mood for more Crimson Romance?
Check out *Scrimmage Gone South*
by Alicia Hunter Pace
at *CrimsonRomance.com*.

About the Author

Eva Shaw, Ph.D. is the ghostwriter and author of more than seventy award-winning books.

Her latest novels include *Games of the Heart* (a best-selling novel for Crimson Romance Books) and *Doubts of the Heart* (also for Crimson Romance Books) and the ghosted novel *Poisoned Fate*, which is scheduled to be made into a major motion picture.

Other books include *Ghostwriting: The Complete Guide*, *Writeriffic 2: Creativity Training for Writers*, *Write Your Book in 20 Minutes*, *Shovel It: Nature's Health Plan*, *What to Do When a Loved One Dies*, *For the Love of Children*, *There's No Business Like Show Business*, *Insider's Guide to San Diego*, *The Sun Never Sets*, *My Affair with Art*, and many more.

She was selected as one the country's premier ghostwriters and asked to write an article for the *2013 Writer's Market*, called *Ghostwriting 101*. Other articles have been published in a wide range of magazines and publications, such as *Woman's World*, *Shape*, *Country Living*, *San Diego Union Tribune*, *Los Angeles Times*, *Costco Connection*, *Publisher's Weekly*, *Washington Post*, and the *Wall Street Journal* plus she has ghosted more than one thousand columns, articles, and short stories.

Eva is a regular presenter at conferences speaking on writing, grief, and recovery. She teaches six university-level online writing courses (with Education to Go, *www.ed2go.com*) that are available at two thousand colleges and universities worldwide. A breast cancer survivor, she's an active volunteer with causes affecting women and children in her community, church, and internationally as a board member with Days for Girls International. A portion of the profits of this book will be given to the Breast Cancer Research Fund.

Eva lives and writes in Carlsbad, CA with husband Joseph and their rambunctious Welsh terrier, Miss Rosy Geranium.

Eva is available for speaking engagements, conferences, and book discussion events. Contact Eva or her personal assistant, Frannie, at 760-434-6445.

For more information about Eva, her writing, teaching, and ghostwriting, please visit *www.evashaw.com*.